BACK IN BLACK

JULIE MULHERN

Thank you, Edie!

CHAPTER ONE

July 1975
Kansas City, Missouri

"Remind me why we're doing this?" I slid my umbrella into the brass stand that stood near the club's secondary entrance.

"Because we adore Kay." Libba had put together an intimate luncheon for our high school chum Kay Morrison, who was in town from New York.

I well understood why we were entertaining for Kay. She was a delight. "Why Althea?" Kay's cousin took unnatural delight in other's misfortunes. When Henry was alive, she'd barely contained her glee when she patted my arm and told me my husband was having an affair with Madeline Harper (among others). When I'd shrugged (his infidelity was hardly news), her disappointment was palpable. She'd hoped for tears. Instead, she got a smile that was half-sweet and half-indifferent. Then I said,

"How kind of you to tell me." I never let her (or anyone else) see the anger that seethed inside me.

"I know. I know. She's awful." Libba slipped her trench coat from her shoulders revealing a black shirt dress best worn to a cocktail party. I kept that thought to myself.

Outside, the rain was gentle, a soft gray haze that did little to affect the heat or humidity of the July afternoon.

Inside, the air-conditioner blew cold, and I was glad for the sweater tied loosely around my shoulders.

Libba shivered in the chilly air. "Kay asked me to invite her, and Lois and Tish will be there. You like them."

I did like them, but not enough to make up for Althea. "Do we have place cards?"

"For six?" Libba tilted her chin and narrowed her eyes as if my question was unreasonable. "No."

"If I end up next Althea, I won't be happy."

She rolled her eyes. "It's two hours, not the rest of your life."

"It's Althea." I smoothed my skirt and walked toward the dining room, passing the men's grill where golfers who were waiting out the rain nursed their drinks.

"I had no idea you disliked her so much." Libba followed me. "We both know she can be amusing."

Althea twisted other people's tragedies into dark comedy. She'd done it to me, and now, as the hostess (which required falling on a sword) it seemed inevitable that I'd be stuck sitting next to her. "She dines out on other's misery."

Together, Libba and I entered the dining room. "Oh, dear," I murmured.

"What?"

I nodded toward Myra Lawrence and Hazel York. Widows, the two women were several years older than Mother and three times as disapproving. They wore matching sour-puss expressions.

"You're on your own," said my best friend.

Myra tried for a smile as I approached their table. It didn't reach her eyes. "Good afternoon, Ellison."

"Good afternoon, it's nice to see you both." Politeness would save me. Maybe. Probably not. Since their husbands' deaths, Myra and Hazel had become inseparable. They took pleasure in terrorizing almost anyone who crossed their path (Mother, of course, was immune).

"It looks like you're having a party." Myra waved at the table set for six next to picture windows that looked out on the dreary terrace and sodden golf course. In defiance of the weather, the table was covered with a sunny lemon-yellow cloth. A floral arrangement featuring bright pink Gerbera daisies sat in its center. On a nearby stand, two bottles peeked their gold-wrapped necks above the rim of a silver ice bucket.

"A small luncheon for Kay Morrison."

"Her mother is ill," Hazel spoke slowly as if she questioned my intelligence.

"Yes, ma'am."

"And she has time for a party?"

"Now, Hazel, don't judge. I'm sure Kay needs a few hours away. When Oliver was ill, I sat with him so you could have a break." Hazel's husband Oliver had been a lovely man. Sitting with him was hardly onerous.

"I won't keep you from your lunch," I retreated a step.

"It's nice to see you, Ellison. Tell Libba we don't bite." Myra's accompanying smile was shark-like.

"I will." I hurried to join Libba.

"You survived."

"Barely." I nodded at our table. "The flowers are pretty."

"Mhmm," Libba agreed.

I peeked inside the closest bucket. "Champagne. You ordered Champagne." If Myra and Hazel noticed us drinking Champagne when Kay was in town because of her mother's failing health, they'd pillory us for sure.

"We see Kay so seldom; we have to celebrate." Easy for Libba to say, Hazel York wouldn't be calling *her* mother.

"Ellison? Libba?" Kay stood at the entrance to the dining room. She looked impossibly thin and utterly chic in a black silk blouse paired with drapey black slacks. A silk scarf in a geometric print in shades of ebony, crimson and white draped around her neck. She wore her dark hair shoulder length and sported blunt bangs. Her lipstick matched the red in her scarf. I expected nothing less than perfection from Kay—after all, she had worked for Halston before taking a job with Bill Blass—and she didn't disappoint.

"You're here!" Libba opened her arms and hurried across the dining room toward our guest. The two women hugged, but not so tightly as to wrinkle each other's clothes.

I followed at a more sedate space, taking a few seconds to really look at our friend. Despite her fabulous ensemble, Kay looked tired. Even stressed. And she was too thin. "How are you?" I asked as we kissed the air next to each other's cheeks.

"Never better," she lied. "You look marvelous."

"I had to up my game for you." I wore a sleeveless white sheath with tiny black polka dots.

Kay smiled as if I were joking. I wasn't.

"How long has it been since the three of us were together?" she asked.

"Too long," Libba claimed her elbow and walked toward the table. A table that suddenly looked terribly provincial. We should have used crisp white linens, and a silver Revere bowl filled with orchids.

"How gorgeous," Kay declared. "Glorious color is just what I needed on such a gloomy day. And Champagne? I adore Champagne. You think of everything."

That's why everyone loved Kay; she was effortlessly charming and always knew exactly what to say. It was why I'd endure Althea for a whole luncheon. It was why I ignored Myra and Hazel's disapproving glares (I didn't see their glares, I *felt* them).

"How's your mother?" I asked.

Kay's expression clouded. "Her mind is gone."

I winced. Seeing Mother without her faculties would break my heart. Suddenly the tightness around Kay's eyes made perfect sense.

She bit her lower lip then produced a smile. "I hoped we'd eventually mend fences. Now, that isn't an option."

Mother and I had a fraught relationship, but it was placid compared to the one Kay and her mother, Sybil, shared. They were oil and water, night and day, chalk and cheese. Sybil Morrison was stodgy. Kay was a free spirit. Sybil wanted a comfortable, safe marriage for her daughter. A doctor or lawyer or CEO. Kay wanted excitement and independence. She'd moved to New York, found a job in fashion, and married a restaurateur.

I'd dragged Henry (kicking and screaming) to the small cere-mony at city hall followed by a much larger reception at Harvey's restaurant.

A horrified Sybil had refused to attend.

When Kay and Harvey divorced a year later (as Henry fore-told), Sybil was the first to say, "I told you so." Henry was the second. Fortunately, he only said it to me. Althea was probably the third.

Sybil expected her divorced-at-twenty-four daughter to run home with her tail between her legs.

Kay had stayed in New York, disappointing her mother again.

I was a dab hand at disappointing Mother, but no matter how many times I did it, it never got any easier. The burn of guilt. The moment of self-doubt. *What if Mother really did know best?* And the tone of her voice, dear Lord, the tone when she said my name. *Ellison.* I'd shattered her hopes and, worse, embarrassed her. Again.

Mother might bemoan my finding bodies. She might struggle to keep her opinions of my second husband to herself. But she was proud of my success.

Kay couldn't say the same. Sybil took Kay's wildly successful career as a rejection of traditional values and wasn't shy about sharing her disapproval. It did not foster warm and fuzzy feelings between them.

"I'm so sorry."

Her eyes misted. "Let's talk about something else."

"I want to hear all about the Battle of Versailles. I hope you're not tired of talking about it."

Kay had attended the already legendary fashion show at Versailles where French fashion designers Yves Saint Laurent, Pierre Cardin, Emanuel Ungaro, Marc Bohan, and Hubert de Givenchy had gone head-to-head with upstart Americans Bill Blass, Anne Klein, Stephen Burrows, Oscar de la Renta, and Halston. The Americans with their energy and modern take on fashion had stolen the show.

Her eyes lit with enthusiasm. "I'm so glad it raised as much money as it did. Versailles is a mess. The ceiling leaked in the room where they put Halston. He pouted. He threw a tantrum. They brought him a bucket. The window in Bill's workroom wouldn't fully close." She rolled her eyes. "The French designers had three times the space we did, and—"

"Kay!"

My shoulders tightened at the sound of Althea's voice.

And then she was upon us, hugging her cousin. "Good heavens, you're thin. How do you expect to attract a man if you're nothing but skin and bone?"

Kay escaped Althea's embrace. "I don't need a man."

Althea snorted then turned toward Libba and me. Here chin

tilted as if we'd presented her with a puzzle. "Libba, I thought you were seeing Charlie Ardmore."

"I am."

Her gaze lingered on the number of buttons Libba had failed to fasten. "I see. Ellison, someone told me you married a police officer."

"A detective."

"How convenient for you. Thank you for inviting me."

"We're delighted you could join us," Libba replied through gritted teeth.

"And the table, isn't it cute?"

Puppies were cute, and little girls with pigtails, and fluffy bunnies. Ladies' luncheons were supposed to be elegant.

"So summery," said Kay. "And cheerful. And there's Champagne!"

Althea wrinkled her nose. "Is there anything stronger?"

"Of course," Libba replied. "What would you like?"

"A gin martini. Extra dry."

Libba caught the waiter's eye. "What kind of gin?"

"Gordon's will do."

The waiter arrived at the table where we stood waiting for Tish and Lois.

"A dry Gordon's martini for Mrs. Dodson, please."

"Extra dry," Althea corrected. "Two olives."

Kay's lips thinned as if she disapproved of drinking gin at noon. Or maybe Althea's atrocious manners stole the smile from Kay's face.

Althea's gaze scanned our cute table a second time. "The table is set for six. Who else is coming?"

"Tish and Lois," Kay supplied.

"Really? They only stay in touch so they have a free place to stay when they're in New York."

"Neither of them has ever stayed with me."

"Then they want you to get them discount couture."

"They're two of my oldest, dearest friends. And neither of them is remotely interested in high fashion." Kay was right. Libba might push the fashion envelope, and I might try to stay *au courant*, but most of our friends were more comfortable in Lilly Pulitzer or St. John than Stephen Burrows or Bill Gibb.

As if to prove the point, Tish entered the dining room wearing a Lilly shift. The fabric, pansies in varying shades of turquoise, royal blue, and white, was familiar. I'd bought the same dress four years ago. She'd paired it with pearls, Bernardo sandals, and a Nantucket friendship basket. Her only make-up was a swipe of pink lipstick. She saw us, and her steps faltered. "I'm under-dressed."

I hurried to her side. "Are you kidding? You're perfect. That blue brings out the color of your eyes."

"I agree," said Kay, who wrapped her friend in a warm hug. "You're perfect, and I am positively thrilled to see you."

The waiter appeared and served Althea her martini, and Libba asked him to open the Champagne.

"This is such a treat," said Tish. "I was dying to get out of the house. I swear, on rainy days, the walls press in on me."

"You should find a hobby. Take up exercise. I'm sure your husband would appreciate it." Althea took a sip of her martini and nodded her approval. At least the gin passed muster.

Tish, whose Lilly shift was looking a bit tight, narrowed her eyes. "Althea, I didn't expect to see you today."

Althea and her soon-to-be-ex-husband were close to signing the papers on an ugly divorce. If anyone asked me (fortunately, no one did), I'd have told them that Frank Dodson was a saint to put up with Althea as long as he did. Another sip of martini, then Althea said, "Why not?"

"You've had a trying summer."

"I'd say it's Frank who's had the trying summer." She lifted her glass in a one-person toast. "Thank heavens our grandfather —" she tipped the edge of her glass toward Kay "—had the good sense to put our inheritances in trusts. Frank couldn't get a dime."

"Yoohoo! I'm here! So sorry I'm late." Lois blew into the dining room, pausing as she took in the women already gathered around the table. Then, she hurried toward us. She kissed cheeks, exclaimed over the flowers on the table, and oohed and aahed over how her friend was as chic as all get out. "Goodness, Kay. If I tried to wear that, Skip would laugh at me. But you look like ten million dollars. What's your secret?" She didn't pause for an answer. "You've always had a sense of style. Ellison, too. But you, you look like you should be lunching with Babe Paley, not us. Have you lunched with Babe Paley? I see her picture in *Town & Country*, and I think she's the most elegant woman alive. Some will tell you Jaqueline de Ribes has more elegance, but I say it's Babe. Oh, my gracious! You must know the countess. She was at the Battles of Versailles."

"It was an enormous party. I didn't meet everyone."

Lois wrinkled her nose. "Too bad. Tell me you know Babe Paley. Pleeaase."

"I hate to disappoint, but we run in different circles."

"Drat. I wanted you to tell me all about her."

"Do you ever stop talking?" Althea fixed a curious gaze on Lois's tanned face.

"Althea!" Kay sounded scandalized.

Althea seemed unconcerned. "I'm a straight shooter."

"Declaring that you're a straight shooter isn't a free pass to say whatever you want."

I agreed. "Oh, good." I accepted a glass of Champagne from the waiter. "Shall we toast Kay?"

Libba raised her flute. "Welcome home, Kay. Make new friends but keep the old. One is silver, the other gold. You, my dear, are gold, and we're so glad you're here with us."

We clinked rims and drank and ignored Althea's sour expression.

"Where do you want us?" asked Tish.

"Why don't you sit next to Kay?" Libba suggested. "Kay, you sit here." She tapped a chair.

Kay took her seat, and Tish sat on her left. Althea claimed the chair on the right. I sat next to Althea. Lois sat next to me. And Libba took the remaining chair.

Over the salad course, the entrée (trout served with rice pilaf and steamed broccoli), and dessert (raspberry sorbet), Kay kept us entertained with stories from New York and Paris.

The waiter was pouring me a second cup of coffee when Althea leaned toward her cousin and whispered, "There's something I must tell you. It's about…" her voice trailed as she spotted someone in the hallway outside the dining room.

I turned my head to see the person who caught Althea's attention and quieted her tongue, but they were already gone.

Althea sat back in her chair, crossed her arms, and positively glared at me. "You dated Hunter Tafft." She made dating him sound like a crime.

I blinked at her. Why did she care about the men I'd dated? "Hunter and I went out for dinner a few times."

"You're still friends," she accused.

Why the ire? "Yes, we're friends."

"Wait." Kay's wide eyes sparkled, and she wagged a finger at me. "You dated Hunter Tafft? Why am I just hearing about this now?"

"She was too busy finding bodies to tell you." Althea offered me a tight, unpleasant smile. "She didn't have time to brief you on her love life."

Kay waved away the bodies with a flick of her elegant wrist. "You were dating Hunter and fell for someone else? How could you? Hunter has that hair."

Hunter's hair was brightly polished sterling and pretty fabulous. "I'm aware."

"Oh, my gracious," Lois pressed her palms to her chest.

"Ellison's husband looks just like Steve McQueen. Except his eyes are brown. And he's better looking. Less smirky. And he's here. And he's real. And—"

"Steve McQueen?" Kay cut off Lois's list of Anarchy's attributes. "When can I meet your husband? I must see the man you chose over Hunter."

"Come by for a drink tonight."

"What time?"

"Five-thirty?"

"I'll be there."

"Be prepared to forget all about silver hair," said Libba. "Anarchy is...let's just say Lois is not wrong. We all understand why Ellison picked him."

My husband had coffee brown eyes, a lean face, and a smile that made my knees weak. He had quiet charm, quiet strength, and conspicuous good looks. I was a lucky woman.

"More coffee, Mrs. Jones?" The waiter stood at my elbow.

Silly question. "Please."

He poured, and I searched for a new topic. "It looks like the weather is clearing." Outside, the clouds had parted to allow the sun to peek through. It probably felt like a sauna.

"Thank heavens," said Tish. "Maybe Bob can get out on the golf course."

Althea turned to her. "Is that where you think he goes in the afternoons?"

"Where else would he go?" I spoke through gritted teeth. I knew first-hand the pain of having a husband's infidelity thrown in one's face. I wouldn't wish that on Tish.

"Althea." Kay caught her cousin's wrist, pulled her close, and whispered in her ear. When she finished, Althea's cheeks mottled. "Ellison, Libba, thank you for a wonderful luncheon. I can't think of an afternoon I've enjoyed more."

"It was our pleasure."

She glanced at her watch and her brow furrowed. "I hate to

be the one to break up the party, but I promised the nurse who stays with Mother that I'd be back by two-thirty."

Everyone rose from the table and exchanged hugs and kisses and promised that we'd do this again soon. Well, everyone but Althea. She looked ready to spit nails.

When I hugged Kay, she whispered, "Five-thirty?"

"We'll count on you."

Our guests left us, and I turned to Libba. "Never again."

"You didn't have to sit next to her."

"If I put Lois next to her, Althea would have spent the entire luncheon insulting her."

"That assumes she'd be able to get a word in. Maybe she'll get better,. Now that she's divorced."

Since when did Libba wear rose-colored glasses? I raised my brows in disbelief. "I sincerely doubt it." Mean-spirited people didn't get any nicer when they found themselves alone.

"Do you want to take the flowers?" asked Libba.

I glanced at the colorful arrangement. "You don't want it?"

"If they go home with you, Aggie will change the water every day. They'll last for a week. If they go home with me, they'll be dead by Monday."

"I'll take them." I picked up the arrangement. "Walk me to my car?" I had an unhappy relationship with the club's parking lot. Too many bodies. Too many murder attempts.

"Let me get my coat."

A few minutes later, I settled the floral arrangement on the passenger side floorboards. "Drat."

"What?"

"I forgot my umbrella."

Libba huffed her annoyance before asking, "Do you want me to go with you?"

I scanned the nearly empty lot for threats. "No. Go see Charlie. Also, you're both welcome to come for drinks tonight."

"I never turn down a drink." She hopped into her Mercedes,

rolling down the window to offer me a jaunty wave goodbye, then sped down the club's drive.

I walked back to the clubhouse, claimed my umbrella, and decided a trip to the ladies' room wouldn't be amiss.

The white paneled door that opened onto the ladies' lounge was closed, which was unusual. I pulled it open, and my stomach plunged to my ankles. "Althea?"

Althea didn't answer. She couldn't. Not with a knife sticking out of her chest.

CHAPTER TWO

The trout almondine I'd eaten for lunch threatened to make a reappearance, and I took deep gulping breaths in an effort not to throw up at a crime scene.

Althea lay on the peach hued carpet—not peach hued anymore, the crimson carpet—and stared sightlessly at the ceiling. The table set for bridge in the corner, the floral club chairs, the pastel paintings hanging on the delicately hued walls—they were all at odds with violent death.

Violent death didn't care.

I staggered into the hallway and spotted a waiter carrying a tray of dirty dishes from the men's grill. Seeing the stacked plates reminded me that we'd been away from the table for no more than ten minutes. Althea was freshly dead. "Excuse me," I called.

His head turned my way.

"I need to see the manager. Immediately," I squeaked out the need for urgency.

"Yes, Mrs. Jones." He paused, taking a long hard look at me. "Are you okay?"

No. I wasn't. I'd found another body. At. The. Club. Mother's head was going to spin like Regan's in *The Exorcist*. "Please. The manager."

"Of course." He pushed open the kitchen door and disappeared.

A moment later, the manager joined me outside the ladies' lounge. "Problem, Mrs. Jones?" He looked nervous, as if he was worried that I'd found a body.

He was right to be nervous.

"Althea Dodson has been murdered."

He paled.

"Her body is in the lounge." Thank God it was the casual lounge. If I'd found a body in the lounge on the other side of the club, the lounge Mother preferred, she would have combusted. Not that I had anything to do with where people got murdered. Or where I found their bodies.

"You're joking."

I cracked the door, and he stuck his head inside, quickly stumbling backward.

"She's dead." He sounded winded.

"Yes. We need to call the police. My husband."

"The homicide detective?"

"That's right."

"He'll be discreet?"

"We're not talking about the bookkeeper who embezzled from the capital fund," a secret that everyone seemed to know (so, not discreet). "We're talking about murder."

He made no move to call the police. "Dodson. I don't recognize that name. She's not a member."

"No." I offered an apologetic shrug. "She was a guest at the luncheon I just hosted."

If looks could kill, I'd be as dead as Althea.

"Perhaps you'd like me to make the call?" I offered.

"Please," he snapped.

There was no reason for him to be so terse. It wasn't as if I'd killed Althea.

"You'll guard the door?"

He gave a curt nod, and I hurried to the walnut phone booth down the hall, pressed a button for an outside line, and called home.

"Jones' residence." My housekeeper sounded positively chipper.

"Aggie, it's me. May I please speak with Anarchy?" Normally, Anarchy worked on Fridays, but he had the weekend off. We'd planned on a family dinner. Tomorrow night, we had a wedding to attend.

"He's outside playing catch with Beau."

"It's important."

"Did you find a body?" She was kidding.

I let silence answer for me.

"Lord love a duck. Again? I'll get him right away."

Less than thirty seconds later, Anarchy was on the line. "Ellison? Where are you? Are you okay? Safe?"

"I'm fine. I'm safe. I'm at the club. Someone murdered Althea Dodson. I found her."

"Who's Althea Dodson?"

"She was a guest at the luncheon I just hosted."

"Hell."

"Just wait till Mother finds out."

"Who else knows?"

"Right now, just the club manager. He's guarding the door to the ladies' lounge. That's where I found her. She's been stabbed."

"I'll call it in, then I'm on my way."

"Thank you."

"Stay safe." He hung up.

I lingered in the phone booth. As soon as I exited, there'd be questions to answer. Aspersions would be cast. Fingers would be pointed. The news would reach Mother.

I should be mourning Althea, instead the only thing I felt was exhaustion. Why, why, why had I decided I needed a trip to the bathroom? I was only five minutes from home. If I'd ignored my bladder, I could be sitting on the patio right now, enjoying the rest of my Friday afternoon with my family.

I took a bracing breath, emerged from the phone booth, and returned to the manager. "My husband is on his way."

He grunted at me.

Well, then.

We waited in itchy silence. I was silent because I had nothing to say. I suspected the club manager held his tongue because he had too much to say, and none of it pleasant.

An eternity (seven minutes) later, Anarchy arrived. His hands closed around my upper arms and his gaze searched my face.

"I'm fine. I opened the door, saw her, asked for the manager, then called you." I wasn't fine.

He gave a brief nod, then opened the door to the lounge.

The coppery smell of blood wafted into the hallway, and my stomach lurched.

I was being terribly selfish, bemoaning my bad luck, worrying about Mother's reaction—all while poor Althea's death scented the air.

Anarchy let the door fall closed. "The crime scene techs and the photographer are on their way. Can you tell me what happened?"

I ignored the sudden swelling in my throat. "We finished lunch, and everyone headed their own way."

"Everyone?"

"Kay, Lois, Tish, and Althea," I replied. "Libba and I walked to the parking lot together, and I realized I'd forgotten my umbrella. I came back for it and decided to stop by the ladies' room. That's when I found her."

"How long between the end of lunch and when you found her?"

I propped myself up against the nearest wall. "Ten minutes."

Anarchy rubbed his chin. "When you say everyone headed their own way, what did you mean?"

"Kay said she had to get home to relieve her mother's nurse. I don't know where Tish or Lois went."

"Did they leave the club?"

"I assume so, but that's what I thought about Althea." And she hadn't left.

Anarchy nodded as if I'd made a good point. "Do you need something to drink? You look pale."

I nodded and, to my horror, my eyes welled. Why was it that kindness made me cry? I swallowed a lump and said, "Yes, please."

"Water or something stronger?"

"Water is fine." I glanced at the manager. "Or iced tea."

"Bring her iced tea," Anarchy told the manager. "With extra lemons and those little pink packets of sweetener." He turned to me, "You know, you could just add lemonade."

I managed a weak smile. "Too much sugar."

The manager scowled at us both, then left to fetch my iced tea.

When he was out of earshot, Anarchy asked, "What can you tell me about the deceased?"

"She's going through an ugly divorce."

"Ugly enough for murder?"

"I don't know. Although, if you ask me, it's a wonder they stayed married as long as they did."

"Oh?"

"Althea was unpleasant." I didn't like speaking ill of the dead, but there was no point in pretending that Althea was the sort of woman who nursed orphaned kittens with droppers of milk. She wasn't kind. She wasn't charitable. And she didn't have much use for other people.

"Why did you invite her to lunch?"

"She's Kay's cousin. Was Kay's cousin."

"Did anything odd happen while you were eating?"

"Not at all." I frowned.

"What?"

"Althea said she needed to tell Kay something."

"Did she?"

"No. Someone walked by in the hallway, and Althea abruptly changed the subject."

"To what?"

"My relationship with Hunter Tafft."

Anarchy frowned at me.

"Now, Kay wants to meet you."

"Oh? Why?"

"She thinks Hunter is dreamy and wants to meet the man I picked instead of him."

Anarchy's lips quirked. Smirked. Was he...preening? Then his lips were at the shell of my ear. "I thought I picked you."

I tilted my head and smiled into his coffee brown eyes. "I'm so glad you did. So glad we picked each other."

"Are you done making moon eyes over a corpse?" Peters, Anarchy's grumpy partner, had found us, and he was as rude as ever.

I didn't let myself react to his tone or his words. I kept my voice calm. Even. "The body—" corpse seemed such a harsh word for a woman with whom I'd just lunched "—is in the lounge. We're in the hallway."

Peters scowled at me. "Semantics."

"Reality. Althea is in the lounge."

"I should have figured you'd know the stiff." His narrowed gaze took in the elegant hallway, my Gucci handbag, the pearls at my neck, then, not surprisingly, he sneered.

"You're in a sunny mood."

"Wasn't our turn," he grumbled. "We had the weekend off. But you called, so we're up."

I looked to Anarchy for an explanation.

"Homicide detectives are on a rotation," he explained. "When a call comes in, whoever is at the top of the rotation or 'up,' catches the case."

"Unless you call." Peters, who wore his usual wrinkled raincoat, glared at me. "If you call, we're up."

I called a lot.

"If I hadn't called?"

"Harris and Miller," Peters replied.

"And what would you be doing?"

"Yardwork."

"Well, then—" I offered him an extra-bright smile "—I did you favor."

He growled at me.

Anarchy held up his hands in a plea for peace. "Peters, let's take a look at the body."

"If you don't need me, I'll go home."

Anarchy hesitated. "You're okay getting to the car?"

Peters rolled his eyes.

"I'll be fine."

My husband rubbed his palm across his chin, a sure sign he was unhappy. "I'll walk you."

"She said she'll be fine."

"And she's been attacked in the parking lot before."

Peters grunted, unable to argue Anarchy's excellent point.

"I'll be back in five." Anarchy rested his hand at the small of my back and guided me down the hallway.

Outside, the air was humid enough to puddle in my lungs, and the parking lot was filling up with golfers eager to play a quick nine holes despite the soggy, cart-path-only conditions.

Anarchy opened the car door for me. "You didn't lock it?"

"I must have forgotten." I frowned. "Do I cause you more work? By calling, I mean."

"No. We'd still catch cases."

"But you catch the high-profile cases because of me?"
He nodded.

"And Peters doesn't enjoy the limelight."

"There's more pressure," he admitted.

"Ellison?" My father climbed out of a Mercedes parked a few spaces away. A warm smile curled his lips, and his eyes sparkled.

"Daddy." I closed the distance between us and kissed his cheek.

"How was your luncheon?" He frowned as he held out his hand to Anarchy, as if he couldn't quite imagine why my husband might be there.

They shook, and my father's frown deepened as he took in Anarchy's serious expression.

"The luncheon was fine."

"Why do I hear a 'but' at the end of that statement?"

"Because I found a body."

"Murder?"

"Yes."

Daddy raked his fingers through his silver hair. "Does your mother know?"

"Not, yet."

He closed his eyes with his hands still on his scalp. "Who?"

"Althea Dodson."

His eyes flew open. "Jonbie Dodson's daughter-in-law?"

I nodded as Anarchy asked, "Jonbie?"

"John Ballester Dodson," I explained. "He comes from a long line of John's and his parents decided to use his middle name. But John Ballester is a mouthful, and, at two, his younger sister shortened it."

"That's his car." Daddy pointed to a black Cadillac Fleetwood.

"How did he feel about his son's divorce?"

Daddy's expression tightened. "Always the cop."

"A woman is dead."

My father nodded. Slowly. Unhappily. "And everyone's a suspect."

"Let's call them persons of interest."

Daddy huffed and scowled into the middle distance. "Jonbie was mad as hell. He and Lilly gave John and Althea a cabin in Michigan as a wedding gift. The cabin has been in the Dodson family for generations—at least four Johns. Althea demanded the place as part of the divorce settlement. Jonbie calls her a grasping, money-grubbing harpy, and that's when he's feeling charitable. After a few drinks, the description got more colorful."

I bet. Lilly Dodson spent her days keeping Jonbie wrapped in a bubble of contentment. She adjusted her schedule to suit his needs and took up every unpleasant task—from gathering paperwork for the accountant to making sure their backyard, occupied by two enormous Newfoundland dogs, remained pristine. She told Mother (and Mother told me) that her life was easier when everything went Jonbie's way. His temper was not to be trifled with.

When I'd reasonably pointed out that Jonbie was an enormous man-child, and Lilly acted more like his mother than his partner, Mother had pursed her lips and muttered something about learning how to keep a husband happy.

I adored my husband and wanted him to be happy, but not by turning myself into a buffer. I'd been down that road with my first husband, and I hadn't enjoyed it. If Anarchy couldn't deal with life's small inconveniences without descending into a foul mood, I'd married the wrong man. Anarchy dealt with murder without descending into a foul mood. I'd married the right man.

I tucked a strand of hair behind my ear and dug my keys out of my handbag.

"Was Dodson's car here when you brought out the flowers?" Anarchy asked.

"I can't remember." I'd been chatting with Libba and scanning for possible threats, not cataloging the cars parked the next row over.

"Are you meeting him for golf?" Anarchy asked my father.

"Not today."

A white panel van pulled up to the clubhouse.

Anarchy watched it park. "The crime scene specialists. I should go. Harrington, always a pleasure." He bent and brushed a kiss across my cheek, then nodded to the open car door. "See you at home."

I said goodbye to my father and drove home at a sedate pace, in no hurry to receive an angry phone call from Mother. She remained convinced that I put out cosmic energy that led me to bodies. All I needed to do was fix my aura, or qi, or karma, and I'd stop tripping over corpses. Maybe she was right, because I'd lost count of the bodies, and that couldn't be normal.

I parked in the circle drive in front of the house, carefully lifted the flower arrangement off the floorboards, and, with my hands full, jabbed my elbow at the doorbell.

Inside the house, dogs barked, and I heard Aggie tell them to be quiet.

A moment later, the front door opened, and Aggie took the flower arrangement from my arms. "Your mother has called. Three times. She wants you to call her immediately."

"Already? News travels fast."

Aggie, who wore a bright yellow kaftan embellished with crocheted cherries, held up her hands. Her red Napier hoop earrings swung as she said, "Please don't shoot the messenger."

"Never," I replied. "Do you think the messenger might help me sneak out of town?"

"She'd find you."

"You think?"

Aggie gave me a flat look. She was right. Mother would track me down. There was no escaping her. Frances Walford was a force of nature—an F-5 tornado headed straight at me.

"Fine," I ceded. "I'll call her."

With the dogs, Max and Finn, at my heels, I went to the family room, took a seat at my desk, and dialed.

"Walford residence."

"Good afternoon, this is Ellison calling. May I please speak to Mother?"

"One moment, Mrs. Jones." Mother's housekeeper was scrupulously polite. Always. Mother demanded nothing less.

I drummed my fingers on the desk and awaited my fate. Max yawned as his amber eyes took in my distress. Max was smarter than half the people I knew. Unfortunately, he frequently used that intelligence for evil. Next to him, Finn wagged his stubby tail. Finn was a happy dog. His bad behavior wasn't the result of careful consideration. Rather, Finn chased and dug on a moment's whim. I adored them both.

"Ellison Walford Russell!"

I startled before saying, "Jones." Not that she'd listen. Mother all too ready to forget I'd remarried.

"How could you?" she demanded.

I blinked. How could I? I'd found countless bodies. She might not like it, but she should be used to it by now. "It's not the first time."

"And I had to hear about it from someone else!"

I frowned. I almost never told Mother when I found a body, the futile hope that she might never learn about the corpse always stilled my tongue. "Mother—"

"Don't you 'Mother' me, Ellison Russell!"

"Jones."

She growled, "What were you thinking?"

"There's no way I could have anticipated a—"

"Have you lost your ever-loving mind? At your age? You're not a young woman. And you insisted on adopting Beau. The last thing you need is a baby."

I frowned in confusion. "A baby?"

"Yes, Ellison. A baby. What were you thinking?"

I stared at the dogs. They grinned at me as if they appreciated the afternoon's entertainment. "Mother, I'm not pregnant."

Several seconds passed before Mother asked, "Are you sure?"

"Positive." My voice was as dry as dust. "Who told you I was having a baby?"

I could *hear* the steam rising from Mother's ears, practically see the annoyed purse of her lips. "It doesn't matter." She paused a beat, then asked, "What didn't you anticipate?"

I tilted my head, stared at the ceiling, and prepared for Armageddon. "I found another body." I rushed through the words, waiting for the sky to fall.

"Whose?"

I frowned. Where was the outrage? The annoyance? The long-winded diatribe about how unseemly it was to find corpses? "Althea Dodson's."

"Dreadful woman."

"Be that as it may, I found her in the lounge at the club."

"Ellison!" Now, Mother sounded properly scandalized.

"The casual lounge."

"Thank God for small favors. What happened?"

Max sighed and rested his chin on his paws. He'd expected fireworks, drama, a melting telephone. Instead, Mother sounded almost reasonable.

"Someone murdered her," I replied

"Was there blood?" Did I detect a hopeful lilt to her voice?

I pictured the scene. Althea. The knife. The pool of crimson. "Lots of it."

She hummed as if she approved. "The carpet looked tired. It needed replacing, and I never cared for that God-awful peach color. I'll call Janet Crane." Janet was married to David, the chairman of the house and grounds committee. "Men don't care about carpet, especially not carpet in the ladies' lounge. This is our chance to replace it with something more neutral."

Mother wasn't usually so cavalier about murder. "Althea's barely cold."

"It's not as if she was a member. Maybe with new carpet, we can also paint the walls. Do you think Janet could talk David into recovering the furniture?"

"Mother!"

"What, Ellison?"

"I found a body. Don't you care?"

"Of course, I care. I always care. But my caring never makes a difference. You just keep finding bodies. Today, I'm choosing to look on the bright side."

"There's a bright side?" Althea was dead.

"This is an opportunity to redecorate the lounge. And, more importantly, you're not pregnant."

If Mother wasn't upset with me, I wasn't about to argue, no matter how callous her attitude toward Althea's murder. "Not pregnant," I parroted.

"You're not...trying?"

"We are not."

"Finally, you're showing some sense."

I showed plenty of sense. I'd married a wonderful man, raised a fabulous daughter, and welcomed the sweetest boy on the planet into our family. And now, I showed enough sense to bite my tongue.

"I have a call to make."

I bet she did. I wouldn't want to be the woman who'd mistakenly told her I was pregnant. Or Janet Crane.

"Goodbye, Mother."

"Try not to find any more bodies. Especially at the club. If this continues, people will avoid you." With that bit of advice (one she gave often), she hung up, leaving my smart retort unuttered.

CHAPTER THREE

The dogs followed me upstairs to my bedroom and watched as I changed out of my dress and into a pair of shorts and a polo shirt.

Max watched because he knew me well. He anticipated a coming walk.

Finn watched because he followed Max's lead in most everything.

Their tails wagged as I pulled on a pair of sneakers.

"You want a walk?"

They answered with doggy grins, and Finn whined softly.

"Let's go then."

They barreled out my room and raced down the front stairs.

I took a moment to pull my hair into a ponytail, then headed to the kitchen where the dogs danced with unexpected impatience.

"They haven't been out?" I asked Aggie.

"Not yet." She glowered at the twosome as if they'd been up to mischief in my absence.

Knowing them, it was a certainty.

"Grace said she'd take them for a run."

"Grace got an emergency call to babysit. Your friend Daisy was desperate." And a desperate Daisy paid top dollar.

"I see. Where's Beau?"

"Anarchy took him to his friend Joey's after you called from the club."

She'd been left alone with two dogs in need of exercise. I grabbed the leashes from their hooks and attached them to their collars. Not an easy task since Finn hopped around like a Mexican jumping bean.

"Finn! Sit."

He reluctantly lowered his haunches.

"Everything okay with your mother?" Aggie asked.

"She's so thrilled I'm not pregnant that she didn't care about the body." No need to mention Mother's eagerness to redecorate the lounge. Her focus on new carpet didn't cast her in the best light.

"Pregnant?"

"Idle gossip." Anarchy and I had each other, and Grace and Beau. We didn't need a baby to make us a family.

Aggie's earrings (twice the size of her ears) bobbed as she nodded her understanding. "Did you know her well? The dead woman."

I grimaced. "Well enough."

"You're not sad." A statement, not a question.

"No. I don't suppose I am."

Woof. Max barked his displeasure. We'd talked long enough and were needlessly delaying his constitutional.

"Shush," I told him. "I'm sorry she's dead. But I won't miss her."

"She was murdered?"

Max tugged on his leash, and I frowned at him before replying, "Yes."

"Who do you think killed her?"

"She was in the middle of an ugly divorce."

"The husband?" Aggie wrinkled her nose. "Seems so obvious."

Unhappy spouses weren't always guilty (I was living proof of that), but more often than not, they were. "Anarchy is investigating."

Woof. Max gave me a disgusted look.

"I should go." I let the dogs pull me toward the back door.

Once outside, they pulled harder.

"No." I pulled back. "Behave yourselves."

They gave me indulgent doggy smiles and walked like gentlemen—down the driveway, down the sidewalk, all the way to the corner. So, three minutes. Then, Finn spotted a squirrel. In his canine opinion, said squirrel was far enough from the nearest tree to give him a fighting chance at capture. He lunged, ripping the leash from my hand.

"Finn!"

He ignored me as he raced toward the squirrel who ran as if his life depended upon the speed in his little legs.

It did.

The squirrel reached a tree with less than a second to spare. Reaching the safety of a branch, the animal chittered angrily.

Finn circled the trunk as if the squirrel might be foolish enough to climb down.

When Max and I reached Finn, I told him, "Bad dog."

Finn, whose pink tongue lolled out of the side of his mouth, didn't care what I called him.

I successfully reclaimed his leash and yanked him away from the tree. "Come. Now."

He huffed his disappointment but allowed me to lead him back to the sidewalk.

We turned the corner and headed toward the park.

"Ellison! Ellison, is that you?"

I recognized the voice and kept walking.

Max crossed in front of Finn, tangling their leashes and giving me less control.

"Drat," I said under my breath.

"Ellison!"

I glanced over my shoulder and saw her. If we weren't near a busy street, I'd have let go of Finn's leash just to have a reason to chase him.

"I know you hear me!"

I turned. "Hello, Prudence." Prudence Davies was a horse-toothed harpy who'd had an affair with my late husband.

Finn growled, deep in his throat. Max bared his teeth.

She eyed my dogs and retreated a step. "Is it true?"

"Is what true?" Did the whole town think I was pregnant? I resisted placing my hand on my stomach. Was I looking poochy?

"Did you find Althea Dodson's body at the club?"

Oh. That. "Yes."

She smirked. "Your mother must be so pleased."

Little did she know that Mother was so excited that I wasn't pregnant and so enthused about the new carpet, she hardly cared that I'd found a body. "Mother is heartbroken that someone lost their life." Two could play at sarcasm.

Prudence snorted. Something she ought never do. It made her sound like a hog nosing slop. "I heard your husband is investigating."

Finn growled deeper. Longer.

"Yes."

She eyed Finn warily. "Does he have any suspects?"

As if I'd tell her. "Why do you ask?"

"No reason." The sudden flush on her cheeks said different.

Woof. Max's bark usually demanded walks or treats or pets. This bark said he'd like to take a bite out of Prudence's skinny calf.

She retreated another step. "Can't you control your animals?"

I had death grips on their leashes, and they hadn't bitten her.

Yet. "I heard you were spotted at dinner with John Dodson." I'd heard no such thing, but the deeper flush on Prudence's cheeks was gratifying. I'd hit an unexpected mark.

"What if I was?"

It meant that John had terrible—truly terrible—taste in women. Getting rid of Althea only to take up with Prudence was criminally stupid.

This was my chance to learn more about the divorce, information I could share with Anarchy. "I also heard that Althea was being difficult."

"Difficult?" Prudence planted her hands on her bony hips. "She was being completely unreasonable." And Prudence had stepped in as John's shoulder-to-cry-on. Probably holding tight to the hope that she'd be the next Mrs. John Dodson. Of course, the longer the divorce dragged on, the better the possibility that John came to his senses. There were scads of women better than Prudence. I'd introduce him. Gladly.

"How so?"

"She wanted things that have been in the Dodson family for generations. She wanted a ridiculous amount of alimony." She took a step closer, then reconsidered, retreating two. "She wanted to see John suffer, and she's the one who asked for the divorce."

That was new information. I'd assumed John was divorcing Althea.

"I wonder why."

Prudence snorted again, and I thought of Petunia Pig. Although, the cartoon was much better looking than Prudence. "She was almost forty."

"Not usually a reason for divorce," I observed.

Prudence scowled at me. "She would have received the money from her grandmother's trust at forty. If she and John weren't married, he'd have no claim. Meanwhile, she tried to take him for every penny she could." Prudence's livid tone made me wonder if her relationship with John pre-dated Althea's request for a divorce. It wouldn't be the first time that Prudence took up with a married man.

"Where were you this afternoon?" I asked sweetly.

Her cheeks mottled. "How dare you?"

Both dogs growled, pulling on their leashes.

"Sit," I told them. When they planted their doggy butts on the sidewalk, I returned my gaze to Prudence. "You can tell me, or you can tell Anarchy."

Her lips thinned. She had no intention of telling me anything.

"Never mind," I told her. "I'll tell Anarchy how invested you are. He'll be in touch."

The dogs and I left her on the sidewalk, and I made a list of questions. How long had Prudence been seeing John Dodson? How much did Althea stand to inherit? What happened to the money now?

We reached Loose Park. The park was originally a private golf course, the land leased to the club members for a dollar a year plus taxes. When the club members bought land of their own, Ella Loose bought the golf course they'd leased and gifted it to the city in honor of her late husband. The city converted the course to a park, complete with a none-too-clean pond (I was all too familiar with its dirty water), a rose garden, tennis courts, a playground, and a walking trail of just over a mile. On a sunny Friday afternoon, especially after a morning filled with rain, the park was full.

The dogs and I circled the walking trail three times. Their tails wagged each time we met another dog, and they kept their eyes out for squirrels. But the squirrels we encountered at the park were savvy. They stayed near the trees, and the dogs seemed to know that chasing them would be a waste of time.

"Last lap," I told them.

Their short tails wagged in tandem.

"Ellison?" A man's voice called my name.

I glanced over my shoulder and spotted Perry Brandt walking

his dog Goldie, an adorable mutt that he and his wife Liz had adopted from rescue.

We stopped, and he caught up to us, kissing my cheek while the dogs sniffed each other's nether regions.

"Nice afternoon for a walk," he observed.

"These two were driving Aggie nuts."

My unrepentant dogs grinned at me.

Perry rubbed the back of his neck. "I heard you found a body at the club."

News traveled fast. "I did."

"Althea Dodson?"

The police cruisers parked outside the club's entrance would have attracted attention. Immediate attention. Rubbernecking from the golf course I understood. But how did everyone know I'd found the body? Did they just assume? Given my track record, I couldn't exactly blame them. And how did they know I'd found Althea? "Yes. Why?"

"My firm was representing John."

"Really?" I raised my brows. Perry was the managing partner at a corporate law firm. "I wasn't aware your firm handled family law."

"We don't. We made an exception because of his other dealings."

"Well, she's gone. The cabin stays with the Dodsons."

He winced. "You heard about that?"

"Ugly divorce? People talk." I tightened my grip on Finn's leash since he seemed to be tracking a squirrel who'd wandered dangerously far from its tree. "You have criminal attorneys?"

Perry's fingers flexed, and he quickly jammed his hand in his pocket. "John's a suspect?" He sounded only mildly curious. I wasn't fooled.

Aside from his abysmal taste in women, I had nothing against John Dodson. We'd chatted at cocktail parties, occasionally attended the same dinner parties, and he and my late husband had taken turns inviting each other to play golf. "I assume so. Hopefully, he has an alibi."

"What time did you find her?"

I shook my head. "Sorry, Perry. Anarchy's investigating." And I would not be handing out case details like candy on Halloween.

He nodded as if he'd expected me to clam up. For all their faults, lawyers understood confidentiality. "I don't think he did it."

"I hope you're right."

Woof. Finn barked at the squirrel.

"I should get going."

He nodded. "Call Liz. Let's get together for dinner. Better yet, how about a round of golf?"

"I'll call her."

He dropped another kiss on my cheek, then he and Goldie headed in the opposite direction.

The dogs and I headed home. When we reached the back-yard, I took off their leashes and watched as they carefully checked their yard for squirrels, rabbits, or foolish cats. Finding none, they joined me at the back door.

I stepped inside and took a moment to enjoy the dry, cool air. It wasn't terribly hot outside, but the humidity hung heavy.

Aggie looked up from chopping celery. "You're home."

"Hopefully we took the edge off. What are you making?"

"Etouffee. Beau says it's one of his favorites."

"Sounds delicious." We were so lucky to have Aggie in our lives. Despite my best efforts, I couldn't cook. If I were respon-sible for nightly dinners, we'd live on frozen pizza and take-out. I took a pitcher of water from the fridge and poured myself a glass as the dogs emptied their water bowl.

"Your mother called."

My shoulders stiffened. "Again?"

"She wanted to confirm you're not pregnant."

"What did you tell her?"

"That you were drinking martinis with Libba just last night. I also told her that, despite my best efforts, you haven't gained an ounce since I started working here."

"And?"

"I think she took me at my word."

"Sorry about that." Dealing with Frances Walford, especially when she was in a mood, wasn't easy.

Aggie shrugged. "She's a mother. She worries."

"Did Anarchy call?"

She pulled an apologetic face and shook her head. "Sorry. No."

"I'm sure he's busy interviewing the staff. They'll know who was in the clubhouse when Althea was killed." I put my empty glass in the dishwasher. "Although, I suppose one of them might have killed her."

"Motive?"

"She was frequently rude."

"Rude enough to justify murder?"

I shrugged. "Quite possibly."

"Ellison?" Libba's voice carried from the front hall.

What was she doing here? I glanced at the wall clock. "Oh. Dear. Lord."

"What's wrong?" asked Aggie.

"Kay is coming for drinks. So are Libba and Charlie." I'd completely forgotten.

Aggie wiped her hands on the purple apron covering her yellow kaftan. "I'll throw together some hors d'oeuvres. What time is your friend coming?" She meant Kay. Libba, who barged in whenever she felt like it, didn't count.

"Ellison?" Libba was louder this time.

"We're in the kitchen," I called.

Libba burst into the kitchen. "Did you really find Althea's

body?" She looked at me and her eyes narrowed. "What are you wearing?"

"I took the dogs for a walk."

"Kay will be here any minute."

"Keep Aggie company. I'll go change."

Despite my excellent suggestion, Libba followed me up the stairs. "So, is it true? Did you find her?"

"Yes." I turned and scowled at my best friend. "Why do you sound surprised? I find bodies all the time." And I hated it.

Her expression softened, almost as if she could sense the horror and the sadness and the why-me angst that took over each time I found a fresh corpse.

"Don't." I turned my back on her.

"Don't what?"

"Be sympathetic. If you're nice, I'll cry."

"I'm always nice."

"Right." I climbed the remaining stairs.

"Kay will be here in ten minutes," she said. "And you look like a midwestern mom." So much for Libba being nice.

"I am a midwestern mom," I replied.

"And Kay hangs out with Halston and Andy Warhol. Up your game." Libba followed me into the bedroom, then the bathroom.

I glanced in the mirror. There was no saving my hair. If I took out the band, I'd have that odd ridge. I left it in a ponytail.

"Really? A ponytail?"

"Out." I pointed to the bedroom, then washed my face and applied fresh mascara and blush.

When I emerged, Libba sat on the edge of my bed with my open jewelry box in her lap. "What are you going to tell Kay?" she asked.

The air whooshed out of my lungs. *Kay, so glad you could make it. Anarchy's not here. He's investigating Althea's murder.*

By the way, I found her with a knife in her chest. May I fix you a martini?

"Well?"

"I don't know." I changed into a Lilly shift and spritzed my wrists with Rive Gauche.

Libba, who wore a black sheath, was unimpressed. "You still look like a mom."

I shrugged. I'd known Kay most of my life. It was too late to impress her. Also, chances were good, she'd be too distracted be her cousin's murder to care what I wore. "Maybe she already knows about Althea." Prudence had. Perry had.

Libba considered that for all of five seconds before shaking her head. "She's been gone too long. She doesn't have a network."

"You don't think some helpful soul called her?" Helpful soul. Ha! Far too many women delighted in being the first to know and share the latest gossip. Especially when the gossip was salacious.

"That would be an awkward conversation." She pushed aside a string of coral beads. "*We haven't spoken in twenty years, but I wanted to offer my sympathies on your cousin's murder. You hadn't heard? So sorry to be the bearer of bad news. By the way, Ellison found her.* Here." She held out a strand of pearls.

I fastened the pearls around my neck. "It's not outside the realm of possibility."

"Is this new?" She held up a diamond pendant.

"Anarchy bought it for me on our honeymoon."

"The man has good taste. Excellent taste. Why haven't I seen you wear it?"

I grimaced, slightly embarrassed. "The diamond is…big."

"The diamond is huge. I'd never take it off. Besides, if you wore this and told people who gave it to you, everyone would know Anarchy is more than just a cop."

I scowled at her before consciously smoothing my features. It wasn't Libba's fault that the people we knew considered a man's profession before forming an opinion. As for Anarchy, I was fairly certain he was more comfortable being 'just a cop' than heir to a California-size fortune.

"He wouldn't have bought it for you if he didn't want you to wear it."

"Fine." I took the pendant from her and fastened it around my neck.

"About that dress, are you sure you won't change? You have closets full of beautiful clothes."

"I'm wearing something comfortable."

Libba huffed her displeasure. Loudly.

"You sound like Mother."

"That's just mean. Take it back."

Not bloody likely. "Come on," I opened the door to the hallway. "I could use a drink." Or three. And for once, I didn't mean coffee.

Libba grinned at me, the comparison to Mother forgiven thanks to the offer of chilled vodka. "You're speaking my language."

"I'll ask Aggie to make a pitcher. I'm sure Kay will need one, too."

CHAPTER FOUR

"Do you think Kay is coming?" Libba, who sat on the settee in my living room, glanced at her watch, then swirled the liquor in her glass.

"It's five-forty." Well within the window to avoid being rude. Still, it was odd. The Kay I remembered from our youth was never late.

"I wonder if she found out about Althea." Libba didn't sound terribly curious. She sounded bored. She'd been by my side for too many bodies. Murder no longer horrified her. "She might be upset."

"Might be? Althea was her only remaining family on her mother's side."

"Althea was Althea. Unkind. Mean-spirited. Sharp-tongued."

I couldn't argue that. Not when I agreed with every adjective. Rather than speak ill of the dead, I changed the subject. "Where's Charlie? I thought he was joining us."

"He has a patient in the hospital who has him worried. He stayed late to keep an eye on him." Charlie Ardmore, my next-door neighbor and Libba's boyfriend, was a cardiologist at St.

Mark's Hospital. "Say, that reminds me. How closely do you look at your club bill?"

"What does my club bill have to do with Charlie working late?" I held up my hands. "You know what? Never mind. I don't look closely. I hardly have time to look at the total."

"You don't review the chits and tally them?"

I sent an are-you-kidding glare her way. "They sent the June bill in a manilla envelope." A bulging manilla envelope. I'd given the contents no more than a cursory glance. The kids had ordered drinks and snacks and lunches, plus there were charges for tennis and golf lessons, swim team fees, the cocktails Anarchy and I drank, dinners, bottles of wine, and the occasional charge for a new box of golf balls or having a racket restrung. "If I went through every chit, I'd be busy the whole month of July. Why do you ask?"

"I got charged for a new putter. One I didn't buy."

"Did you call the bookkeeper?"

"I did, and she apologized and took it off my bill. But it made me wonder what other mistakes they might make. I can't help but—"

Ding, dong.

"Finally." Libba drew out the word as if we'd been waiting for hours.

I stood. "I'll get it."

Libba stretched out her perfectly tanned legs and lazily lifted her glass.

The dogs met me at the front door. Their tails wagged in perfect sync, and they bounced with excitement.

"Behave yourselves," I told them.

They grinned as if I'd said something amusing.

With a sigh, I opened the door and watched Max bury his nose in Kay's crotch.

Her eyes widened. "Well, hello there. Usually, I make a man buy me dinner first."

"So sorry, Kay." I grabbed Max's collar and dragged him away, which allowed Finn an opportunity to sniff Kay's bits. "Bad dog."

Finn's stubby tail wagged faster

"Aggie?" My cry was slightly desperate.

She appeared at the kitchen door. "Max. Finn. Come. Now."

They immediately lost interest in Kay and trotted toward the kitchen.

"I am so, so sorry about that."

"Don't be silly. Do you remember my parents' Labrador?"

"Buster?"

"He spent half his life sniffing people's nether regions. It drove Mother mad, but neither she nor the trainer Daddy hired could break him of the habit."

"I'd forgotten." I ushered her into the foyer. "We're in the living room. May I get you a drink?"

"Of course." She smiled at me, and I realized she was entirely too upbeat for a woman who'd just lost a family member. No one had told her about Althea.

"Libba and I are drinking martinis, but I have most anything you'd like."

"A martini sounds marvelous." She followed me into the living room and smiled at Libba. "Don't you look chic?"

Libba smirked at me. "You as well."

Kay wore the same flowy black silk blouse and pants she'd worn to lunch, but she'd replaced the scarf with a king's ransom of gold chains.

"I told Ellison she needed to up her game. But did she listen?" Libba pointed at my Lilly shift. "She did not. Humans are the only species where females compete to find a mate. Every other species, it's the male that puts forth the effort. Male peacocks with their bright tail feathers. Cardinals with their red feathers. Lions with their manes. Females sit back and pick the best mate. But not humans. Nope. Women spend hours on their make-up and hair and clothing. We wear high heels and seamed stockings. We attract the males."

"What does that have to do with my Lilly dress?" I handed Kay a very full martini glass.

"Here's the thing. Once a woman has a man, she stops trying so hard. Her roots show. Her mascara, if she even bothers with mascara, smudges. And the sexy dresses that caught his attention give way to floral shifts."

"Are you saying I've given up?"

"I'm saying that dress—" she wagged her finger at my blameless shift "—doesn't show much effort. It's frumpy."

I gasped as if she'd stabbed me.

Kay, who'd been following our exchange, smiled so brightly it hurt to look at her. "I love Ellison's dress. It's quintessentially American, and I love American fashion. Also, it's colorful. Perfect for an artist. This spring, I spent and few weeks in Palm Beach and I met Suzie Zuzek. She's utterly delightful."

Libba frowned. "Who's Suzie Zuzek?"

"She designs the prints for Lilly, and she's a genius. If I'm not mistaken, that print is called 'flora.'"

I smirked at Libba, then waved Kay toward a wingback chair. "Please, sit."

Kay perched and sipped and glanced around my living room. "Your home is as lovely as ever."

"Thank you," I replied.

"When do I get to meet the man who beat out Hunter for your affections?"

Oh, dear. "He's investigating a murder."

Libba snorted into her martini.

Kay's brows lifted.

I drank. Deeply. "About that…"

"Did you know that Ellison finds bodies?" Libba didn't wait for a response. "She's found them in swimming pools and haunted houses and under the bleachers at Grace's high school."

Kay stared at me like I'd grown an extra head.

"I'm afraid it's true." I swallowed a lump. "In fact, I found a body today."

"Oh, Ellison." Kay leaned toward me, reaching out to grab my hand and give it a squeeze. "How awful for you."

"Kay—" I offered her an apologetic smile "—I found Althea."

The sympathetic expression fell off Kay's face, splashing into her chilled vodka. "Ellison, that's not funny."

"Not remotely," I agreed.

She put her glass on the coffee table and stared at me. Interminable seconds passed as she studied my serious expression. "You're not joking?"

"No." Regret colored my voice.

"When? How?"

"I found her in the ladies' lounge after our luncheon. She was murdered."

Kay turned pale beneath her weekends-in-the-Hamptons tan. "Murdered?"

"Yes."

"How?"

"The police are investigating." Anarchy wouldn't appreciate me sharing the details of a murder. I kept the knife in Althea's chest to myself.

"No." Kay shook her head. Denial was everyone's first reaction to murder. "That can't be right. Why would anyone kill Althea?"

Libba snorted again.

Kay flashed her a scowl. "I know she wasn't the easiest woman. She could be prickly. But murder?" She shook her head with more vigor bordering on belligerence. "There must be some mistake."

With impeccable timing (we needed a break in the tension), Aggie stepped into the living room. "I made a few canapés." She bent and put a platter on the coffee table. "We've got a cheese ball and crackers, stuffed olives, and tuna-fish salad on cucumber rounds."

"Thank you, Aggie. This looks delicious." And miraculous, given the brief window I'd given her to prepare.

"My pleasure." She retreated to the hallway.

Kay, who wore a slightly stunned expression, watched her go. A few seconds passed before she asked, "Who was that?"

"My housekeeper, Aggie DeLuca."

"Quite a kaftan."

"You should see the lime green one," said Libba.

Kay slumped in her chair and stared at me. "You truly found Althea?"

"I did. I'm sorry for your loss." I refrained from offering her an olive or urging her to try the cheese ball. "May I refresh your drink?"

"Please."

I refilled her glass.

Libba leaned forward, claimed a cucumber round, popped the hors d'oeuvre into her mouth, and moaned. "Oh my God, this is fabulous. Kay, you have to try one."

I gaped at her.

So did Kay.

"A little decorum?" I suggested.

"What? You didn't even like Althea." She pointed at me, then shifted her finger to Kay. "And you only tolerated her because she was your cousin. I've known you since we were old enough to toddle. If she wasn't blood, you'd have had nothing to do with her. Don't pretend regrets you don't feel."

I resisted the tuna fish salad on cucumber. "We can still mourn her death."

"I don't have much family left."

I winced on Kay's behalf. Family might be awful, but they were still family.

"Daddy was an only child, and Mother had one sibling. Althea was my only cousin. When Mother goes, it'll be just me."

"Sometimes the family we choose is better than the one we're born with. I can guarantee you that Ellison is closer to Karma than Marjorie."

Kay frowned. "Who's Karma?"

"Ellison's illegitimate half-sister." Libba held up her hand to stop Kay's questions. "It's a long story. I'll tell you later. And there's Beau."

"Beau?"

"The little boy from the across the street. Ellison and Anarchy are adopting him. Also, me. Ellison and I are closer than sisters. Her family is bigger than mere blood. It's built on shared laughter and tears, love and annoyance." She caught my stare and added, "Extreme annoyance." When Kay didn't respond, Libba continued. "A year ago, Ellison's family included a man who cheated on her, a teenage daughter with a burgeoning attitude problem, and parents who controlled her by withholding their approval. Now she has a man who adores her, Grace is a joy, Beau is a delight, and she stands up to Frances on the regular. Just because Althea's gone doesn't mean you'll be without a family."

I blinked back the prickle of tears.

"Or look at me," Libba continued. "A year ago, I was alone. Well, except for Ellison. Now I have Charlie and his two teenagers, both of whom resent the hell out of me."

I shifted on the settee. "They're mellowing."

Libba's mouth twisted in a wry grin. "I'm sure we'll be great friends by their thirties."

I ran my hand across my mouth to hide my smile. "What Libba forgot to say was that you have both of us."

"She's right." Libba nodded. "Ellison adopts willy-nilly, and I need a sister with actual style."

"One day in Lilly, and you act like I'm always frumpy."

Libba wrinkled her nose. "You can do better."

"By wearing black?"

"You did find a body."

My hands, laced loosely together in my lap, tightened into fists. Did she have to take us back there?

"I'll have to make arrangements," Kay murmured. "She and John were at each other's throats. If he's in charge of planning, he'll buy a pine box, toss her in a hole, and cover her with dirt."

"I can help," I offered.

Libba nodded with enthusiasm. "She planned Henry's funeral last summer, and it was a humdinger."

I scowled at my best friend.

"What?" She offered me a too sweet smile. "Not even Frances could find fault."

Mainly because Mother had a heavy hand in the planning.

"What do I do first?" asked Kay.

"There will be an autopsy, so it may be a few days. In the meantime, you could write her obituary. Unless you think John…"

"No. He wouldn't write anything kind." She stared at her lap for long seconds before lifting her head and catching my gaze. "Do you think he killed her?"

"I think Anarchy will question him. And you."

"Me?" she squeaked.

"Where did you go after the luncheon?" If she'd gone immediately home as she said, she was in the clear.

"I called home after I left you. A new nurse was there. They didn't need me. So, I went shopping on the Plaza."

"How long were you in the clubhouse after the party broke up?"

"Ten minutes. Fifteen at most."

I swallowed a sigh. "Did anyone see you? Did you talk to anyone?"

"No." Her answer was immediate.

"This is serious, Kay. You're sure you didn't see anyone?"

"You're scaring me."

"I want you to have an alibi."

"I'd like to have one, too. But I didn't speak to a single soul."

"Anarchy or Peters will ask you the same questions."

"Who's Peters?"

"Anarchy's partner," I replied.

"Imagine heavy brows and a droopy face, sort of like Abe Vigoda in *The Godfather*, except shorter, and with darker hair and a bad mustache." Libba let her surprisingly accurate description settle. "Then add Columbo's raincoat after he's slept in his car." That was charitable. Peters' raincoat looked like he'd wadded into a ball and used it as a pillow. "Also, he has the personality of a bear awakened from hibernation in mid-January."

"I'm a suspect?" Kay's cheeks paled, and her chin quivered.

"Only until they can determine you didn't do it," said Libba.

I shot her a look. "You're not a suspect. You're a person of interest. So is everyone else who was in the clubhouse when she died."

"Even you?"

"Even me," I lied. "Although, I was with Libba until I found Althea."

"You could have killed her, then called for help."

"Thanks, Libba. What's my motive?"

She frowned as if I'd ruined her fun. "You don't have one. Neither does Kay."

"Actually, I do."

We turned toward her. "With Althea gone, I'm the sole beneficiary of my grandparents' trust."

"How much?"

I was glad Libba was crass enough to ask.

"Millions."

Somehow, I maintained a neutral expression. Kay had no alibi and an excellent motive. The combination was not good. For her.

CHAPTER FIVE

"I t looks like a used tissue." Beau tilted his head and narrowed his eyes. "Or a small brain."

"The first pancake never turns out." I sprayed more Pam onto the skillet and turned up the heat. Then I poured more batter.

"Anarchy usually makes the pancakes."

"He's investigating a case and didn't came home till late. I let him sleep in."

"You found another body." Beau nodded sagely, as if finding a body was old hat, even to him.

"I did."

"Was it scary?" Did he imagine she stumbled across the killer, too?

"My heart rose in my chest."

Beau's eyes were the size of silver-dollar pancakes. "What did you do?"

"I closed the door, so I didn't contaminate the crime scene, then called for help."

He deflated. Obviously, he'd expected something more exciting. "But what if the murderer was still there?"

"He wasn't."

"But what if he was?" Beau insisted. It was sweet how he assumed the killer was a man. In my experience, women could be equally vicious.

"I would have run."

His forehead wrinkled.

"I mean it. If you're ever around someone who wants to hurt you—seriously hurt you—run. Proving you're brave won't help you if you're dead."

"Anarchy doesn't run."

"Anarchy is a grown man with a badge and a gun."

He nodded and pointed to the skillet where the pancake was smoking.

"Drat!" I reached for the skillet's handle.

"Wait!" Beau pointed to the oven mitt I'd left on the counter next to the stove.

"Thanks." I grabbed the mitt, picked up the blackened skillet, and scraped the burned pancake into the sink. "Third time's a charm."

His face puckered with doubt. "Maybe we should wait for Anarchy."

Undaunted, I pulled out a fresh skillet, sprayed the Pam, and poured more batter.

"Doesn't it have to heat up first?"

I frowned. "Does it?" I turned up the heat.

He nodded. "What do you do if you can't run?"

I hit people with skillets. In my hands, they were better used as weapons. "Often times, Anarchy saves me." On occasion, I saved him. "I try to avoid bad people. I know you and Grace are counting on me."

He nodded.

"I need more coffee." I crossed to Mr. Coffee and refilled my mug.

"I think the pancake needs to be flipped."

I abandoned my coffee, hurried back to the stove, and found a pancake that was neither burnt nor misshapen. In short, a miracle. Quickly, I grabbed the spatula. Anarchy did a fancy flick of his wrist when he flipped pancakes. I knew better. I eased the spatula under the cake and turned it. The dratted thing landed on the edge of the skillet. Half in. Half out. One hundred percent ruined. I swallowed a string of expletives.

"You're really bad at this."

I couldn't argue. "I'm sorry."

"It's just pancakes. Besides, you're good at other stuff. Painting. Reading stories. Picking me up on time." That last one was heartbreaking. Beau's first family had regularly forgotten him.

"Problem?" Anarchy stood in the entrance to the kitchen wearing faded jeans and a tee-shirt that showed off the broad expanse of his chest. His hair was still sleep mussed and his grin was slow.

Relief flooded my chest. "See, Beau? Like I told you, he's always rescuing me." I smiled at my husband. "I'm having a slight issue with the pancakes."

He joined me at the stove and stared into the batter bowl. "Why is it so lumpy?"

"I followed the directions." Ish.

He brushed a kiss just behind my ear. "Why don't I start fresh?"

"But—"

"We're almost out of coffee."

My head whipped around to check the level in Mr. Coffee's pot. Anarchy was right. There was less than a quarter of a pot left. I poured him a mug, then busied myself refilling Mr. Coffee's reservoir.

Anarchy rinsed the mixing bowl, taking long seconds to stare at the burned skillet I'd left in the bottom of the sink. Finally, he shook his head and tore his gaze away. "Beau, check the fridge. I think we have blueberries."

Now he was just showing off.

"Grab the milk and eggs, too."

Beau carried everything Anarchy requested to the counter, then asked, "What time did you get home last night?"

Anarchy cracked an egg into the bowl. "After eleven. We need butter, too."

Beau turned toward the fridge, and I gave Anarchy a look. He'd returned at one. I'd glanced at the clock when he slid into bed.

Beau lined the butter dish up next to the milk. "Did you catch the killer?"

"Not yet."

"Do you think it's someone who belongs to the club?"

"Are you worried about the killer?" asked Anarchy.

Beau shifted his gaze to me, then ducked his head.

"You don't need to worry about me, Beau. People who commit murder have a motive."

"Like what?" he asked.

Anarchy and I exchanged a quick glance, then I opened the coffee can and measured a scoop. "Money or jealousy or to protect their reputations."

"I bet lots of people are jealous of you."

"It's more like a husband or wife who gets jealous."

Beau's expression cleared, and he nodded sagely. "Cheaters."

Anarchy and I exchanged another glance. Given Beau's family history, how should we reply?

"There are also gang-related murders." Anarchy dumped a carefully measured cup of Bisquik into the bowl, then began whisking.

"Perhaps we could find a less ghoulish subject," I suggested. "Beau, are you excited for camp?" I'd spent the past week buying everything on the list while Aggie sewed nametags into all of Beau's clothes. We planned on putting him on a plane for Minnesota tomorrow morning.

"I guess." He spoke with all the enthusiasm of a convicted killer walking toward the gallows.

"You can always come home." We'd alerted the camp to Beau's situation, and they'd monitor him closely.

"They have catamarans. For sailing." He nodded as if he'd made an important decision. "Sailing is awesome."

What would Mother say if we left town the day after Christmas? We could rent a place in Key West or go farther south to Lyford Cay. We could charter a sailboat. I took a contemplative sip of coffee. Could Anarchy get time off work? I'd have to discuss it with him.

"Hey, Beau, would you finish mixing the batter while I prep the pan?" Anarchy held out the batter bowl. When Beau took it, Anarchy put the skillet (the last clean skillet we owned) on the stove, turned on the heat, then dropped a pat of butter onto its surface.

"Not Pam?"

"I prefer butter. What are you doing today?"

"The only thing on my calendar is the Wade wedding, and that's not till eight."

He grimaced.

"You forgot?"

He nodded. He had a case. He forgot most everything when he was trying to catch a killer. "Can you come to the station?"

"Official questions?"

He nodded again. "Also, we'd like you to look at something we booked into evidence. Beau, let's see that batter." He peered into the bowl. "Looks perfect. Why don't you add some blueberries?"

"How many?"

"As many as you'd like."

Beau dumped the container, then gave the batter another stir before giving the bowl to Anarchy.

Anarchy poured the first pancake onto the skillet and watched its surface. "See those bubbles?" he asked.

I eyed the pancake. "Yes."

"When they pop, it's ready to flip."

Anarchy's first pancake was perfect. So was the second. And the third. The fourth did the impossible—it lured Grace out of bed before nine on a Saturday.

"Pancakes?" Anarchy asked her.

"Please."

He made a stack for Grace, who claimed the stool next to Beau's at the kitchen island.

She moaned her approval, and Anarchy winked at me. "This one's yours." He waved his spatula over yet another perfect pancake.

I topped off our coffee mugs, then pushed Mr. Coffee's buttons to start a fresh pot.

A moment later, Anarchy handed me my plate. "Nice necklace."

My free hand rose to my throat.

"It looks good on you."

"It would look good on anyone. It's gorgeous."

"It looks especially good on you."

Grace looked up from her pancakes. "You don't usually wear diamonds to breakfast."

"The clasp is stuck. I wore it to bed."

"I'll fix it before I go to the station." He poured more batter onto the skillet. "Anyone want seconds?"

"That one is for you," Beau replied.

We were together. Happy and whole. So why did the thought of going to the station niggle at me? I smiled brightly at my family and ate pancakes that felt like lead in my stomach.

∼

Anarchy escorted me into the station, and I wrinkled my nose at the overwhelming odor of stale cigarette smoke, burned coffee, and desperation. "This way." His hand pressed against the small of my back as he guided me to his desk and pulled out a chair.

I sat, crossing my ankles, and lacing hands in my lap.

His lips quirked as if he knew that I defaulted to Mother's rules on deportment when I was nervous. And I was nervous. Even though it was Saturday, the squad room was busy, and I felt the other officer's eyes on me.

I was Anarchy's snooty wife. The one who didn't host back-yard barbeques. The one who didn't know the other detectives' wives or girlfriends. The one who didn't fit in.

"Are you okay?" he asked.

I smiled brightly and lied. "Fine."

"I'll be back in a few minutes. Do you need coffee?"

I wasn't desperate enough for police coffee. "No, thank you."

He nodded briefly. "Five minutes. No more."

He left me to study the surface of his desk. It held a type-writer, a picture from our wedding day, a picture of Grace and Beau, a chipped coffee cup filled with pens and pencils, and a wire bin jammed full of loose papers.

The back of my neck prickled, and I turned to find Peters scowling at me. "Good morning," I ventured.

"You think you can make it more than a week without finding a body?" he snarled.

My hackles rose, and a sharp retort rose to my lips. Then I remembered my call to Anarchy had ruined Peters' weekend. "I'll try," I said sincerely. "I'm sorry if Althea's murder upset your plans."

His eyes narrowed, and he tilted his head, searching for sarcasm or attitude. Finding none, he grunted at me. "Coffee?"

"No, thank you."

"You don't like our coffee?" He'd thrown down a gauntlet.

One I refused to pick up. I'd had police coffee and was willing to bet the glass coffee pot hadn't been washed since early 1974. "I woke up early, and I've already had four cups." Which was nothing. Hardly a cup per hour. But it sounded better than telling him the station's coffee tasted worse than battery acid. Not that I'd tasted battery acid, but I had an imagination.

He grunted again. A suspicious grunt this time. "Where's Jones?"

"Anarchy is fetching something from the evidence locker."

"The scarf. It was under the body. Maybe you can identify it."

I thought back to Althea's clothing at the luncheon. She'd worn a powder blue suit with a white silk blouse. I didn't remember a scarf. "I'll try."

The door at the far end of the room opened, and I swallowed a sigh of relief. Anarchy had returned. He held a manilla envelope. When he reached his desk, he poured the envelope's contents onto his desk.

My breath caught, and I gripped the arms of my chair.

"You recognize it?" he asked.

I stared at the black, white, and crimson scarf. "You found that under Althea's body?"

Anarchy's brows lifted as he shifted his gaze to Peters.

Peters shrugged. "I told her."

"Do you recognize it?" Anarchy asked again.

I swallowed a sigh and stared at the length of silk. Blood had discolored much of the white, leaving it a rusty brown.

"Ellison?"

Finding bodies was terrible. Fingering friends as potential suspects was worse. "Kay Morrison wore it to lunch."

CHAPTER SIX

The church wasn't air-conditioned. Was. Not. Air-conditioned. A trickle of perspiration tickled the valley between my breasts.

"You didn't know?" asked Anarchy.

"I did not." Most of the weddings I attended were at blessedly cool Episcopalian or Presbyterian churches. This church, with its soaring ceiling, gothic architecture, stunning stained-glass windows, and five altars, was not. Five altars. If Mother were here, she'd grumble about why any church needed five altars. And, given that I was melting faster than the wicked witch in *The Wizard of Oz,* I wouldn't argue with her. Fewer altars. More AC. Please.

Anarchy mopped his brow. In his tux, he had it worse than I did. At least my dress was a light chiffon and backless. "Not the place for a summer wedding."

"They assumed it would be cooler this late in the evening?" Proof that assuming made an ass of you and me. Or a puddle. In this case, assuming made a sweaty puddle.

It didn't help that the large church was packed.

"Remind me how we know these people," Anarchy

whispered.

"I'm not sure you've met them." We sat on the bride's side of the aisle. "Linda and Chuck Wade. It's their daughter, Lindsay, getting married."

The woman on the other side of Anarchy leaned into our conversation. "Chuck's nickname in college was 'Cash.' He played wide receiver, and if he caught the ball, he took it to the bank."

"You went to college with him?" I asked.

"Before that. We went to grade school together. I'm wondering how the young man Lindsay's marrying ever got his blessing."

I didn't know the woman from Adam, but that kind of speculation, especially at the actual wedding, was beyond rude. It was the prickly heat that made me say, "You mean everyone's wondering if she's pregnant?"

Her lips curled in a tight smile. "Tomato, tomahto."

"Linda has been planning this for a year."

"Pfft." She sat back in the pew and side-eyed me, disappointed with my reluctance to let facts get in the way of juicy gossip.

I waved the program in front of my face, hoping for a breath of air. "This is dreadful. Hopefully, the minister will be quick."

"The priest, not the minister." The woman gave a small chuckle. "Don't go to many Catholic weddings, do you?"

"No."

"They're never quick."

I gave her a tight smile, then watched as the groom and his groomsmen filled in, each one looking increasingly miserable. "Is it me, or does the groom look a bit green around the gills?"

Anarchy studied the young man for a minute. "I wonder if he's sick."

"Maybe he's nervous," I ventured.

"Ha!" Our third wheel dismissed those theories with a decisive shake of her head. "The boys went out after the rehearsal dinner. He's hungover."

"It's eight o'clock at night.",

"According to my daughter, she's one of Lindsay's brides-maids, they stayed out till six this morning."

"I didn't know there were bars open that late."

Anarchy patted my hand.

The music started, and we watched as Linda and the groom's mother were escorted to their seats.

The assembly stood and turned.

Lindsay wore a silk organza gown. The dress's neckline featured a deep vee edge with an enormous ruffle. Her hair was swept into a Gibson girl chignon. She looked lovely.

Chuck tucked her hand farther into the crook of his arm, and, together, they walked down the aisle.

The priest, a portly man with red cheeks and fly-away hair, met them at the front of the church. "Who gives this woman's hand in marriage?"

"Her mother and I." With a scowl, Chuck transferred Lind-say's delicate fingers from his arm to the groom's. Then, he joined Linda in the first pew. The stiff set of his shoulders suggested ire. Annoyance that his future son-in-law's cheeks were the color of boiled asparagus? Although, I imagined everyone in the church was cranky. Prickly heat and sweating through your tux or gown will do that to people.

Next to me, Anarchy pulled out a handkerchief and dabbed at his temples.

"Never again," I whispered. "I promise."

"I'll hold you to that," he whispered back.

The priest, who was looking ruddier with each passing second, held out his hands. "Let us pray."

The groom, whose name was Billy, was still the color of overcooked vegetables. He stood at the front of the church and swayed as if there was a stiff wind.

"Uh-oh," Anarchy murmured.

The young man held up his hand, as if he needed a moment. "Sorry!" He turned away from Lindsay and ran.

For a brief second no one moved. Everyone too shocked to react.

Chuck recovered first. He burst out of his pew and gave chase. The father-of-the-bride, who'd played football in college and stayed fit despite the passage of years, was the faster man. And for an instant, I thought he might tackle the groom.

The church was enormous, filled with five altars and hundreds of sweating people, but you could have heard a pin drop.

"You no-good bastard. No one leaves my daughter on the altar." Chuck's words boomed through the silent church.

Billy groaned, then escaped through a side door. Chuck followed.

I shifted my gaze from the door Chuck had left open to the altar where Lindsay pressed her hand to her mouth. The poor girl's shoulders shook, and her eyes watered. I tilted my head. Was she crying or laughing? Not that I'd blame her for either. I hoped she was laughing. Sometimes, when life slapped you across the face, a good bout of laughter took away the sting.

Linda had disappeared from the front pew. I half-stood, searching for my friend. She hadn't disappeared. She was bent over with her head between her knees.

The congregation remained deadly quiet, no one was quite sure of the correct response to a runaway groom or how to comfort a bride who stood alone on the altar.

Gak!

The sound came from the open doorway. Someone was retching. Violently. My stomach twisted in sympathy. I opened my eyes wide and took shallow breaths. I would not be sick. I would not be sick. Also, there was almost nothing I wouldn't do for a cool glass of water.

"You're pathetic." Chuck's voice carried, and standing alone in front of her friends and family, Lindsay winced. If she did end up getting married, holidays were going to be awkward.

"The best man doesn't look so good." Anarchy nodded toward a young man with light brown hair.

A sheen of sweat covered his face, and his skin looked wan beneath his tan. As I watched, his eyes rolled back in his head, and he collapsed onto the marble stairs. Fortunately, his head landed on the plush carpet-runner that led to the altar.

The congregation, at least those who weren't trying to peer into the room where Chuck muttered not-suitable-for-church curses as his maybe-future son-in-law tried to relocate his innards, gasped.

The priest's mouth opened and shut, but no words came out.

An ugly, small, overheated part of me wanted to stand up and say that none of this would have happened if they'd installed air-conditioning. I gripped the edge of the pew and kept my seat.

It was Lindsay who faced the congregation and asked, "Can we get a doctor up here, please?" Her voice was strong and steady. The girl had grit.

Several men hurried to the front of the church. We sat close enough to hear their diagnosis—dehydration and heat exhaustion. They conscripted the other groomsmen and carried the unconscious man away, presumably to a smaller room with a window unit. It was then that I realized the sound of vomiting had ended.

Given that we were in church, I said a silent prayer of thanks.

"Find me a damned towel, then get your worthless ass out there and marry my daughter." Chuck needed a towel. Had the groom thrown up on him?

Oh, dear Lord.

I didn't envy Lindsay during the holidays. Not one bit.

"This is one we won't forget," I muttered.

"Amen, sister," said the woman on Anarchy's other side.

~

THEY MARRIED. LINDSAY WADE TOOK BILLY HALPERN TO BE her wedded husband as steam rose from her father's ears. When it was over (Anarchy's neighbor was right—the service was not quick), we hurried to the car and I fiddled with the vents, not caring what the airflow did to my hair. "Should we go home and change?" Our clothes were damp with sweat.

"I only have one tuxedo." Meaning he didn't have a change of clothes. He rubbed his hand across his chin. "Unless you want to skip the reception."

I heard the hopeful note in his voice and hated to disappoint him. "We have to go."

"You're certain?"

"After that service? I can't abandon Linda."

He chuckled. Anarchy wasn't usually the type to laugh at other's misfortune, but pack hundreds of people into a stifling church, then hit them with more drama than a soap opera, and even my perfect husband turned a little dark. "It's too bad no one thought to get the rings from the best man before they took him to the hospital."

Linda and Chuck had practically thrown their rings at the priest when they realized there was another hiccup.

"I'm sure the reception will be lovely." Linda had put so much time and effort into its planning.

"If the air-conditioning is out, we're leaving."

I lowered the visor, checked my makeup in the mirror, and used the pads of my thumbs to erase my smudged mascara. "Don't even joke."

"I'm not joking."

Entering the club felt like walking into an icebox. I breathed a happy sigh and grabbed a highball garnished with lemon from a passing waiter. "What am I drinking?" As long as it was cold, I didn't particularly care.

"Vodka and lemonade with a splash of seltzer."

I handed my glass to Anarchy and took another. "Cheers."

"I shouldn't drink."

"After what we just endured?"

"Just one."

We clinked glasses, then moved past the club's foyer.

"The flowers are lovely." Arrangements of peach roses, white hydrangea, and delphinium graced each table. The buffet table featured an enormous vase carved from ice. It too was filled with flowers.

"Are Libba and Charlie here?"

"No. But Liz and Perry will be here. And Jinx and George. Also—"

"Ellison!" Lois surged forward and kissed the air next to my cheek. "I heard you found Althea's body. How dreadful for you! For Althea, too! But she's gone, and you're the one who'll have nightmares about her murder. I heard she was strangled." Her fingers rose to her own throat. "To think, a killer somehow snuck onto club property. It's terrifying." She glanced around, taking stock of who stood nearby. Then, she lowered her voice. "Did you make it through the whole service? Skip made me leave when they couldn't find the rings. That poor girl. Can you imagine so many things going wrong?" She thrust her hand toward Anarchy. "You probably don't remember me, but we met at your wedding. I'm Lois Wortham."

"You were having lunch with Ellison before Althea Dodson was killed. I've been trying to get in touch with you."

"Have you? I've been dreadfully busy. Besides, I don't know a thing. When we left the table, I went home. End of story."

Something flickered in Anarchy's eyes.

"Did you see anyone in the parking lot when you were leaving?"

Her gaze shifted to the left, catching on the ice sculpture. "Honestly? I can't remember." She shrugged as if her faulty memory ended the discussion. "Have you ever been hotter in your life?"

I'd melted on tennis courts and golf courses. I'd sweated through my clothes watching Grace play field hockey on an unseasonably hot spring day. Yes, I'd been hotter. "Never inside."

"Poor Linda. She put so much into planning this, and then…" Lois shook her head.

"The reception is gorgeous."

"It is." Lois nodded with enthusiasm. "I should find Skip. He hates it when I disappear."

She left us, and I turned to my husband. "She lied?"

"She lied," he confirmed.

"Thank you for not making an issue of it here." I wish my friends realized how lying made them look guilty. After I'd identified Kay's scarf, Anarchy went to her mother's house. She admitted the scarf was hers but claimed she'd misplaced it at the club.

When he'd asked her why she didn't look for it, she'd told him it was Vera, not Hermès.

Now Kay was due at the station first thing Monday morning. I couldn't help but wonder if Lois might not come right after her.

"No more shop talk." Anarchy took my elbow and guided me to the bar where he ordered me another vodka-lemonade spritz. We mingled. We told Lindsay how beautiful she looked. We endured what seemed like a hundred questions about Althea's death.

Yes, I'd found her.

No, Anarchy couldn't comment.

No, we didn't know when the police tape would be removed.

Yes, we understood it was a terrible inconvenience.

"Ellison, thank heavens I found you." Leslie Vance's hand clamped onto my arm, then she turned to Anarchy. "You're the cop, right?"

"Homicide detective," I replied. I didn't care for Leslie. And as far as I knew, the feeling was mutual. We were cordial. Nothing more.

"I need you." She tugged on my arm. "I need you both."

"What's wrong?" Had she found a body?

"There's a prostitute in the ladies' lounge." Leslie was given to dramatics. Her son had a hang nail. Infection! Amputation! Or at least a trip to the emergency room. A call from the principal's office once sent her into a tailspin. Her son's permanent record was ruined. Ruined. He'd never get into Harvard. It wasn't just his permanent record that was ruined, it was his whole life. The teacher who sent him deserved to be fired. Immediately.

"Seems an odd place for a prostitute," Anarchy remarked, not quite hiding the quirk at the corner of his lips.

Leslie frowned at him. "What do you mean?"

"Not many potential clients in the ladies' lounge."

"Please." She tugged on my arm again. Harder this time. "Go look."

"Fine."

Leslie turned her attention to Anarchy. "You should go with her."

"I'll lurk in the hall."

I stepped into the lounge and spotted the woman immediately. She stood in front of the bank of mirrors at the back of the lounge. Her dress was short. And tight. And shiny. Her make-up —especially her eye make-up—was heavy handed. Her straight hair hung all the way to her bottom. If she were Lindsay's age and had a twenty-three-year-old body, she might have pulled it off. But she was older. Deep lines cut into the skin around her mouth and eyes, and she carried too many extra pounds to wear short or tight or shiny.

I touched up my lipstick and smiled at her in the mirror. "It's a lovely party."

"I hope they're happy together." Her consonants and vowels

slurred together. "I'm so glad that Billy is feeling bitter. Butter." She shook her head. "Batter."

"Better?"

"That's it. He had a hangover, and it was hot in the church. But he's better now."

"How do you know Billy?"

"I'm his aunt."

"My congratulations to Billy and your family. Lindsay's a wonderful girl." I nodded at her reflection.

"I'm Dawn."

"Ellison. It was a pleasure meeting you."

When I emerged, Leslie pounced on me. "Well?"

"She's the groom's aunt."

Her eyes widened to a comical size. "You're kidding."

"I am not."

"I wonder if Chuck met her before he gave his blessing."

"I don't imagine we'll ever know." I stepped away from her and glanced at my watch. "I bet they're almost ready to cut the cake."

"I love cake." Anarchy claimed my hand and led me away from the lounge.

"Ellison." Whoever called my name was behind us.

I pasted on a smile and turned. "Louise, how nice to see you. Have you met my husband?" Louise was one of Mother's friends. Not one of her close friends—Louise was too given to idle gossip—more of a sub-for-bridge friend. "Anarchy, this is Louise Danner."

"Pleased to meet you." He held out his hand.

"You're the detective?"

Anarchy offered her a charming smile as they shook. "Yes, ma'am."

"I know who murdered Althea Dodson."

"Oh?"

"Tish Hart killed her."

I blinked back my surprise. "What makes you say that?"

"Althea was making it impossible to ignore Robert's wandering...eye." Louise expected a gasp or a demand for more information. Then she'd smile coyly and declare she wasn't a gossip.

I held my tongue, hoping silence would keep Louise talking.

"You're speechless."

I shrugged. "Not really. I just assumed you'd have more to say."

"I'm not a gossip."

"Of course not, but there must be a reason you think Tish is a killer." I smiled sweetly. "I know you'd hate to commit slander."

Louise's cheeks darkened. "I saw Tish leaving the ladies lounge."

"Yesterday?"

"Yes, yesterday," she snapped. "I forgot we'd canceled bridge. When no one showed up, I called Beth Coombs to find out where everyone was. When I came out of the phone booth, I saw Tish leaving the ladies' lounge."

"And you think Tish killed Althea because..."

"Tish doesn't want a divorce. Now that Althea's dead, Tish can go back to ignoring Robert's infidelity."

"It's an interesting theory," said Anarchy. "We'll be questioning Mrs. Hart."

Louise looked pleased. No, smug.

"Of course, now that we know you were at the club near the time of the murder, we'll have to question you as well."

The smirk ran away from her face.

"If you'll excuse us—" Anarchy reclaimed my hand "—we're in search of cake."

"Did you know about Tish?" I whispered as we walked away from a gaping Louise.

Anarchy's jaw firmed. "I did not."

CHAPTER SEVEN

We checked Beau's duffel bag to Minneapolis, leaving him with a backpack filled with word-search books and comics. Then, we walked him to his gate.

The quickness in his steps brought a smile to my face. He was excited to go. Sending him to camp was the right decision.

When we arrived at the gate, I nodded to the other parents putting their darlings on the plane. A senior counselor would meet the boys at the airport in Minneapolis, load them onto the camp bus, and drive them two hours north.

Beau's camp was on a lake. He could swim and kayak and sail the camp's small catamarans. He could hike and go horse-back riding. He could play tennis or baseball. There would be campfires and songs and s'mores. He'd have a marvelous time.

I gave him a tight hug as the plane began boarding. "You can call us."

"I know."

I smoothed his blond hair. "You're going to have loads of fun."

"I know." He spoke in the long-suffering tone of children whose parents pointed out the obvious.

I hid my smile against the top of his head. "I'll miss you."

"I'll miss you, too."

My throat tightened, and I blinked back the sudden wetness in my eyes.

"Here." Anarchy held out a box of Milk Duds, Beau's favorite candy. "Eat them on the plane. You're not supposed to take candy to camp."

Best not mention the three boxes I'd tucked into Beau's duffel. Sneaking candy into camp was a time-honored tradition.

I gave Beau one last squeezy hug, then watched as he passed through the door to the jetway. I pressed my hand to my heart and blinked back a second round of tears.

"You, okay?" Anarchy wrapped an arm around my shoulders and pulled me against his side.

I sniffled. "I'm fine. You?"

"Fine." I didn't miss the extra rumble in his voice.

We were walking toward the exit when I spotted Lindsay.

She saw me, too.

We smiled at each other and stopped to speak.

I gave her a quick, no-wrinkle hug. "You're married now."

She gave an enthusiastic nod. "I am! I'm so glad the wedding's over. Mom stressed over every detail while Daddy grumbled over every penny she spent. There was a dark cloud hanging over the house. Now they can go back to their happy-go-lucky selves."

I wasn't sure anyone had ever described Chuck Wade as happy-go-lucky.

"It was a beautiful reception, and you were a beautiful bride."

Lindsay's eyes crinkled with amusement. "Not going to comment on the actual wedding?"

Definitely not. "How's the best man?"

"The hospital kept him overnight. He's terribly embarrassed." She glanced over her shoulder as if she were looking for her new husband. "At least he didn't throw up on Daddy's shoes."

"There's that. Where are you going for your honeymoon?"

"My grandparents' cabin in Wisconsin. It's one of my favorite places on earth. So peaceful. And after the past month or two, I need some peace."

Billy staggered through the glass doors carrying what looked like two heavy carry-ons. He blinked when he saw us, and I could see the cogs in his brain spinning, trying desperately to come up with our names. I took pity on him.

"Billy, nice to see you again. Ellison and Anarchy Jones. I'm sure you talked to so many people last night that everyone's names have run together.

He offered me a grateful smile. "A pleasure to see you, too." He dropped the heavy bags and held out his hand to Anarchy. "Leaving for vacation?"

Shaking Billy's hand, Anarchy replied, "We dropped our son off for camp."

Billy reclaimed the carry-ons. "Sweetheart, we need to find our gate, the plane starts boarding in a few minutes."

"We should go," said Lindsay. "I'm so glad you were able to help us celebrate."

"Us too. Have a wonderful time in Wisconsin."

They hurried away.

"Go ahead and say it," said Anarchy.

"I don't know what you mean," I replied airily.

His grinned at me and called my bluff, "Yes, you do."

"Fine," I huffed. "Three years. Tops."

"Ouch. They seem so in love."

"He embarrassed her in front of everyone she holds dear, I'd say two years, but Lindsay's the stubborn type. She'll give it her all and then some just to prove everyone wrong. By three years, she'll realize being happy is better than being right. Also, she's taking him on a honeymoon, not the other way round."

"You paid for things in Italy."

"I might have bought the occasional dinner, but you bought the plane tickets and took care of the hotels." Anarchy had spent a small fortune making sure I had the honeymoon of my dreams. I touched the diamond pendant he'd given me.

He took my hand, and we stepped outside into morning's building heat.

"Are you working this afternoon?" I asked. He'd already taken a great deal of time away from the investigation. Enough to make Peters extremely grouchy.

"I am. What are you doing?"

"I thought I might go to the pool."

He cocked a brow as he opened the car's passenger-side door. "If you hear anything…"

"Of course, I'll tell you. But last night's wedding may eclipse Althea's murder."

Anarchy slipped behind the wheel, slid the key into the ignition, and turned on the engine.

I immediately adjusted the vents.

"Promise me something?"

"Anything."

"Don't wander around the club by yourself."

Two hours later, I was at the pool, stretched on a lounge chair. My friend Jinx occupied the chaise next to mine. With swim season over and camp and vacation seasons begun, the pool deck was quiet. A handful of teenage girls in tiny bikinis clustered near the diving well, several older women sunned themselves as they flipped through the latest issue of *Vogue* or *The Independent*, and by the baby pool, mothers with young children splashed in the shallow water.

"Are you and Anarchy traveling this summer?" asked Jinx.

"Anarchy used his vacation time for our honeymoon. What about you?"

"Colorado for the month of August." Jinx and her husband owned a second home in Vail. "You should come out for a long weekend."

"We'd love that."

"Then we'll get it on the calendar."

I felt her appraising gaze from behind her dark sunglasses. "Yes?"

"Murder or wedding?" she asked.

"Wedding."

"I don't even know where to begin. Did you see the expression on Chuck's face when he was chasing the groom? The man was positively murderous."

"Quite memorable."

"I'm scarred." Jinx pressed a hand to her tanned chest. "Scarred. I'll never attend another wedding at that church again."

Here, beneath the unrelenting rays of the afternoon sun, I was cooler than I'd been last night. "Certainly not in the summertime. I never dreamed they'd be without air-conditioning."

"Me either."

"The reception was lovely." We needed to say something positive. Or at least I did.

"It should have been. They spent thirty-thousand dollars."

If it were anyone but Jinx, I'd dismiss the ridiculous number. But Jinx got her facts straight. I turned in my chair and stared at her. "How?" According to the evening news, the average American made just over seventy-five hundred a year. Spending thirty thousand on a wedding was excessive. Showy. Pretentious. "What did they spend it on?"

"They served tenderloin and lobster and caviar. They flew in the band from Chicago. The flowers. The dress. Top-shelf liquor. Veuve Champagne. It all adds up."

"But thirty-thousand dollars?" Could they even afford that?

Chuck was a highly successful estate attorney, but that amount was exorbitant. "No wonder they went through with the wedding."

"Did you meet the groom's family?"

"I did,"

"The groom's father owns a plumbing company."

"Honorable, honest work."

"If you don't mind fiddling with other people's toilets. Did you meet the aunt?"

"I did."

"Then there's nothing left to say. Murder?"

"What about it?"

"Stabbed or strangled? I've heard both."

"Active investigation."

"I'm betting stabbed with lots of blood. They're talking about replacing the carpet. If she'd been strangled, they'd just have it cleaned."

"I can't fault your logic." It was as close to a confirmation as I'd come.

"Why Althea?" Jinx shook the Styrofoam cup that held her iced tea. "I assume John is a suspect."

I gave her a flat look.

"Of course he's a suspect. Has Anarchy talked to him yet?"

"I honestly don't know." But I'd find out. John had a better motive than Tish.

"Then there's Kay Morrison." Jinx lowered her sunglasses and stared at me over the rims. "She was at the club. And with Althea gone, she'll get all of her grandparents' trust."

"How do you know that?"

"I have my sources."

"I don't get the impression Kay is hurting for money."

"Maybe. Maybe, not. But living in New York is expensive." Jinx stretched and yawned. "I assume you heard about Tish's motive?"

"I did."

"Then there's Lois."

"Lois?" I spoke loud enough to attract attention. The teenagers on the other side of the pool gaped at us. I lowered my voice. "What do you mean?"

"She and Althea hated each other."

"They did?"

Jinx nodded. "Althea blackballed Lois at Kappa."

"We're long past sorority rush."

"Lois made sure that Althea couldn't get into the garden society."

"Hardly motive for murder."

"Althea tanked Lois's application to the DAR."

How had I missed all this? "I see a pattern, but—"

"There's more. Lois made sure Althea's name never appeared on the ballot for CSO." Children's Support Organization was hard to get into even when a candidate could get their name on the ballot.

"I get it. They hated each other, but—"

Jinx held up her palm. "I'm not done. Althea was pressuring Chuck to fire Skip."

I squinted my eyes against the sun and tried to imagine a world where Althea Dodson could influence who did or did not work for a large law firm. "Why would Chuck consider such a thing?"

"That trust is huge. Managing it, even if Kay took half, would generate a ton of money for the firm."

"With Althea dead, Skip's job is safe."

"Exactly."

"Basically, everyone at that luncheon but Libba and me had a reason to want her dead."

Jinx held out her hand and examined her manicure. "There's a couples' scramble on Tuesday night. I want you and Anarchy to play with George and me."

I gaped at the sudden change in direction. "Pardon?"

"Golf, Ellison. You're good at it."

"Anarchy's in the middle of an investigation." He didn't have time to chase a ball around a golf course.

"He's investigating a murder that happened at this club. Tish and Lois are playing with their husbands."

"I'll ask him. He's not much of a golfer."

"It's a scramble, Ellison. We tee off at six, play nine, then the club will serve us dinner on the patio. There will be drinking." She was right. Only the most competitive of players took couples' scrambles seriously. Everyone else imbibed. "Since it's hot, there will be lots of drinking. That means loose tongues."

When she put it that way, how could we refuse?

"YOU'RE GLOWING," SAID ANARCHY.

We sat, just the two of us, at the dining table. Grace had gone to a movie with friends.

"I got the perfect amount of sun."

"Who was there?"

"Jinx. She wants us to play in a scramble on Tuesday evening."

"Golf?" He'd taken a few lessons and played a handful of rounds with my father, but Anarchy had not embraced golf as a pastime.

"Golf. Tish and Robert Hart are playing." I took a breath before I pointed a finger at yet another friend. "And Lois and Skip Wortham."

He looked up from his plate. Aggie had paired grilled salmon with asparagus and a butter lettuce salad dressed with a home-made citrus vinaigrette. "Skip and Robert were both at the club when Althea was stabbed."

"You have the complete list?" I asked.

"I think so. Including the staff, there were forty people in the clubhouse when she died."

"That many?"

"The six of you in the dining room, plus Myra Lawrence, and sixteen men in the grill. Your mother's friend Louise. A foursome playing bridge in the cardroom, none of whom left the table anywhere near the time of the murder. Then, the staff—the bartender, two waiters, and a large contingent in the kitchen. They were prepping for the Wade wedding reception."

I took a large sip of wine. It was cool and crisp, and I took a second sip before I said, "Lois and Skip had a motive."

He paused a forkful of salad halfway to his mouth. "Oh?"

"Lois and Althea hated each other. Althea was pressuring the firm that manages her grandmother's trust to fire Skip."

"Why now?"

"The trust is set to distribute when Kay and Althea turn forty. Althea's birthday is in October. She was insisting they fire Skip. If they didn't, she'd take her portion and find other management."

"Jinx told you?"

"Yes."

Anarchy rubbed his jaw. "She's sure?"

"It's Jinx." My friend had her flaws, but her information was one-hundred-percent reliable. I took a bite of salmon.

"Let's walk through what you remember from your lunch. Did you notice any tension between Lois and Althea?"

"Not especially."

"Did anyone leave the table?"

"Kay and Tish excused themselves just before dessert was served. They weren't gone more than five minutes."

"Try and remember, you've got a good eye for details. When Kay came back, was she wearing her scarf?"

He'd asked that before, but I closed my eyes and tried to the picture the six of us seated around the table. I gave an apologetic shrug. "I can't remember."

"That's okay. You finished lunch, then everyone stood and pretended to kiss each other's cheeks and promised to get together soon. What then?" Anarchy had us pegged.

"They left."

"The four of them together?"

"Althea left right away. Then Lois and Tish. Kay lingered to thank us for hosting the luncheon. When she left, Libba and I decided that I'd take the flowers, then we went to the parking lot."

"Peters spoke with Tish. She said that she and Lois separated just outside the dining room. Lois needed to grab something from the locker room. Tish claims she went straight to her car."

"But, according to Louise, she went to the lounge." I hated to think my friend might be a killer. "What about the men in the grill?"

"As the weather cleared, they began to disperse. As your lunch was breaking up, there were still eight men in the grill, including Skip Wortham, Chuck Wade, Perry Brandt, and Robbie Smart."

"Where was Robert? You said he was still in the clubhouse."

"He says he was in the men's locker room."

"Have you talked to Perry?"

"That's how I know who was in the grill. He was having a late lunch with Robbie, but he admits that anyone could have left without him noticing."

"Did the bartender notice anyone leaving?"

"No, but he was busy fixing drinks and busing the recently vacated tables."

"So, we can add Skip to the list of suspects without alibis. Did anyone see Robert in the locker room?"

"No."

"Where did the knife come from?" I should have asked before now.

"It's a hunting knife, available at any sporting goods store."

I'd expected him to tell me it was a steak knife or chef's knife stolen from the kitchen. "If someone brought a hunting knife to the club, they planned on killing her."

"Exactly what we were thinking."

"Fingerprints?"

"Wiped clean."

"Althea wasn't a club member; how did they know she'd be there? Wait." I hated to voice the horrible thought in my head. "Do you think her murder was random?"

"We've considered the possibility, but we believe she was the target. Who knew Althea would be at the club on Friday afternoon?"

"Kay, for sure. She added her to the guest list. I don't know about Lois or Tish. Mother knew I was hosting a luncheon with Libba, and I told her who was coming. I don't know who she might have told. We can ask her. Same with Libba, she might have mentioned it to someone. Also, Althea. She could have told people she was invited."

Anarchy groaned. "So, there's no telling."

"Probably not."

"What else?"

I closed my eyes and tried to remember more. "Tish!"

"What about her?"

"Her purse was tiny. Chanel. The one with the chains instead of straps. Also, her dress was too small."

"Meaning?"

"Where would she hide a knife?"

He nodded. Slowly.

"The other purses?"

"Lois carried a tote. Kay had a big slouchy shoulder bag."

"Would you talk to Tish? Maybe she noticed something she doesn't feel comfortable telling the police."

Anarchy needed my help. With an investigation. I hid my smile behind my napkin. "Of course. I'll call her when we finish dinner."

CHAPTER EIGHT

Tish and I met at André's. "I just love a prix fixe menu," she'd said when she suggested the restaurant just south of the Country Club Plaza.

I found three courses for lunch to be two too many, but I'd happily agreed to meet her there. Mainly because I adored the chocolates they sold near the front entrance. I'd say their dark chocolate hearts were to die for but given my track record that seemed like tempting fate. Also, André's made fabulous quiche. Even better than Aggie's, not that I'd ever tell her that.

Tish and I arrived at André's at the same time and followed the hostess to a corner table in the Swiss-chalet-decorated restaurant. She handed us the *carte du jour* and her smile brightened. "Daphne is your waitress, today. She'll be with you shortly."

I glanced at the menu and quickly decided on the green salad and chicken crêpes.

Tish studied the piece of paper as if her life depended upon it. She was so engrossed that she startled when our waitress put down two water glasses and said, "Good afternoon, may I get some drinks started for you?"

"Wine?" I offered Tish an encouraging smile.

"I shouldn't."

"It's been a rough few days."

"You're right. You pick, Ellison."

"Something dry and white. A pinot gris or Sancerre."

"Yes, ma'am. I'll give you a few more minutes with the menu." Daphne left us.

"I always have a terrible time deciding," said Tish. "I bet you already know."

"Their crêpes are always delicious."

"True. But they have stroganoff, today. I love a good stroganoff."

I took a sip of water and held my tongue. For me, heavy meals and summer heat were a bad combination. I'd spend the rest of the day napping.

Tish put down her menu. "You've never asked me to lunch before. This is about Althea."

I offered an apologetic shrug. "I know you didn't kill her."

Tish couldn't have looked more shocked if I'd leaned across the table and slapped her. "People think I killed Althea?"

"I don't."

"What about your husband?"

"You couldn't have done it."

She stared at me open-mouthed, as if my declaration of her innocence had short-circuited her brain. "I don't have a solid alibi, and Althea and I had a...problem."

"Are you trying to change my mind?"

"No! No. Not at all. I'm relieved."

"You went to the ladies' lounge after lunch."

"Did I?" She frowned. "If I did, it was just a trip to the bathroom. I don't remember."

I believed her. "Why did Althea have a problem with you?"

Tish swirled the water in her glass, seemingly fascinated by the liquid. "It started about six weeks ago."

"Any idea what set her off?"

"None."

"Did you see her often?" I could go for months without crossing paths with Althea.

Tish grimaced. "We sat on two of the same committees this spring—a fundraiser for the hospital's burn unit, and we're both on the cookbook committee for the League." Tish put her glass down and folded her hands in her lap. "She never missed an opportunity to comment on my weight or hint that Robert was carrying on." She rolled her eyes. "As if I didn't already know."

"You knew?"

"Pfft. For years."

"Years?" I couldn't hide my surprise. I'd know about Henry's cheating and had resolved to stay with him until Grace graduated from high school. I'd had an end date in mind.

"You're wondering why I stayed. I can see it in your eyes."

"I never question another woman's marriage." Okay, not strictly true. But I tried to keep judgment at bay.

"Robert and I have been together since our freshman year in college. He was everything my parents wanted for me. Nice family. High-earning potential. Stability. We got married the week after we graduated."

The waitress appeared and poured our wine.

We ordered our lunches, then Tish took a large sip of Sancerre. "This is good."

I sipped and nodded, hoping she'd continue.

After a second sip, she put down her glass. "I've never worked a day in my life. Well, not a paying job. Raising kids is definitely work. I don't have a talent. I can't paint or write or decorate houses. I have no marketable skills. If Robert and I divorced, and I had to find work, I'd end up at a retail counter. Or, worse, I'd have to join the horde of divorcées selling real estate. Neither is appealing."

She shifted her gaze to another table where four women were celebrating a birthday. Small gifts wrapped in beautiful paper and Champagne glasses dotted the table's surface. As we watched, three of the women raised their glasses and toasted their friend.

"Robert knows I'll never give him a divorce. To be honest, I don't think he even wants one either. If we ended our marriage, the settlement would mean he'd have to sell assets. The capital gains would kill him. Plus, he can blame his unwillingness to commit on me. I'm sure he tells those women I'll never give him a divorce.

"Are you happy?"

"I'm not unhappy. Robert and I are...well, we're not friends, but we're cordial. We both adore the kids. He gives me a generous allowance. What more do I need?"

"Aren't you lonely?"

"No." Her response was so immediate that I believed her.

Daphne returned, putting a green salad in front of me and a creamed soup at Tish's place. Then, she took the wine from the bucket and topped off our glasses.

"Thank you," I murmured.

When she left, Tish continued, "For years, I had the kids. Now that they're in college, I can do whatever I want."

That was well and good, but not the same as having a man who loved you.

"I take vacations by myself. A spa. A skiing trip. Robert hates to ski. I'm considering a European river cruise."

"All alone?"

A tiny smile curled her lips. "One meets people on vacation."

"And not one man has made you consider divorce."

Her expression turned dreamy. "Not a man."

I nearly choked on my wine.

Tish's eyes widened as she realized what she'd given away. "You won't tell anyone?"

"Not a soul."

"I don't care for me. I am what I am. But the children..."

"No one will ever hear it from me. Does Robert know?"

"We've never discussed it, but I assume so."

"You could go to New York or San Francisco." Henry had a maiden aunt who'd set up house with another woman in Carmel. They'd seemed very happy.

"My life and my friends are here."

"You could find a partner."

"Not everyone gets a fairy tale, Ellison." A reminder to hold tightly to mine. She glanced around the crowded restaurant. "Perhaps we should talk about something else?"

"Did you notice anything odd the day Althea was killed?"

"Besides Althea being there? Kay knew how much she and Lois hated each other."

"I wonder why she included her."

"No idea. Maybe she thought they could act like adults for a few hours." Tish spooned her soup.

"Anything else?"

"Not that I can think of."

We chatted our way through three courses, then I claimed the check.

"Thank you for lunch, Ellison. You're a good friend."

"Is there any chance that Robert and Althea..."

She wrinkled her nose. "Lord, I hope not. I like to think my husband has better taste than that."

"It would explain her antipathy."

"You'll have to ask Robert."

I stopped at the front counter and bought an embarrassing number of chocolates.

"Anything else for you, Mrs. Jones?"

"An assortment of petit fours, please." I'd take them to Mother and Daddy's for dessert. (Mother had called to insist we join them before I left to meet Tish for lunch). I watched the girl behind the counter box up a dozen pastries masquerading as art, then I paid for the sugar none of us needed, turned, and walked straight into a man's chest. "Oomph."

His hands grabbed my arms, steadying me.

"I'm so sorry, I didn't realize you were standing behind me." I tilted my head and looked up at John Dodson. John was tall, with salt and pepper hair and brown eyes. Not coffee brown eyes like Anarchy's. Muddy brown. And right now, those eyes radiated worry.

His grip on my arm tightened. "I need to talk to you."

He'd searched me out. A chill ran down my spine.

"I called your house."

"Oh?" I found it hard to believe Aggie would give a suspect in a murder investigation my location.

"Your daughter told me you'd met a friend for lunch at André's."

Grace and I would have words when I got home. "What do you want to talk about?"

He glanced around the crowded area. "Can we go someplace more private?"

There was no way I was leaving André's with him. I shook my head.

"You think I'm guilty. You think I killed her."

"An unhappy spouse is always a suspect." I knew that from experience.

"I didn't kill Althea. I was nowhere near the club when she died." He kept his voice low, but a woman standing nearby gaped at us.

"Then you have nothing to worry about."

He released me and raked his fingers through his hair. "We both know that's not true. Please, Ellison. Can we at least sit?"

"Why talk to me? If you have information, tell Anarchy."

"Please?"

We were attracting more *looks*—two people suspected of killing their spouses openly discussing murder. Well, one of us was a suspect. I'd been proven innocent. The fact that John was lurking around André's meant that Anarchy didn't have enough to charge him. I wished, fervently, that we'd spent more time discussing Anarchy's suspicions in regard to Althea's estranged husband.

"Fine," I ceded.

John walked me to the hostess station. If she noticed I was back around so soon, her face didn't show it. Instead, she led us to the corner table I'd recently vacated.

"Menus?"

"Not for me, thank you." She gave a brief nod and left us in peace.

Daphne, who I'd already tipped generously, replaced her. Her eyes widened slightly when she saw me.

"Tab, please. Two limes."

"And for you, sir?"

"Iced tea."

She made a note on her order pad and hurried away.

"I didn't kill Althea."

"Anarchy is good at his job," I rested my laced fingers on the edge of the table. "So is Peters."

John put his elbows on the table and sank his head into his hands. "Everyone thinks I killed her."

"That will go away when the real killer is caught."

"And if he's not?"

Then John would live under a cloud of suspicion for the rest of his life.

"What do you want from me?"

John's lips thinned to a tight, angry line. "Althea kept score. Always. She tallied slights and perceived insults and dollars." He looked tired, as if the weight of Althea's death was slowly crushing him. "God help me if she spent more on our anniversary or Christmas than I did. She never used her accounting degree in a professional capacity, but in her personal life..." His voice trailed off to nothing.

"What are you saying?"

"Althea and I were even. Done. I wanted her out of my life, not dead."

"She wanted your family's cabin."

John shook his head, as if the idea annoyed him. "Not enough to drag out our divorce. If it went too long—until her birthday—she'd get her trust, and I'd have a claim. No way would she let that happen."

"With her dead, you don't pay alimony, you don't split property, and you keep the cabin."

"I was at work when she was killed. In a meeting with ten people."

How convenient for him. "You could've hired someone."

"A hitman?" His voice went unnaturally high. "Where would I find a hitman?"

I assumed the question was rhetorical.

He shook his head. "Even if I knew where to find a killer-for-hire, it's not like a stranger could just wander around a country club searching for their victim."

Not strictly true. If someone looked like they belonged, wore the right clothes, used the right words, no one would think anything was amiss.

"I think she was seeing someone."

Althea? Uptight, unhappy, unfashionable Althea? "Who?"

"I don't know."

Daphne served us our drinks. "May I get you anything else?"

"No," John snapped.

The woman retreated a step. "No, thank you," I told her. "We have everything we need."

She offered me a brief smile and hurried away.

I scowled across the table at John. "Really?"

"What?"

"Biting the waitress's head off?"

He glared at me for a few seconds before his face crumpled. "You're right. You're right. I'll apologize before we leave."

I suspected that apology would come in the form of a twenty-dollar tip for a two-dollar tab. "Why am I here?" He hadn't told me anything of substance.

"I thought you might understand..." He'd thought I'd feel sympathy and somehow intercede on his behalf.

"Investigations take time."

"Meanwhile, everyone in town is whispering that I killed my wife."

"Not everyone. There are other suspects. Other gossip."

"Really?" He sounded ridiculously hopeful.

"Who else might have wanted her dead?"

I was flabbergasted when he pulled a list from his pocket and handed it to me.

THE CHANDELIER IN MOTHER'S DINING ROOM HAD TEN ARMS AND dripped with hundreds of crystals, every single one sparkled brighter than the Hope diamond.

Daddy sat at the head of the table, Mother at the foot. Karma sat across from Grace and me. Anarchy had taken John's list from my hands, scanned the names, and sent his regrets.

Lucky man.

"Tell Karma about the wedding, Ellison," Mother prompted.

"The church isn't air-conditioned. It was a black-tie wedding in a blast furnace."

Karma offered a sympathetic grimace.

"Tell her the rest," Mother directed.

"The groom and his groomsmen were suffering the effects of too much to drink."

"At the wedding?" Karma asked, raising an eyebrow.

Mother noted it as if she approved of Karma's slightly judgmental question.

"Apparently, they stayed out late the night before the service. The groom had to remove himself from the front of the church."

"Ellison makes it sound almost civilized." Mother lifted her water goblet to her lips and took a dainty sip.

Given that I'd rather talk about the wedding than Althea, I gave up a few more details. "He removed himself at a dead run, and the bride's father chased him."

Mother put down her goblet. "The whole church heard Chuck tell that boy he was pathetic."

"Billy did throw up on Chuck's shoes."

Grace giggled.

"Then the best man passed out."

"No!" Karma sounded horrified.

"Someone took him to the hospital, but they forgot to get the rings. When the priest asked for them, no one knew what to do."

"Who are these people?"

"The Wades? Linda is a Ledbetter," Mother explained. "She found Chuck at college."

"Found him?" Karma asked.

"He was a football star. Big man on campus. A nice change for him."

"What does that mean?" Karma asked.

It meant Mother didn't approve of Chuck's blue-collar background.

"He's not exactly our kind," Mother replied. "At any rate, he thrived on the adulation—people yelling his name from the stands." She sniffed. "They called him 'Bank,'—no, that's not right. They called him 'Cash.'" She nodded, please that she'd remembered. "He graduated and went on to law school. Then he and Linda came home to Kansas City. Her father got him a job at his law firm."

Chuck wasn't my favorite, but out of loyalty to Linda, I added, "He's a good attorney. He made partner on his own."

Karma offered me a smile. "It's quite amazing that the wedding wasn't the most memorable part of your weekend."' 1

"Althea Dodson. Dreadful woman." Mother picked up the silver bell next to her water goblet. In the blink of an eye, the housekeeper appeared. "You may serve the main course."

"Yes, Mrs. Walford." She began to clear our salad plates.

"The Morrison family made their money manufacturing pig feed. Bing Morrison sold the company for a fortune, but my grandmother remembered when he arrived in Kansas City. He didn't know a soul and had hardly two nickels to rub together. He started that company and married a salesgirl from EBT. Maude was a beautiful woman but dumb as a box of rocks. That's why Bing put his money in trust. He didn't have any faith in Maude's ability to handle large amounts of money. He knew she'd squander everything he'd made. That same distrust extended to his children. The trust distributes to his grandchildren." Mother's lips twisted into a wry smile. "He never dreamed he'd have granddaughters." She patted her lips with her linen napkin.

"Kay has always been a good friend." And I'd never cared that her money was new.

Mother sniffed.

"Was Lindsey a pretty bride?" Grace asked. Lindsey was one of our regular babysitters when Grace was little—her favorite. They came up with a game called "Big Bad Buffalo." As far as I could tell, the rules involved Lindsey chasing Grace around the house until she dropped from exhaustion.

"She looked beautiful," I replied. Then I described her dress.

Mother scoffed. "Chuck never should have let her marry that boy. I give it three years, tops." She looked at me, daring me to argue.

I kept my mouth shut and gave a silent thanks that Anarchy wasn't here to hear her.

"Grace, I hear you're dating the Kettering boy. What's his first name?"

I turned and stared at my daughter. She'd said nothing about dating Jonathan Kettering. Not. A. Word.

Her cheeks flushed. "Jonathan. And we're not dating. A group of us went to the movies last week. That's all."

"His grandmother and I have been friends since we were girls." In other words, she approved.

"It wasn't really a date, Granna."

"Did you go to the movies with him?"

"Yes, but there were ten of us."

"Did he buy your ticket?"

"Yes, but—"

"Did he hold your hand?"

The color on Grace's cheeks darkened.

"Grace, sit up straight. You're a lovely girl, but posture is important. No boy wants a shlumpy girlfriend."

Grace stiffened her spine and managed a sickly smile.

I decided to save her. "Anarchy and I are playing in the scramble at the club tomorrow night."

"Is he wearing plus-fours?" asked Daddy.

"Good Lord, no."

"Why not?"

I stared at my father. "Can you honestly imagine Anarchy in knickers?"

"But it's a Bonnie and Clyde themed event."

"It's themed?" I could happily wring Jinx's neck. She hadn't told me, and a theme wasn't the kind of detail she missed. "I imagine we'll stick with argyle."

"You should put forth some effort," said Mother. This from a woman who'd dressed up as Betty Ford last Halloween. On any given day, the two women wore similar helmets of hair. Their clothes were similar, tasteful and conservative. Mother dressing up as the First Lady was like Grace dressing up as a teenager.

I gritted my teeth and smiled. "Getting Anarchy to play took plenty of effort. Themed clothing is a step too far."

"Your mother used to be such fun," Mother said to Grace.

And I'd gotten grounded for it.

"I'm not asking him to wear knickers. He only agreed to play because most of the suspects in Althea's murder will be there."

"Ellison!" Mother pressed a hand to her chest. "How could you?"

"How could I what?"

"Exploit the club like that."

"I'm fairly certain everyone at the club wants the killer caught."

Mother sniffed. "Just imagine if you hadn't found the body."

"Althea would still be dead, and there would still be a murder investigation. Look at the bright side, Mother. I hear your getting new carpet in the lounge."

She couldn't quite hide her satisfaction. "Well, even tragedies have silver linings."

"I'm not sure if Althea would agree."

CHAPTER NINE

The dogs were waiting for me when I got back from my morning swim. They danced around the kitchen, pushing each other out of the way in their bids for my attention. It was too early for this, especially after a restless night.

I gave them a bleary-eyed glare and pushed Mr. Coffee's button. "Calm down."

They didn't.

"Out!" I shoved them outside into the backyard and watched as they policed the fence line. Satisfied that no rabbits or cats had invaded their territory, Max stretched out on the patio, and Finn barked at a tree. He'd never done that before, I felt suddenly guilty. Did Finn need more of my attention with Beau gone?

"Does Finn seem sad to you?" I asked Mr. Coffee. "Do you think he misses Beau?"

It's not your job to keep everyone happy. And Finn's a dog.

"But I don't want him to be sad."

Not your job. Also, he's a dog.

"Dogs have feelings."

Finn will be fine. And again. Not. Your. Job.

It was a sweet thing to say, but I'd spent much of my life trying to do just that—to keep Henry or Mother or Grace happy. It felt like my job. Rather than reply, I measured out the kibble for the dogs' breakfasts.

Mr. Coffee gurgled.

"Anarchy got home late again." I hadn't truly slept until he joined me in bed.

Does he have any suspects?

"Too many suspects. And I know and like them all."

Who?

"There's Kay and Tish, and Lois. None of them have alibis, and all of them have motives. Although we don't see how Tish could've had access to the murder weapon."

Who else?

"John Dodson."

The husband?

"That's right. At least he has an alibi. Then there's Skip Wortham—Althea was threatening his job. He had motive and opportunity."

Is that all?

"John Dodson gave me a list of people who might have wanted Althea dead."

How many?

"The list took up a whole sheet from a legal pad." I took a cup from the cabinet and helped myself to coffee. "Anarchy is looking into each name. I imagine that's why he was so late." I sniffed the cream, then added a jot to my cup.

Who do you think killed her?

"She was having an affair. Maybe it was her lover?"

Who was he?

"That's a mystery."

A pitiful bark from the backyard had me opening the back

door. The dogs dashed inside, totally fixated on the bowls waiting for them on the counter.

"Okay, okay," I told them. "Sit."

Grudgingly, they lowered to their haunches.

I put down their bowls, and they raced to see who could inhale their food the fastest.

Footsteps on the back stairs caught my attention, and I wore a welcoming smile when Anarchy opened the door into the kitchen.

"Good morning," he said as he stepped forward and kissed me.

I allowed myself to melt into his chest. "You worked late."

He groaned. "According to John Dodson, half the people Althea knew wanted her dead."

"Coffee?" I crossed to Mr. Coffee and filled a mug, taking the opportunity to top off my mug as well.

"Thanks," he said, accepting the cup of coffee. "How was dinner?"

"We rehashed the wedding and the murder. Grace is dating Jonathan Kettering and..."

"Wait, what?"

"Tonight's golf event is themed." I spoke rip-the-Band-Aid-off quickly.

"Themed?"

"Bonnie and Clyde."

He blinked slowly and a certain hardness fell across his features. "A woman was murdered in the clubhouse on Friday, and their theme is a couple suspected of numerous ruthless killings?"

When he put it that way, it sounded worse than plus-fours.

"More Warren Beatty and Faye Dunaway and the clothes from the film, less murderous bank robbers."

Anarchy pinched the bridge of his nose. "She was pregnant."

"Bonnie Parker?"

"Althea. We got the medical examiner's report, and she was pregnant."

"She was forty." Having a baby in my twenties had been exhausting. And I'd had lots of help. A nanny who came three days a week, and Mother who stopped by twice a day to offer me unsolicited advice.

"Be that as it may, she was expecting. Any idea who the father might be?"

"Not John. I'll call Jinx. She might have an idea."

"I'd prefer this not get out."

"She's a vault," I assured him, then glanced at the wall clock. "It's too early to call, but at the stroke of nine, I'll get her on the phone." I settled on the closest stool, shaking my head in near disbelief. "Pregnant?"

"Ten weeks," he clarified.

"It makes it so much worse," I said, my stomach knotting. I'd been operating under the assumption that Althea did something or knew something that got her killed. Not that she deserved to die, no one deserved to be murdered. But a baby...I felt sick to my stomach.

Anarchy wrapped his arm around my shoulders and, despite the ache in my heart, I felt a little better.

Anarchy left for work at eight-thirty. At nine, I called Jinx.

She answered on the third ring. "Hello."

"It's Ellison."

"What's wrong? You sound upset."

"If I tell you something, it has to stay between us."

"Of course."

"Althea Dodson was pregnant."

"John's? No. That can't be right."

We thought about that for a moment, and the silence stretched like saltwater taffy.

"Are you sure about this?" she asked. "Althea? Pregnant?"

"I'm sure. Do you think Robert might be the father?"

"Robert? As in Tish's Robert?"

"Yes."

"Robert Hart?"

"Yes." I'd hoped she'd tell me I'd lost my mind.

"You're asking because Althea took against Tish?"

"Yes."

I could almost see the furrow between her brows deepen as she considered. "It's possible."

"Drat."

"You wanted me to tell you that he'd never stray?"

"Not so much that." I knew well how husbands cheated. "But Althea?"

"Henry cheated on you with Prudence. That's proof there's no accounting for taste."

In truth, I'd been more upset by my late husband's choice to cheat on me with an unattractive woman than the cheating itself. "I don't get it, if you're going to risk everything, why not pick a pretty woman?"

Jinx snorted. "Please. Prudence's biggest selling point was, and is, her lax morals. It's not as if Henry was actually attracted to her."

"Could've fooled me."

"I'm just saying, men on the prowl aren't always discerning."

I wasn't going to argue that. "Althea and Robert. Is there a way to confirm they were having an affair?" Short of confronting Robert.

"Let me make a call. I'll get back to you as soon as possible."

Before I could remind her about the importance of discretion, she hung up.

"Mom?" Grace had slipped into the kitchen while I was on the phone with Jinx.

I returned the receiver to the cradle. "Good morning."

"I'm sorry about last night," she said. We'd driven separate cars to Mother and Daddy's, and Grace had met up with friends when dinner concluded. We hadn't had a chance to talk about Jonathan—not that there was much to talk about. Grace went on lots of dates. She'd go gaga for a boy on Monday, then, by Friday, the boy was a drag.

Jonathan had told his mom. Presumably his mother had told his grandmother, who told Mother. But it hadn't helped his case. Not with Grace. She didn't like getting surprised by Mother any more than I did.

"I'd prefer to know who you're dating before your grandmother does. Getting blindsided by Granna is never fun."

Mothers and daughters. Were my interactions with Mother teaching Grace reticence in all things? I'd learned at an early age that anything I shared with Mother was ammunition in a future argument. I'd stopped telling her things. A distance grew between us.

I was the artsy daughter, the one she couldn't quite understand, the one who played her cards close to her vest.

I loved Mother. I did. And I'd strived my whole life to please her, but over the past year, our relationship had changed. I was less interested in earning her approval and more interested in being my own woman. That meant telling her things she didn't want to hear. That meant lifting my chin and standing up for myself when she used my words against me.

We were a work in progress.

"I said I was sorry." Grace opened the fridge and stared inside, finally selecting an apple. "Have you heard from Beau?"

"The head counselor left a message on the machine while we were at dinner last night. He's having the time of his life." Which was a huge relief. "He spent all afternoon on a catamaran."

"I'm glad." She took a bite of her apple

Brnng, brnng.

I picked up the receiver.

"It's me," said Jinx. "Are you ready for a field trip?"

～

JINX PULLED INTO MY DRIVEWAY A FEW MINUTES PAST ONE.

I begged the dogs to behave, called a goodbye to Aggie, and slipped out the front door and into the passenger seat of Jinx's butter-yellow Coupe Deville. "Where are we going?"

She braked at the bottom of my drive. "How much cash do you have?"

"Sixty dollars."

"Not enough. We have to stop at the bank."

"How much do I need?" What kind of field trip was this?

"At least a couple hundred."

"For?"

"It never hurts to encourage a motel clerk's memory."

"You bribe motel clerks?"

"We're not going to the Alameda, Ellison. Motels hire people who'd sell their grandmothers if the price was right."

"How do you know which motel Robert frequents?"

"Funny story. When Ellen Bailey thought Oliver was cheating, she hired a private detective. The PI took pictures of Oliver and a blonde in a tube top and short shorts. In the background, he also caught Robert."

"Ellen shared the picture with you?" That was surprising.

"The blonde looked familiar, but she couldn't place her. She wanted to know if I recognized her. She didn't notice Robert in the background."

"Did you recognize the blonde?"

Jinx nodded.

"Who was she?"

"A waitress at the club. Ellen got her fired." Ellen had also filed for divorce, which was probably why Jinx felt comfortable sharing the story.

"So, we know where Robert met Althea." I pulled my checkbook from my purse and wrote myself a check for five-hundred dollars. "How should I get the cash?"

"I find hundred-dollar bills are the best for loosening tongues."

"That's what I'll ask for."

I endorsed the back of the check. A moment later, when we pulled into the drive-through at the bank, I handed the check and my driver's license to Jinx.

"Really?" she asked. "You give them your driver's license?"

"It's the rules."

"It's your bank."

It was Grace's bank, but I was the board chairman until she was old enough to take an active role. "Which is why I follow the rules."

Jinx turned her head, lowered her sunglasses, and peered at me over the rims. "You and Anarchy really are perfectly matched."

I wasn't sure she meant it as a compliment, but I chose to take it as one.

The friendly teller sent out five crisp hundred-dollar bills and my license in a bank envelope. "Have a nice day, Mrs. Jones."

I leaned over Jinx and spoke into the microphone. "Thank you. You, too."

Jinx put the car in drive and pulled away. "So, Grace and Jonathan Kettering?"

Did the whole world know before me? "I guess so."

"You don't sound happy."

"Grace's relationships are ephemeral. Here and gone in the blink of an eye."

She shrugged. "Teenagers. How is Beau doing at camp?"

"He's having fun."

"Good. That poor kid deserves it." She headed the car south. And west.

"Where exactly are we going?"

"A motel on Metcalf."

"We should have brought pictures."

"I did. Look in the backseat."

I twisted and looked over my shoulder. Several copies of *The Independent* lay on the seat. The society magazine was mostly pictures and pithy asides.

"I picked copies with pictures of Robert and Althea."

"You are a genius."

She nodded her agreement. "I try."

Contrary to Jinx's prediction, the clerk at the motel seemed nice. She had gray hair, sharp blue eyes, and a ready smile. Her nametag read "Ethel."

"Checking in?" she asked.

"No," Jinx replied. "We need your help." She flipped to a dog-eared page in *The Independent*. "This man is one of your regular customers."

Ethel glanced down at the page, and Jinx tapped her fire engine-red fingernail next to Robert's face.

"He kind of looks like Ben Franklin." Ethel wasn't subtle. Which was fine. I preferred a direct approach.

Jinx gave a tiny nod, and Ethel said, "Yeah, I've seen him."

"How about this woman?" Jinx flipped through a different issue until she found a photo of Althea at a ladies' luncheon.

The clerk scrunched her face. "Maybe."

"Ellison." Jinx's tone made it clear she wanted money.

I handed over two hundred-dollar bills, and the clerk watched our exchange with avid interest. Jinx slid the money across the counter but kept her fingers firmly pressed against Ben's face. "You've seen her?"

"She's been here."

"Have they been here together?" I asked.

The clerk shifted her gaze from the money already on the counter to my handbag.

I withdrew another hundred.

"Tuesdays and Thursdays. They arrive around three; he leaves by six."

"Thank you." I put the bill on the counter. "The police may follow up."

"The police? No police! This is a family-friendly hotel." She waved at a display filled with brightly colored brochures advertising local attractions: Worlds of Fun, the Kansas City Royals, Crown Center, and the Country Club Plaza. Then, she pointed to the tiny pool in the center of the parking lot as if a square of tepid water proved her point.

Jinx held up her hands. "They may not come." Her voice was soothing, even as she shot me a glare.

"Right," I backtracked, realizing my mistake. "No police."

We left the clerk three-hundred dollars richer and walked back to Jinx's Cadillac.

"Rookie mistake, Ellison. Never, ever mention the police."

"Lesson learned. But Anarchy will send someone out to interview her."

"You don't have to tell her that." Jinx slid behind the wheel.

I buckled my seatbelt. "Althea and Robert. Pregnant. It's quite a motive for murder."

"For Tish?"

"And, depending on how he felt about the baby, for Robert."

CHAPTER TEN

"Your clubs are already on the cart, Mrs. Jones," said Benji, one of the assistant golf pros. Like the titular dog in the movie, he had shaggy hair and kind eyes. "May I take those for you, sir?"

Anarchy allowed Benji to take his golf bag.

"You know you can store them here." I waved in the direction of the pro shop.

He shook his head. "I've been sneaking off to a public course to practice."

I looked up at my husband, speechless.

His cheeks flushed. "I'm not very good. If I'm going to make a fool of myself, I'd rather do it around people I'll never see again."

"Daddy says you have potential."

"Golf takes time, Ellison."

In more ways than one, a round of golf took several hours. But the practice—the swings, the strokes, learning to read a putt, making adjustments to grips or stances until the club pro was satisfied, aim—that took years. I'd spent years. As a kid, I'd done my time playing endless rounds with Daddy, junior golf, even my high school's girls' team.

Anarchy hadn't.

I reached for his hand. "I'll sneak off with you."

A slow grin lit his face. "Are we still talking about golf?"

My cheeks, already flushed from the late afternoon heat, grew warmer. "We could work on your hip movement."

"Could we?" His eyes twinkled.

"And your hands. Grip is very important."

"How import—"

"Ellison, there you are," Jinx's strident tone made it sound like we'd kept her waiting.

"Anarchy," she lifted up on her tiptoes and kissed my husband's cheek. "Did Ellison tell you what we learned at the motel?"

"She did. Peters is probably there now. Thank you for your help."

"Anytime," Jinx tossed a sheet of paper at me. "Have you seen this?"

I scanned the page. "Longest drive with a marshmallow?"

"Look at six. They've put out opposite-hand drivers." Her eyes narrowed. "Why aren't you in costume?"

"Celebrating murderers less than a week after a murder isn't in the best taste."

"The theme was chosen long before Althea got herself killed." She waved my concern away.

"I'm a homicide detective, Jinx. I'm not dressing up like Clyde Barrow."

Jinx shook her head as if Anarchy was being deliberately obtuse. "It's about the clothes, not the man."

There was a metaphor in this conversation—one that didn't reflect well on club's membership.

"How many are playing?" asked Anarchy, deftly changing the subject.

"Thirty-six," she replied.

I scanned the growing crowd and spotted Tish in conversation with Lois. Had Tish ever shared her secret with her best friend? My gaze shifted, and I found Jinx's husband, George. He clutched a beer and spoke with Chuck. "The Wades are playing?"

"A united, happy front after that disaster of a wedding."

"The reception was lovely." My reply rang hollow, mainly because she was right. The wedding had been *The Towering Inferno*, *The Poseidon Adventure*, and *Airport* all rolled into one. The only thing missing had been Charlton Heston or Burt Lancaster starting a fist fight.

"Sure about that? How would you feel if Grace got married and your friends mistook a member of the groom's family for a hooker?"

I'd smile and pretend I didn't hear the tittering whispers, exactly what Linda and Chuck were doing. I returned my attention to the paper in my hand. There were prizes for the longest drive, closest to the pin, and low score.

"Have you played lately?" Jinx asked Anarchy.

"No."

"Neither have I."

"Tennis is Jinx's game," I noted.

"Do you think we have time to go to the range?" she asked.

I glanced at my watch. "Probably not."

Jinx took the sheet of paper from my hand. "What's this? On the seventh hole—" Jinx pointed "—we're only allowed our seven irons."

The seventh hole was a challenging par five, and using a seven-iron made reaching the green in three nearly impossible.

"No putter?" Anarchy asked.

"It says not," I confirmed.

George, who wore baggy pants, a vest over his white shirt (I didn't envy him in the heat), and a newsboy cap, joined us, handed Anarchy a beer, then said to his wife, "Anarchy and Ellison don't look like fools."

"Don't complain," Jinx smoothed the bias-cut skirt which hit her mid-calf. She'd paired it with a form-fitting sweater and beret. "If Jim Higgins hadn't worn plus-fours, we might've won for best costume."

"Honey, Katie and Jim Higgins always win for best costume. It's a wonder anyone else even bothers to dress up."

"That's a defeatist attitude, George."

"That's reality." George was right, not that I'd ever admit that within Jinx's hearing. The Higginses went all out. It was a point of pride for Katie.

The four of us walked toward the long line of golf carts, stopping in front of the two with our names on cards on the front. The men climbed into the drivers' seats, and Anarchy handed me the scorecard.

I opened the bottle of water one of the pros has left in the cup holder. "Looks like we tee off on five."

Anarchy frowned. "Maybe you should drive."

It dawned on me; he didn't know how to get to the fifth hole. "Just follow George."

A slight breezed ruffled my hair as we drove. It was refreshing. All too soon, we reached the par-three fifth hole and teed off. It was then I realized that Daddy was right; Anarchy had potential. His drive landed on the green within a few feet of the hole.

Maybe golf could be our new thing—better than our current thing, which involved finding bodies and solving crimes.

"Nice shot," said George, who'd driven his ball into a bunker, drained his beer can.

Jinx, who didn't drink, scowled at her husband.

We climbed aboard our carts and drove to the ladies' tee where Jinx and I took our shots. Mine landed on the green, but not as close to the hole as Anarchy's.

"How often do you practice?" I asked when I climbed back into the cart.

"Lucky shot."

At the green, we watched as George put a fresh beer in the cart's cup holder. He pulled his sand wedge from his bag, tripped through the soft sand, and glared at his ball, which was deep in the bunker. An impressive spray of sand accompanied his swing, but the ball hit the bunker's rim and dribbled back to his feet.

"Move, George," Jinx muttered. Her drive had been well short, and they'd decided to play George's. She pitched the ball onto the green and leaving it a foot away from the hole.

We ceded the putt, and Jinx gave her husband a tight smile. "I'm driving the cart."

He gave her a happy wave and headed toward the passenger seat.

We struggled to drive a marshmallow more than a few yards, we discovered we were terrible with opposite-hand drivers, we wiped sweat from our brows, and we laughed.

When we came off the course, George, who'd waved down the beer cart twice, was schnockered. And he wasn't alone. Anarchy, Jinx, and I were among the few sober golfers.

The club had set up a bar on the patio. An assortment of tables covered with white linens and mason jars stuffed to bursting with daisies and Queen Anne's lace sat in front of a buffet laden with chafing dishes.

Jinx and I immediately headed to the bar. She ordered a club soda with a splash of cranberry and a lime twist. I ordered a gin and tonic.

"Everyone's lubricated." She waved at the bleary crowd. "Go. Investigate." I followed the tilt of her still-extended hand to my husband, who was deep in conversation with Skip Wortham. The inference was clear. He was pumping our friends for information about the murders while I lazed at the bar.

"You're okay on your own?" I asked.

Jinx lit a cigarette and blew a plume of smoke into the humid air. "I'm fine."

I wrinkled my nose at the smell.

Jinx rolled her eyes.

I left her, drifting toward Robert Hart, who was chatting with Linda and Chuck Wade. Linda smiled when I approached.

"I'm so glad to see you, Ellison. How did you shoot?"

"Four under. You?"

She glanced at Chuck. "Driving the marshmallows proved challenging. And that seventh hole? We double-bogeyed."

"It's hard to putt with a seven iron."

"You used your iron?" she asked. "We switched to putters."

Robert's blurry gaze met mine. "You found Althea." He made it sound like an accusation.

"I did."

"You're bad luck."

"I have bad luck. The people I find would be dead no matter who discovered their bodies."

"That's very cold." As was the look he gave me.

"Maybe," I allowed. "But I'm truly sorry she died."

"She wasn't the nicest woman," Linda ventured. "Chuck manages her grandfather's trust, and he says she was demanding. Even difficult."

"Now, dear," Chuck murmured. "Let's not speak ill of the dead."

"That's just silly." Linda hiccupped. "You didn't have anything nice to say about her when she was alive."

"She wasn't all bad," said Robert.

Linda and Chuck stared at him like he'd just insisted pigs could fly.

"She could be fun," he insisted.

Their incredulous expressions grew even more pronounced.

Lois, who'd approached quietly, clutched my arm. "Good

golly, that was fun." She offered us a lopsided smile. "And hot!" She waved her hand in front of her face, and her eyes crossed.

"How did you do with the marshmallow?" I asked.

"Better than the opposite-hand driver. We got to the ladies' tee, and there it was, waiting for us. A torture device."

I twitched.

"You okay, Ellison?" Chuck asked.

"Fine." I held up my drink and lied. "Just thirsty."

"It was nothing but pre-meditated cruelty," Lois continued. "They left those drivers hoping we'd fail."

"They didn't," I murmured.

Lois frowned at me.

How could she know I was talking about a knife, not a driver? Someone could have hidden a knife in the ladies' lounge, in a side-table drawer or under the settee's cushions. If Althea hadn't visited the lounge, she'd still be alive. But she had ducked into the lounge, and the killer had been ready. They hadn't failed.

I'd been wrong to dismiss Tish as a suspect. She'd had the opportunity to kill Althea. Heck, Louise had seen her leaving the lounge. And given what we knew about the baby, her motive was stronger than ever.

CHAPTER ELEVEN

Brnng, Brnng.

I glared at the phone, as if it were responsible for someone calling before I'd finished my first post-morning-swim cup of coffee.

Brnng, brnng.

Are you going to answer that? Mr. Coffee's tone was curious, not judgmental. If I let the machine pick up, he wouldn't think any less of me.

Brnng, brn—

I snatched the receiver off its cradle. "Hello."

"Ellison, it's Kay on the line."

I forced warmth into my voice. "Good morning." I sipped my coffee and waited for her to explain why she was calling so early. Several seconds passed in silence. She wasn't speaking, but her silence felt heavy—whatever she wanted, she was afraid I'd say no.

The vase of Gerber daisies on the kitchen island caught my eye. As expected, Aggie had religiously changed the water in the vase. The flowers from Kay's luncheon were still vibrant.

"The police are going to release the body, and I don't know

what to do," Kay said, her voice breaking. Althea. She wanted help with Althea. "I've been up all night worrying."

"Did Althea leave any instructions?" I asked, though I doubted it. People in their forties didn't usually expect to die.

"I need to look. Would you go to the house with me? Please?"

"The police said it's okay to enter her house?"

"They did."

"Then I'll go with you."

"Thank you, thank you, thank you."

I raked my fingers through my hair, wondering what I'd gotten myself into. "When do you want to go?"

"This morning, if you're free."

I glanced at the clock. I needed a shower, the dogs needed a walk, and Lord only knew what Grace needed. "Ten o'clock."

"I'll pick you up."

"Fine. See you then."

I hung up the phone, sighing. I didn't really want to do this, but I would—because Kay needed me.

Why didn't she call Libba? Mr. Coffee's amused tone cut through my self-pitying thoughts.

Sorting through a dead woman's belongings in search of funeral instructions wasn't something you called just anyone for. Especially not Libba. Burial or cremation? What should she be buried in? Actually, Libba would be good at that part. What hymns at the service? Who would give the eulogy? If you asked me, planning a funeral was almost as much work as planning a wedding.

But I'd offered to help, so I'd be combing through Althea's desk or nightstand soon enough.

You're a good friend. And it won't be as bad as you think. I promise. Mr. Coffee always knew how to lighten my mood.

Woof, woof. The dogs barked at the back door, demanding to be let in.

I opened it, and Finn barreled past me. Max, sensing my stress, lingered. He pressed against my legs, allowing me to stroke his silky ears. I needed that.

He wriggled with happiness when Anarchy, who was dressed and ready for work, joined us in the kitchen, dropping a quick kiss on my cheek. "Who was on the phone?"

"Kay. She wants me to go to Althea's with her. She thinks Althea may have left funeral instructions."

He searched my face. "You don't want to go."

"Not particularly."

"Uniforms have already been through the house. They didn't see anything to indicate that Althea thought she might die. Nothing about her final wishes." His expression clouded with worry. "I have a terrible feeling you'll be planning her funeral."

"Kay doesn't have anyone else, and her mother is dying."

"What about her other friends?"

"They're suspects in Althea's murder."

His lips thinned.

"That leaves me."

"She and John are still married. He could plan the funeral."

"Very funny."

"Since Althea's death, I've talked to people—she wasn't well liked. I'm not even sure anyone would attend."

"Be that as it may…"

"You're certain Kay won't ask John for help?"

"I'm certain. I promised I'd be there for her, and I can't abandon her the first time she asks for my help."

We both grew quiet. The unspoken expectations of parents, families, and friends tied my tongue. Women gave and gave and gave. Not because we were givers but because giving was expected of us. I thought back to my first marriage. When it fell apart, my mother told me it was my fault—that it was my job to put my husband's needs first. But Henry never put me first, not even once. I'd grown sick of all the giving.

But Anarchy...he was different. He rearranged his schedule to play in a golf scramble, took time off to drive Beau to the airport, and even made pancakes when he should've been at the station.

"I love you," I said, suddenly overwhelmed with gratitude.

He frowned, puzzled. "What brought that on?"

"Just remembering how lucky I am."

He took the coffee mug from my hand, gathered me in his arms, and dropped a kiss on my nose. "I'm the lucky one, and I love you too."

I rested my forehead against his chest, letting the warmth of his presence soothe me.

"We haven't cleared Kay," he said, his voice growing serious. "If you go with her, please be careful."

"About that...what if someone put the knife in the lounge before Althea arrived?" Rather like leaving a wrong-handed driver at the tee box.

"The cleaning crew was running late on Friday. Dolly and Toni didn't finish with the lounge until almost noon. They're sure there was no knife."

"You know the cleaning people's names?"

"As often as I've investigated at the club? I know the staff better than I know the members. Dolly and Toni are good people. Trust me. The knife wasn't there."

I wasn't convinced.

ALTHEA AND JOHN HAD SHARED A LARGE HOME NEAR LOOSE Park. It had the under-furnished feel of a broken marriage. No table in the dining room. No furniture in the walnut-paneled study. A missing coffee table in the family room and empty spaces where two chairs once sat.

"I'll have to clean all this out." Kay sounded utterly defeated.

"John may want some of it."

"One can hope."

"If not, I have the name of a woman who arranges estate sales."

Kay sank onto the nearest chair, one of two remaining in the family room. "I can't believe she's gone." She brushed a lock of hair away from her face. "I should feel sad. I should. But all I feel is exhausted."

"Do you want me to go through her desk?" I nodded toward the sturdy English antique in the corner of the room.

"Would you? Please?"

"I'm not sure what we'll find. The police have already been here."

"We have to look." She meant me. I had to look.

I pulled open the first drawer and found stationery, stamps, an address book, and a variety of pens. The second drawer was empty. "I bet this is where she kept her checkbook and bank statements."

Kay, who'd laced her hands together in her lap, didn't respond.

I pushed the drawer in and felt it catch on something. Pulling it back out, I snaked my hand inside and felt a piece of paper. "They missed something."

Kay looked up from the study of her hands.

I removed the drawer and reached to the back of the desk. Yanking gently, I pulled the paper free.

"What is it?"

I unfolded a sheet of creamy paper and read.

Althea,

Over the years, we've had our differences. You blackballed me at Kappa. At the time, I wanted to be a Kappa more than I wanted my next breath. I was devastated. And angry.

When I had the chance, I kept you out of the garden society. Petty? Yes. But so was blackballing me.

We've had bad blood between us for twenty years, and never, not once, have I considered a course of action that might affect you financially.

What you are doing, demanding that the firm terminate Skip, could ruin us.

I would beg you to stop, but I know my pleas are useless. Instead, I would remind you that I know your secret. If you destroy Skip's career, I will destroy you.

If you do this, I will end you.

Lois

"It's a letter from Lois. Here." I crossed the room and handed it to her.

She read Lois's neat cursive and paled. "I knew they didn't get along, but I had no idea they hated each other." The page fell from her limp fingers to her lap. "What should we do?"

"Give it to the police."

"But it makes Lois look guilty. Can't we pretend we never found it?"

"I don't hide potential evidence from my husband."

She sagged. "How do you deal with…well, you know?"

"Murder?"

She winced. "Yes."

"It's awful. No matter how prickly or difficult or unpleasant Althea was, she deserves justice."

"Even if it's Lois?"

I picked up the letter and scanned it a second time. Why on earth had Lois been so stupid? Committing threats to paper was never a good idea. What secret had she held over Althea? Had she known about Althea and Robert? About the baby?

I returned to the desk, put the letter on its surface, and opened the final drawer. It too was empty. "There's nothing here, Kay. Would you like me to look in her bedroom?"

"Please." She stood. "I'll come with you."

"Are you sure? You look tired. Maybe you could rest. How's your mom, today?"

"Not good. The nurses cost a fortune. I thought Mother had plenty of money, but I stopped by the bank yesterday. She's got a few thousand dollars in cash. I can't find any other assets."

"Her investments?"

"Gone."

"The house?"

"There's a mortgage. A big one. I suppose I could sell the place, but where would she live?" She shook her head. "At least I turn forty in a few days. If I have to, I'll use money from the trust to take care of her."

"I'm so sorry."

She held up her hands as if warding off my sympathy. "I just want to go back to New York and my life."

"I understand." On both counts. New York was her home. And sympathy when I was on the edge of tears made holding those tears back three times harder.

"I can't go home. I can't leave Mother. And Detective Peters told me not to leave town."

"Anarchy and Peters will find Althea's killer. One impediment gone." I winced. Referring to her dying mother as an impediment was thoughtless. "I'm sorry. That came out wrong."

"It's okay." She waved away my apology. "I need a drink."

It wasn't yet noon, but I wasn't about to argue with her. "I think I saw a liquor cart in the living room."

She nodded and stood. "Do you want anything?"

"No. Go get yourself something, and I'll check Althea's bedroom."

"You're a good friend, Ellison."

I gave her an encouraging smile, then climbed the stairs to the second floor.

Althea had kept the master bedroom furniture. Two bedside tables flanked a king-sized mattress. A silver tray filled with perfume bottles sat on the matching dresser. I opened the left side bedside table drawer and found it empty. The right-side drawer held hand cream, a prescription bottle, a manicure set, a pair of reading glasses, and a pen.

I frowned and went back to the bed's left side, opening the drawer a second time.

"Hmm." Why was John's drawer deeper than Althea's?

I returned to the right side, emptied Althea's drawer, and ran my fingers along the bottom. There was a divot. I worried at the imperfection, pushing until the opposite end of the false bottom lifted. I'd found Althea's journal.

There was little to no chance that she'd listed her final wishes in her diary, but I couldn't resist. I picked up the leather-bound book and began to read the more recent entries.

I'm in love. Love. I'd forgotten the swooping feeling in my stomach. I'd forgotten how a woman newly in love can live off emotion instead of food or sleep. I smile for no reason. I count the minutes until we can be together. I save the details of my day so that I can share them with him. He'll leave her. I know he will.

I searched the page for a date and found none.

We snuck away for the weekend. It was marvelous. We dined out without worrying about being spotted. We held hands in public. We made love all night long.

R says T won't give him a divorce.

Unacceptable.

I want to share a bed with him every night.

I want to wear his ring on my finger.

I want him to wear mine.

Had Robert cared for Althea the way she cared for him?

Sybil has taken a turn for the worse. I called Kay and told her she had to come to Kansas City. Sybil is her mother. Sybil is her responsibility. Not mine.

Kay didn't seem happy about leaving New York.

Why should she get a marvelous life when I'm stuck in Kansas City with a man who won't leave his wife? I could tell him about the baby. He'd leave her for sure. But I want him to want me. If he leaves because of the baby, I'll never be sure he truly wants me.

Did that mean Robert didn't know about the baby? I turned the page.

I told him. A child needs a father. He didn't react at first. He sat on the edge of bed in the motel room and stared at his hands. Then, he asked if I was sure.

"I am," I told him.

He asked if I was sure it was his.

I felt like he'd slapped me. I threw a glass at him. It caught his forehead, and shattered, and he swore at me. At me. The mother of his child.

I swore back.

It was our first fight.

R wiped the blood off his face and apologized. He promised we'd work something out. He just needs time to think. I know he'll come around and be as happy as I am.

Reading the journal, I didn't share Althea's optimism.

I always wanted a baby. Always. It's not my fault John couldn't get me pregnant. And now I'm going to have one. I can't believe R suggested I terminate the pregnancy. He tried to make it sound like he was concerned for my health—a first pregnancy at forty puts me and the baby at high risk.

A risk I'm willing to take.

I cried, and he wrapped his arm around my shoulders and promised that everything would be okay. It was the first Thursday since we started meeting at the hotel that we didn't make love.

My heart aches, and I need to talk to someone. Should I tell Kay?

I hadn't liked Althea, but reading her diary, I couldn't help but feel sorry for her. Had she told Kay? I doubted it. Kay wouldn't have included Tish and Althea at the same luncheon if she'd known.

T doesn't know about the baby. R hasn't told her. If she knew, she'd give him a divorce. I'm sure of it. R says he needs more time, but I'm tired of waiting. I want to celebrate this baby not hide it.

R says that no matter what the baby will be illegitimate.

He means that I should be ashamed. Well, it's his baby, too. And if he thinks for one minute that I'll allow him to weasel out of his responsibilities, he's crazy.

I don't understand why he stays with her. She's boring and twenty pounds overweight and the only thing they have in common is their history. If he doesn't tell her, I will.

Althea had been a dangerous mix of insecurity and anger and need. Had she told Tish? I turned the page.

I told R that I'll be showing soon. If he doesn't tell T about the baby, I will. He said he didn't appreciate ultimatums, but this is his fault, not mine. He's forced my hand.

He has three days.

If he doesn't tell her and ask for a divorce, I'll make his life a living hell.

I turned another page, hoping for a resolution, but Althea's promise to make Robert's life a living hell was her last entry.

And an excellent motive for murder.

CHAPTER TWELVE

Lois's letter and Althea's journal, both in marked evidence envelopes, sat on our kitchen island.

Anarchy glared at the envelopes and rubbed a palm across his chin. "I still can't believe the uniforms missed them."

I sat on the stool beside him. Of the two of us, I was in the more forgiving mood. "The letter was stuck at the back of the desk, and the journal was well hidden."

"You found them." He winced. "That came out wrong. You are the most observant person I know. It's no surprise you found them. It's a surprise they didn't."

"They did collect all the financial documents and everything pertaining to her divorce."

"And missed this." He sighed. "I should've gone through the house myself."

I clasped his hand and squeezed. "This isn't your fault. Besides, we have them now." I stared at the envelope holding Lois's letter. "Do you think Lois killed her?"

"You really want to discuss which of your friends killed Althea Dodson?"

"If it helps you, I do." I tapped the envelope with the tip of my finger. "We'll start with Lois."

Anarchy nodded, playing along. "She had a motive, and she wasn't accounted for at the time of the murder. According to you, her handbag was big enough to hold the knife."

"The same could be said of Skip. Well, except for the purse." I tilted my head as I remembered our luncheon. "What was he wearing?"

Anarchy stared at me. "A shirt. Pants."

"It was gray outside. It looked colder than it was. I wore a sweater wrapped around my shoulders. Libba wore a trench coat."

"What are you saying?" he asked.

"It wouldn't be hard to conceal a hunting knife under a golf sweater."

"Fair point. I don't remember a sweater. I'll have to check my notes. Kay?"

I tipped my head and stared at the ceiling. "I really hope my friend didn't kill her cousin," I muttered. Then I lowered my gaze to my fingers and began ticking off everything that indicated her guilt. "She had motive: with Althea gone, she gets the entire trust. And it sounds like she'll need the money to take care of her mother. She had the opportunity. She's unaccounted for after the luncheon. Her handbag was big enough for the knife, and her scarf was found beneath Althea's body. Wait—" I forgot my ticked fingers and held up my hand. "Kay's smart. If she killed Althea, she wouldn't leave her scarf behind."

"Maybe she didn't realize she lost it."

My hand dropped to my lap. "I want her to be innocent."

"I know you do, but we have to follow the evidence. Tish, next?"

Happy to move on, I listed the evidence against Tish. "She was seen leaving the ladies' lounge around the time of the murder. She didn't want a divorce, but Althea was pushing Robert. Hard. She had a motive."

"The knife is the stumbling block."

"Not really," I replied.

Anarchy frowned. "What do you mean?"

"No one would think twice about a woman carrying a gift bag into the clubhouse. She could have carried the knife that way."

"Dolly and Toni were in the lounge until noon."

"Tish was a few minutes late arriving. She could've walked into the clubhouse, gone straight to the lounge to hide the knife, then joined us. Also…

"Yes?"

"She and Kay visited the lounge before dessert. When I asked her about being in the ladies' lounge after lunch, she said she used the bathroom, but she'd been there twenty minutes prior."

"Suspicious," Anarchy agreed. "Unless she has a small bladder."

I smiled briefly and took a sip of iced tea.

He pointed at the envelope that held Althea's journal. "Robert has motive and opportunity."

"I don't know. When I spoke with him last night, he seemed upset. He scolded us about speaking ill of the dead."

"That doesn't mean he didn't kill her."

True. "Any of them could've done it." Frustration made me snarky. "We're missing something."

"Yes."

I stared at my husband, gob-smacked by his easy acceptance.

"We'll find the missing piece. We always do. Hopefully without you putting yourself in danger." He pulled his pager from its clip on his belt and frowned.

"What's wrong?" I asked.

"Hold on." He crossed to the phone and dialed. "Jones." He listened for a moment, then said, "On my way."

When he hung up, I repeated my question. "What's wrong?"

"Hazel York is dead. Murdered. Her cleaning lady found her."

"What?" The dogs, who'd been lounging with their chins on their paws, perked their ears at my pitch. "How long has she been dead? What happened?"

"I don't know." He gave me a quick kiss. "I've got to go. Peters is meeting me there."

The dogs followed him to the door, their tails in sync, matching metronomes. When the door closed behind him, they looked at me expectantly.

"Absolutely not," I told them. "It's a hundred degrees out. You can wait until dusk for a walk."

Max huffed his disappointment.

Finn scratched at the back door, and I let him out into the oppressive heat.

"Do you want to go?" I asked Max.

He rolled his eyes, then stretched out next to the air-conditioning vent.

Which was odd. The two were usually inseparable. Where one went, the other followed.

"Oh, dear."

Max lifted his head and stared at me.

"I have to go." I bribed Finn back into the house, grabbed my keys and handbag, and sped to the Walnuts. The luxury apartments (well, condominiums) were built in 1929 and housed couples (and widows) who no longer wanted to deal with the upkeep on a house. The three buildings were surrounded by ten acres of trees and gardens. I found a spot in the shade of a towering oak and was out of the car as soon as it was in park, running toward the elegant lobby.

"Jimmy!" I gasped for breath. "Is Mrs. Lawrence at home?"

Jimmy had probably seen much stranger things than my mad dash. He offered me an unflappable smile. "Good afternoon, Miss Ellison." The doorman had been calling me "Miss Ellison" since I was a girl visiting my grandparents, who'd lived on the seventh floor. My grandparents had adored Jimmy—so much so that I still remembered him every Christmas.

"Would you call upstairs? Please? I'm worried about Myra."

A frown settled on his face, and he picked up the phone and dialed. After a moment, his face cleared. "Mrs. Lawrence, Mrs. Jones is in the lobby asking after you." He nodded. "Yes, ma'am, I'll send her right up."

My breath steadied, and the tightness in my chest eased. "Thank you, Jimmy."

"My pleasure, Miss Ellison." He stepped out from behind his desk and pushed the button for the elevator. "You take care now."

I rode the elevator to Myra's floor, and when I stepped out, she was waiting at her open front door.

"What's wrong?" she asked. "What's happened?"

"Are you okay?"

The color drained from her face, and her hand clutched the doorframe. "It's Hazel, isn't it? She's dead."

"How did you know?"

"You'd better come in." The invitation was grudging at best. She stepped back, allowing me into her apartment. It was my first time in her home. It looked like she'd hired Sister Parish to decorate. An explosion of chintz met me in the living room— floral upholstery covered every chair and couch and pillow. A cashmere throw in a soft pink that complimented the upholstery was draped over the corner of the sofa. Pink lacquered side tables held ginger jar lamps. Botanical prints covered the walls.

"You have a beautiful apartment."

"Forget the small talk," she snapped. "What's happened to Hazel?"

"Anarchy got a call…"

Her usually firm chin wobbled.

"May I get you something? Tea? Coffee?"

"No." Myra swiped angrily at her eyes. "There's liquor. In that cabinet." She pointed and sank into an easy chair. "A scotch, please."

I hurried to fill an old-fashioned glass with whiskey. Myra drank Hiram Walker Imperial. "Water? Soda? Ice?" Dare I offer a twist? What if she didn't have a lemon?

She held up her palm, rejecting them all. "Straight."

I didn't argue. I handed her the drink, and she poured half the glass's contents down her throat.

"I warned her. I told her she needed to go to the police"

"She saw something the day Althea was murdered?"

"No." She downed the rest of her drink, then held out the glass for a refill. "She heard it."

"Pardon?" I took the glass and poured another finger of scotch.

"Two fingers, dear. Hazel was in the bathroom of the casual lounge." The casual lounge had a seating area where ladies might read or chat or play bridge. One passed through a doorway to the attached bathroom—three stalls, three sinks, and a wall of mirrors.

"She heard the murder?"

"That's what I said. Are you deaf?"

I handed her the two fingers of scotch, hoping eighty proof might mellow her. "Did she tell you what she heard?"

"There was an argument. Hazel recognized Tish Hart's voice. Althea claimed to be pregnant with Robert's baby."

"What did Tish say?"

"She told Althea she'd made a terrible mistake. Then she laughed, probably at Althea's expense. Can you imagine? Getting pregnant with another woman's husband's baby? And at her age. Hazel was struck speechless."

Meaning Hazel was quiet as a mouse to glean as much gossip as she possibly could.

"Hazel heard someone leave, but she was stuck in the bathroom. She could hardly announce herself after what she'd just heard." Because eavesdropping was a nasty habit.

"And then?"

"She heard the door open, and Althea said, 'You can't be in here.' Then Althea gasped and moaned. The door opened and closed again, and it was quiet. She let a moment pass before she peeked."

"She saw the body?"

"She did."

"She didn't call for help?"

"She was in shock. She ran."

"That's all?" According to Myra, Hazel hadn't known enough to get her killed.

"That's all she told me."

Understanding dawned. "She left things out."

"She said she waited at least a minute after he left. Before she peeked, I mean. Somehow, she knew it was a man." Myra stared at her empty glass. "Hazel liked her secrets."

In other words, Hazel had seen the killer, and rather than go to the police, she'd approached him herself.

I frowned, trying to come up with a reason why Hazel would remain silent about a murder. I could think of only two reasons. Either she knew the killer and was protecting him or she'd decided to try her hand at blackmail. Given that Hazel was dead, I was betting on the latter. "Was Hazel having financial difficulties?"

Myra flushed. "That's none of your business."

So, yes. "It is if she was blackmailing a killer."

"Hazel would never!"

"Hazel wasn't killed because she heard Althea tell someone they shouldn't be in the ladies' lounge."

Myra sagged. Slightly.

"I wonder, will the killer wonder about you?"

Her chin jerked upward till she could easily scowl at me. "What do you mean?"

"You and Hazel were inseparable. It would be only natural for her to tell you what she heard…or saw."

"She didn't," Myra's voice quivered.

"Are you sure?"

"She said it was a man. I'm not sure how she knew."

"She peeked. Then she approached him and got herself killed."

Myra gasped as if I'd thrown a bucket of cold water in her face. Her lips thinned. Her eyes narrowed. She shook her head.

"Need I remind you that he may come for you next?"

Her left hand rose to the pearls at her neck and clutched them. Her right hand tightened around the old-fashioned glass—tight enough to whiten her knuckles. "Fine. Yes. She was having difficulties. She was terrified that she'd outlive her money."

"So, she'd resorted to blackmailing a murderer?"

"Don't you dare judge her. Fear makes people do things they wouldn't ordinarily do."

That was true. Sometimes it pushed them toward bravery and heroics. More often than not, it made them stupid. That's what it had done for Hazel.

"I'd like to rest," said Myra. A polite way of telling me to leave.

I nodded. "Is there anything you need? Someone I can call?" Her children had moved away. Her husband was dead. Hazel had been her support.

"I'm fine," she said with more than a little asperity.

"Please, be careful."

"Hmph. You can see yourself out?"

"Goodbye." I rode the elevator to the ground floor and stopped at Jimmy's desk. "Mrs. Lawrence received some bad news. Would you please check on her before you go home for the day?"

His answering smile was both kind and sad. "Will do, Miss Ellison."

With nothing left to keep me, I stepped outside. The heat seemed almost solid, and perspiration immediately dewed my hairline. Since I already had one foot in hell, I decided I might as well go all in. I slid behind the steering wheel and drove the few blocks to Mother's.

I pulled the car around to the back of the house where an elm provided deep shade. Despite the Dutch elm disease decimating other trees in Kansas City, Mother and her arborist were keeping her elm healthy through force of will and the liberal application of fungicides.

Eager to get out of the heat, I opened the back door without knocking. The air-conditioning in the kitchen was heavenly, almost stinging in its icy chill. I enjoyed the cool for long seconds before calling, "Mother?"

Entering without an invitation. Through the backdoor. And raising my voice. None of these things would make her happy.

"Mother?" I wandered into the hallway that led to the front of the house.

She appeared at the top of the steps and glared at me over the balustrade. "What are you doing here?" Her eyes narrowed. "Did you find another body?"

Thankfully I could answer truthfully, "No."

"I hear a 'but.'"

"Hazel York is dead. Her cleaning lady found her."

"Which does not explain why you're in my house without calling first." Mother's eyes narrowed. "Or knocking."

This from the woman who barged into my house whenever she felt the urge.

"Kay Morrison told me that her mother was near penniless. Please don't repeat that." I waited for Mother's grudging nod before I continued. "I just left Myra Lawrence. She told me that Hazel was terrified she'd outlive her money."

Mother descended the stairs like a queen entering her throne room. Chin high. Shoulders and back straight. An air of superiority wrapped around her like an ermine cloak. "Why are you telling me this?"

"I thought they'd be well taken care of. Their husbands were successful..."

"A few bad investments."

That was the easy answer, but, for me, it didn't ring true. "Do you know who manages their money?"

"Heavens no!" She sounded outraged, as if I'd asked if she rifled through their lingerie drawers.

I'd ask Kay.

"What happened to Hazel York?"

"I'm not exactly sure. She was in the ladies' lounge when Althea was killed. I suspect she tried to blackmail the killer."

"She never was very bright." Mother, who'd joined me at the bottom of the stairs, stiffened. Then, she poked me in the chest. "Ellison Walford Russell—"

"Jones," I corrected as I rubbed the spot where Mother had poked me. She poked *hard*. What on earth had I done to deserve it? "Ellison Walford Jones."

"Whatever." She dismissed my second marriage. "You listen to me. You let your husband handle this. The killer has murdered two women in a week. And, I have too much to do to spend time worrying that you're going to be next."

"Mother—"

"I know what you're going to say. 'The police are handling it.' It's what you always say. Then you end up in the killer's sights. You're a painter, not a detective. Go paint."

"Okay."

She blinked at my easy acquiescence. What did she expect?

She was right. Also, it was the first time in my adult life that she'd encouraged me to paint.

"On one condition."

She raised her left brow, a reminder that I was not the one who made the rules in our relationship. "Yes?"

"If you hear of any other widows with unexpected financial woes, you'll let me know."

She didn't respond, her face remained impassive. Regal.

"Please."

"I'm not helping you investigate a murder."

"That's not what I'm asking. Sybil's in trouble, and Kay is worried. If someone is stealing from women unaccustomed to handling their own affairs, we could right a wrong."

Mother sniffed. She might not be the breadwinner in her household, but she knew where every penny was spent. What's more, she probably knew how every dime was invested. That didn't mean her friends were similarly aware. "Fine. If I hear anything, I'll let you know. But if I do this, you steer clear of this investigation."

I held out my hand. "Deal."

CHAPTER THIRTEEN

The afternoon light in my third-floor studio was perfect. I dabbed lemon yellow paint on the canvas, then took a step back—too much lemon, not enough butter. I added the tiniest touch of orange to the paint on my palette, mixed it, and added another stroke.

"Hi."

I had been so engrossed in my work that I hadn't heard Anarchy on the stairs.

I smiled at him. "I didn't expect you back so soon."

"They called us as a courtesy. One of the uniforms recognized Hazel York's name from the list of people at the country club when Althea was murdered."

"What happened?"

He grimaced and looked at the canvas instead of me. "Looks like a B and E gone bad."

"B and E?" I asked.

"Breaking and entering. Someone broke in, and the intruder hit her with a fireplace poker, crushed her skull. The silver is missing—I assume someone like Hazel York had silver—and someone pawed through her jewelry."

"Hmm."

His eyes narrowed. "I know that 'hmm.' You have pertinent information."

"I spoke with Myra Lawrence while you were gone. Actually, I went to see her to make sure she was okay. She and Hazel were pretty much inseparable, and I worried that if something had happened to Hazel, it might've happened to Myra too. But she's alive and well."

He nodded, waiting for me to continue.

"She told me Hazel was in the bathroom when Althea was murdered. She heard an argument between Althea and Tish, and she heard Tish leave. Then someone else came in. Whoever he was, he killed Althea."

"He?"

I put down my paintbrush. "Hazel saw the killer."

"Why didn't she tell the police?"

"I suspect she hoped to blackmail him."

"So, a murder not a robbery." He frowned. "Why would someone like Hazel resort to blackmail?"

"Myra said she was worried about outliving her money. I wonder…"

"What?"

"I wonder if the silver was actually stolen. She might have sold it."

"I'll call Peters. We need to interview Myra Lawrence."

The thought of Peters and his disreputable trench coat on Myra's chintz sofa made me smile. Although, it had been so hot lately that he'd been spotted without it—not that his plaid sport jacket was any better. It was wrinkled and looked like its best days were a decade in the past.

"Anything else I should know?"

"I promised my mother I'd stay out of the investigation."

His eyes sparkled.

"I've said something amusing?"

"Trouble has a way of finding you."

"I know. But I won't go looking for it."

The grin widened.

"I won't!"

"Mom!" Grace's voice carried up the stairs. "There's a phone call for you. It's Kay Morrison. I think you'd better take it. She's crying."

I glanced at Anarchy. "I know you need to go, but would you please wash my brushes?"

"Of course, talk to your friend."

I plugged the phone into the jack (I kept the phone unplugged so I could work without interruptions). "Kay?"

"Will you come over, please?" She gave a long, wet, shuddering sigh. "Mother is gone."

"Oh, no. I'm so sorry."

"I was sitting with her, holding her hand, and she was resting. She opened her eyes and stared at me. Then she said she guessed I'd turned out okay. I asked her if she wanted some water. She shook her head...and died." Kay sounded heartbroken. Her two closest relatives both gone within a week.

"I'm on my way."

I took a few minutes to wash my hands, change out of my paint clothes, and run a brush through my hair, then I drove to Sybil's house.

When Kay opened the front door, her cheeks were tear-stained, her eyes were red, and her chin wobbled.

"I'm so sorry for your loss." I opened my arms.

She collapsed into me, and I rubbed gentle circles on her back as she soaked my tee-shirt.

"I shouldn't cry."

"You should cry. Don't let anyone tell you different. It's the expression of an emotion. Emotions should be experienced, not stuffed down deep inside us because they're inconvenient. Cry. Rage. Do whatever you need to do."

She sniffled through a laugh. "When did you get so smart?"

"Not smart, just experienced."

She pulled away and mopped her eyes with the backs of her hands. "Thank you so much for coming. I don't know what to do next."

"Did Sybil leave any instructions? Which funeral home? Which church?"

"I don't know. I should have looked but...."

She'd been avoiding the realities of her mother dying.

"I'll see if I can find the instructions, then, if you'd like, I'll make the calls."

"You'd do that?" She looked at me like I'd just offered her a kidney.

That much gratitude for something so small made me itchy. I tugged at the scooped neck of my tee-shirt. "It's no problem. Is there anyone else I should call?"

"Her friends?" Kay ground the heels of her hands into her eyes. "I don't know who they are anymore."

"We'll figure it out. Where's her desk?"

"The living room. While you look, I'll make us some coffee."

Sybil's desk was very gilt and very French, and I felt like a royal impostor as I settled into the delicate chair behind it. The surface was littered with mail—letters, cards, bills to be paid—but no invitations. Sybil's friends knew she couldn't socialize.

Had they come to visit? Had they held tightly to the bonds of friendship as Sybil's mind slipped away? I searched my memory for the women I'd seen at the bridge table with her—Theodora "Teddy" Bryant—she deserved a call. What's more, she'd know who else among Sybil's friends I should call.

I opened the desk drawer and found a box of engraved Crane stationery, stamps, pens, paper clips, a roll of tape—nothing remotely resembling instructions for Sybil's funeral.

Where else might they be?

The house was big enough to have a study. I went and found it.

With walnut paneling, plaid carpet, and tweed upholstery on the chairs, I was willing to bet the decor hadn't been changed since the day Kay's father had passed.

I opened the filing cabinet and found neatly labeled files.

Mortgage.

Checking and savings.

Insurance.

Taxes.

Estate Plan.

I pulled out the estate plan file and opened it on the desk. The leather chair creaked when I sat down. "Kay," I called.

She didn't answer.

I gave her a moment, then began to skim through the pages. I breathed a sigh of relief as I read. Kay inherited everything. I wouldn't have put it past Sybil to disinherit her daughter, a final slight from beyond the grave. Chuck Wade was listed as the executor, and if he was unable to fulfill his duties, his firm had the power to appoint a replacement.

I flipped to the end of the document and found what I was looking for—the name of the funeral home she preferred. Her burial plot, next to her husband's, had been bought and paid for, and a list of her favorite hymns was included. It would make things easier.

I rose and crossed to the door. "Kay!"

She appeared in the foyer with two mugs in her hands. "Coffee?"

"Please." I accepted the mug. "I found what we need in a file titled *Estate Plan*. All the documents seem well-organized."

"You haven't seen the mess in the laundry room. When Mom's mind started to go she began throwing anything she deemed important into a wicker laundry basket. It's overflowing. Two years of statements and correspondence."

I went back to the cabinet and opened the brokerage file. The most recent statement was two years old. "I see what you mean. This is dated—" my gaze caught on the account value. "Do you have a more recent statement?"

"I'm sure there's one in the laundry basket."

"Two years ago, there was two-hundred-thousand dollars in this account. If we can find more recent statements, I'll ask Karma to review them."

Kay raked her fingers through her hair. "Why?"

"Someone may have been taking advantage of your mother. I'll probably need bank statements too."

Kay shrugged. She didn't seem to care that someone might have stolen her inheritance. "Whatever you want."

"But first, we need to call the funeral home. They'll take care of your mom."

She drew a sudden, sharp breath, loud enough for me to hear. "You'll call them?"

"Of course, I will."

"Do you mind if I sit with her until they arrive?"

"Not at all. If it's okay with you, I'll collect the rest of the statements."

"Good luck finding them."

"I can also call her friends."

"Thank you, Ellison." She turned away from me, a sudden, brittle movement that revealed the depths of her grief.

When she was gone, I settled behind the desk, located a phone book in the bottom right-hand drawer, and looked up the funeral home's number. The phone was older, with a rotary dial, and my fingers were slow as each digit click-click-clicked.

After I explained who I was and why I was calling, they agreed to send someone.

We hung up, and I took a restorative sip of coffee. Then, I looked up Teddy's number.

This time, my fingers were even slower.

"Bryant residence."

"May I please speak with Mrs. Bryant?"

"Who may I say is calling?"

"Ellison Jones." I swallowed a bit of annoyance with a quick sip of coffee and added, "She may know me as Ellison Russell."

"One moment, please, Mrs. Jones."

I flipped through Sybil's brokerage file while I waited. The account value had steadily grown for years. I knew round-the-clock, in-home care was expensive, but I didn't see any way she could have spent so much.

"Ellison?"

"Teddy. Kay Morrison asked me to call you." Not exactly true, but a lie that might bring Teddy some comfort.

"It's Sybil." Teddy's voice was soft, pained. "She's gone."

"I'm afraid so."

"What can I do?"

"I've called the funeral home, and Kay is upstairs sitting with her mother." Inspiration struck. "You and Sybil were such good friends, would you mind helping Kay organize the funeral. I feel certain you know exactly what Sybil would have wanted."

"You're not helping?"

"I'm helping with Althea's funeral."

"Poor Kay. Of course, I'd be happy to help. Sybil could be particular."

"Yes."

It was as close as either of us would come to speaking ill of the dead.

"Tell Kay I'll come by tomorrow morning around ten. We can get everything organized then. Also, I'll call Sybil's friends."

"Thank you." I didn't know her well, but Teddy Bryant had just earned my highest regard.

~

KARMA SAT AT THE KITCHEN ISLAND WITH A GLASS OF WINE NEAR her hand and Sybil's brokerage statements spread out in front of her. "If someone was stealing, it wasn't the broker. Everything looks in order. The actual sales look fine, and the amounts correspond with deposits made to her checking account." She tapped her nails on a stack of bank statements. "There are large withdrawals from that account. Are you sure she wasn't sending money to one of those evangelists on TV?"

"Not if she was in her right mind." Which, admittedly, she hadn't been. "I've got a bad feeling." I rubbed a hand across my forehead. "I'm worried Sybil isn't the only one."

She swirled the wine in her glass. "What do you mean?"

"Hazel York was worried about outliving her money. I wonder, if we looked at her statements, would we find large withdrawals?"

"Didn't Sybil have dementia?" Karma asked.

"She did," I admitted. "And Hazel seemed sharp as a tack. But something isn't right—I'm sure of it."

"And you're investigating?" Karma prompted.

"I promised Mother I'd stay away from the murders. This is different. If someone is preying on older ladies, I'd like them caught."

"And if the missing money and the murders are related?"

"I don't see how they could be. Althea was young. Well, young-ish. And Anarchy looked at her finances. He didn't find anything amiss. No, I think Hazel was killed because she saw the killer and decided to blackmail him. More wine?"

"Please."

I topped off our glasses.

"How will you investigate?"

It wasn't for nothing I was the board chairman of a bank. "I'll stop by the bank tomorrow. It's possible other older ladies are making large cash withdrawals."

"Did Hazel York bank with you?"

"She did not. Why?"

"Sometimes, people use the note line on a check. You know, if you cash a check to pay the young man who mows your yard, you might write 'lawn,' or if your hairdresser prefers to be paid in cash, you might write 'hair.' I thought if she banked with you, you could look at her cancelled checks."

"Checks are returned with statements, the bank doesn't keep them. But, it's a good idea. I can swing by Sybil's tomorrow and take a look at her canceled checks. Also, I'll tell Anarchy."

"Tell me what?" My husband stepped into the kitchen, nodded at Karma, then kissed my cheek.

"I'm wondering if Hazel made any large withdrawals from her accounts."

He frowned. "You think it might have something to do with her murder?"

"I do not. But I do think someone may have been taking advantage of her."

"I'll see what I can find."

It was sweet of him to offer, but the man was investigating a murder. He didn't have time to review cancelled checks. On this, I was on my own.

CHAPTER FOURTEEN

I pulled into a parking spot and checked my watch. Nine-fifteen. The bank had been open for fifteen minutes, and, hopefully, the morning rush was over.

Or maybe not.

The parking lot was nearly full.

I took a last sip of the coffee I'd poured into a to-go cup, then got out of the car.

Millicent Cushing, who looked like a strong wind might blow her away, stood outside the bank's entrance and scanned the lot. Like Mother, Millicent wore her white hair in a helmet. But Mother's was sleek, even elegant. Millicent's hair was fluffy. Which matched her personality. She was a wispy sort of woman, one who wrung her hands when presented with a problem.

"Good morning, Mrs. Cushing."

She stared at me for long seconds before saying, "Ellison, how nice to see you."

"Likewise. How are you?"

"Fine, dear. Fine. Although this heat is exhausting." She shook her head as if the weather were a personal tragedy.

If the morning had ever held any coolness, it was long since gone. The sun and the humidity promised another day of oven-like temperatures.

"When I was a girl, the summers didn't seem so brutal."

When she was a girl, air-conditioning meant putting a block of ice in a galvanized tub and blowing a fan over it. "Did you summer up north?" Many Kansas City families had second homes in Minnesota or Michigan.

"No. My parents had a place in Platte County." The county to the north and west of Jackson County where Kansas City was located. "The Mississippi ran not a quarter mile from the house, and the breeze off the river kept us cool."

The Mississippi? I wasn't about to correct an octogenarian's geography.

"I remember it like it was yesterday." She stared at the cars whizzing past us, but I got the sense she was looking at something else. "In the evenings, I'd curl up on my father's lap and we'd listen to the radio. My father loved *Abbott & Costello*."

"Is that so?" I added a layer of kindness to my voice. Mrs. Cushing was confused about more than geography. I was fairly certain radios didn't appear in homes until the 1920s. I was absolutely certain I'd listened to *Abbott & Costello* as a child. Bud Abbott and Lou Costello hadn't been alive when Mrs. Cushing was a child on her father's lap. "Who's on first?"

"Who?"

"Who's on first."

"What?"

"What's on second."

She frowned at me, and I realized she wasn't playing along, she was genuinely confused.

"Never mind," I told her. "I'm being silly."

She offered me an indulgent smile. "You young people and your slang."

"It's nice to see you." I moved toward the bank's entrance.

Mrs. Cushing remained on the sidewalk, unmoving, with a befuddled expression on her face.

I paused. "May I help you with something?"

"I can't remember where I parked my car."

"Happens to me all the time. What does it look like?"

"It's black." There were three black cars in the lot.

"What make?"

She blinked.

"What make? Ford? Lincoln? Oldsmobile?"

"Oldsmobile."

"Is that it?" I pointed at a black Oldsmobile Ninety-Eight.

"How clever of you." She dug in her purse, a vintage crocodile handbag, and withdrew her keys.

"You're okay to drive?"

Her expression sharpened. "Of course. Why would you ask such a thing?"

"No reason." I watched her climb into her car and back out of her parking spot. When she turned onto the street, I entered the bank.

"Mrs. Jones." The branch manager, Donna, stepped out of her office to welcome me. "I saw you visiting with Mrs. Cushing."

"She seemed confused."

Donna nodded. "She comes by most mornings and parks in a different spot every time. Then, she can't find her car. Sometimes, she panics."

"That's actually why I'm here. Do you have time to chat with me?"

"Of course." She waved toward her office. "Coffee?"

"Please."

"As I remember, you take cream."

"That's right."

"Please, have a seat. I'll join you in a moment."

On Donna's desk, a neat stack of documents awaited her

attention. The papers shared space with family photos, a silver julep cup filled with pens, a Murano glass paperweight, and a mug of cooling coffee.

Donna offered me a steaming mug, then slipped behind her desk. "You wanted to talk about Mrs. Cushing?"

"Not her specifically, but women like her. Widows who may be a bit confused."

"What about them?"

"I have concerns that someone is preying on them."

"I see."

"Do we have any older customers who regularly withdraw large amounts of cash?"

"Please define large."

"Two thousand dollars or more." Banks kept cash on hand based on the estimated demand in a week. They tended to have more cash in their vaults on the first and fifteenth of the month to accommodate payroll checks. Otherwise, the daily need for cash often matched up with cash deposits. A bank would notice large outlays.

"I can ask the head teller. She's the one who makes sure we have enough cash."

"Please, do that."

"I'll get her." Donna left me, and I sipped my coffee.

When she returned, an older woman with a tight, graying perm and wire-rimmed glasses was with her. "Mrs. Jones, this is Jo, our head teller. Jo, meet Mrs. Jones, the board chairman."

Jo managed a nervous smile. "Donna says you want to know about large withdrawals."

"Yes. Especially older ladies."

Jo scrunched her face and shook her head. "Occasionally we'll get a large withdrawal if someone is going on vacation. Although, we try to talk those customers into carrying travelers checks."

"So, nothing suspicious."

Jo tilted her chin to the side. "I wouldn't say that."

"Oh?" Donna and I spoke as one.

"It might be nothing."

"Tell me. Please."

"We have a couple of older customers who withdraw cash almost every day."

"How much cash?"

"Mrs. Cushing takes out between one-hundred-fifty and two-hundred dollars five times a week. Then there's Mrs. Whittier. She does the same thing."

"Are they the only two?"

"Mrs. Livingston comes in every Monday and withdraws a thousand dollars. I asked her once what she used it for, and she said, 'expenses.'"

I did some quick math. I paid Aggie seven-hundred dollars a week, paid the lawn service fifty dollars a week, and spent less than a hundred on groceries. Sure, there were a few incidentals—the dry cleaners, the occasional prescription, a trip to Winstead's for burgers and frosty malts—but they didn't amount to much. How was a single woman, living in a house that was smaller than mine, spending so much? "What kind of expenses?"

"She wouldn't say."

I glanced at Donna. "Is there any kind of direction about this from the American Bankers' Association?"

"No."

"There should be."

Jo glanced at her wrist. "Mrs. Whittier should be here soon. She usually comes in around nine-thirty."

I glanced at Donna. "I'd like to talk to her."

"She may not tell you anything."

"I'd still like to talk to her."

"She's here." Donna nodded toward the bank's entrance, where Mabel Whittier seemed to be getting her bearings. Mabel was a tall woman with faded blue eyes. She kept her gray hair cut short and never bothered with anything as silly as makeup.

I took a large gulp of coffee.

"She's..." Jo's voice trailed off.

I looked at the teller. "She's what?"

Jo winced. "She has good days and bad days."

"Thanks for letting me know." Hopefully, this was one of the good days. I stepped into the lobby and approached the older lady. "Mrs. Whittier?"

She turned toward me. "Frances, how nice to see you."

"I'm Ellison, Frances's daughter." Did I look like Mother? Surely not. Mother wore her white hair in a helmet. I wore my dark blonde hair at shoulder length. Mother was taller. I was thinner. And I took after Daddy. "It's nice to see you, too."

Mrs. Whittier nodded. Slowly. "Ellison. Of course. You're the painter."

"That's right."

"The one who finds bodies."

I winced. "Not on purpose."

How did one ask an acquaintance how they spent their money? The question was intrusive and rude and necessary. "We've been auditing our cash outlays."

"You work for the bank now?"

"I sit on the board until Grace turns twenty-five." At the moment, that seemed an eternity away.

She nodded. "What about them?"

"We notice that you're withdrawing approximately a thousand dollars a week."

She frowned. "That much?"

"Do you need that much cash?"

"I really don't see that it's any of your business."

"No. You're right. My apologies. How's Ogden?" Her son was about ten years older than me. "Is he still in Chicago?"

"Deerfield. He's the chief executive officer of that company. The one that makes…" her face shuttered in concentration.

"That's right. I remember now. He's been there since he finished at Kellogg. Please give him my regards."

"I will, dear. It's nice to see you."

"Likewise." I retreated to Donna's office. "Is Ogden Whittier on any of his mother's accounts?"

"I can check," she replied.

"Please." I took a sip of coffee and smiled; it was still hot. "Also, please check and see if we have a phone number for him."

"I'll be right back." Donna left me to check on the signature card for Mabel's account. When she returned she gave a slip of paper with two numbers on it. One had a seven-oh-eight area code, the other a three-one-two.

"Ogden?"

"He's on the account. The seven-oh-eight is home. Three-one-two is his office."

"Thank you."

"We may lose the account."

"If we do, it'll be on me." I'd rather lose an account than let Mabel end up like Sybil, down to her last few thousand dollars.

I drove home, took a seat behind my desk, and called Ogden's office number.

"Mr. Whittier's office."

"Good morning. My name is Ellison Jones. I'm from Kansas City, and I'm calling Ogden in regards to his mother. May I please speak with him?"

"Would you hold, please?" She put me on hold without waiting for my response.

I picked up a pencil and doodled a picture of Max and Finn playing. I didn't need real life models, I saw their tussles often enough to know that Finn bent in a near boneless fashion.

"Ellison?" Ogden's voice pulled me away from getting the right angle on Max's tail.

"Ogden—"

"You're calling about Mom. Is she all right?"

"She's fine." I gathered my courage. "I called because I'm on the board of her bank. Are you aware that she's withdrawing a thousand dollars a week in cash?"

"What?" He sounded suitably gobsmacked.

"Recently, I've run across a few ladies' whose assets have been depleted, and we—the bank, I mean—are trying to look out for our customers." I added a few lines to Max's tail. The angle conveyed both playfulness and an absolute determination to win.

"A thousand dollars a week? I've arranged to have all her bills paid. Aside from groceries and dinners or lunches with her friends, what does she spend it on?"

"Honestly, I don't know." I pulled an envelope from my desk drawer. I'd send the doodle to Beau. I bet he was missing the dogs.

"Can you cut her off?"

"Not unless you have her declared incompetent."

He swore softly. "What other ladies?"

"Contemporaries of your mother's."

"I see. I knew she was slipping but—Denise! Cancel the rest of my week and book me on an afternoon flight to Kansas City. Thank you for calling, Ellison. And for looking out for Mom. I appreciate it."

"Ogden, if you happen to find out where the money is going…"

"I'll call you."

I hung up the phone feeling better. I'd done the right thing, at least for Mabel.

～

LIBBA, JINX, AND I SAT AT THE BRIDGE TABLE AND WAITED FOR Daisy. Waiting for Daisy was nothing new, and as Libba idly shuffled a deck of cards, Jinx lit a cigarette.

"Any news on Althea's murder?" she asked.

"No," I lied.

"I heard Hazel York was murdered."

I nodded. "The police's initial assessment is a B and E gone wrong." I adored using Anarchy's jargon. Unfortunately, neither Jinx nor Libba asked me to clarify.

"How's Kay?" Jinx turned her head and blew a plume of smoke away from Libba and me.

I'd gone by Sybil's house after I talked to Ogden. "Not great."

"We should take her to dinner tonight," said Libba. "The last thing she needs is to sit in that house by herself."

"When I left, Teddy Bryant was with her. I got the impression that Teddy has the rest of her day planned out."

"Nice woman," said Jinx. "A straight shooter. I like that."

"I'm late. I'm late. I'm sorry!" Daisy launched herself into the chair across from Jinx. "The kids were—well, the less said, the better."

Daisy had entirely too many kids, and her friends, who'd noticed her recent switch from gin to club soda, worried another was on the way.

"This is the first time I've been in the clubhouse since the murder." She shuddered. "What a day. The rain. The children were climbing the walls. Tom and Louis decided to play catch with an apple in the family room. One of them, neither will admit who, threw high, and the apple ended up caught in the ceiling fan blades. There was apple *everywhere*. Susan and Mary were at each other's throats. The minute the sun came out, I loaded the young ones in the car and came here. Of course, Janie flung open her door and dinged the car next to us. Louise Danner's. And Louise saw it happen. I assured her we'd pay for the damages, but she acted like the kids were little devils."

Louise wasn't far wrong.

"Then, Matthew, who couldn't wait to get to the pool, took off running. He ran into Chuck Wade and got strawberry jam on his golf pants."

"Strawberry jam?" asked Libba. "Why did he have strawberry jam?"

"He didn't have the jar," Daisy clarified. "He had a peanut butter and jelly sandwich. He refused to eat his lunch, and then, when we were ready to leave, he was *starving*. Marvin got a bit tetchy over the June bill, so I've been trying to cut down. I made him the dratted sandwich to eat in the car. Apparently he was covered in jam when he ran into Chuck." She sighed. "At least Chuck was nice about it. Unlike Louise." She turned to me. "How is Beau doing at camp? I've got three leaving next week, and I'm counting the minutes."

"I haven't heard from them."

"I love getting that first post card."

Jinx pushed a made deck toward me. "Cut."

I cut, and she dealt.

"What about you, Libba?" asked Daisy. "Do Charlie's kids go to camp?"

"They're there now. Having the house to ourselves has been bliss."

Daisy picked up her cards and began to sort. "Was anyone here at the Wade wedding?"

"I was," said Jinx. "One spade."

"Two hearts." Libba tapped her cards against the table's edge to close her hand.

"One no-trump," said Daisy.

"You have to bid two," I told her.

She frowned. "Do I?"

"Over two hearts."

"Oh. You're right. Pass."

It was my bid. "Three hearts. And I was also at the wedding."

Jinx frowned at her hand. "Pass."

"I heard the wedding was…" Daisy searched for a word adequate to describe the disaster.

"No air-conditioning. It's your lead."

Daisy led a spade, and I laid down my hand. Ten points. Three hearts. Decent support.

Libba played low from the board, and Jinx played the king.

"Did the groom really throw up on Chuck?"

"He did." Jinx watched Libba play another low spade, then swept the trick.

"Poor man. It was his weekend to get dirty. First the jam, then the vomit."

"Can we not talk about vomit?" asked Libba.

"Fine. But if you had small children at home, a bit of vomit wouldn't bother you."

"I'll take your word for it."

"Speaking of children…" Jinx's brows rose in question.

"I'm not pregnant," Daisy said with a sigh. "That is what you were going to ask?"

Jinx nodded.

"I quit drinking to lose a few pounds. Cutting out gin is easier than cutting out sweets."

Libba looked at her like she'd grown a second head.

"If you think I'm pregnant, my no-alcohol diet isn't working." Daisy smoothed her skirt over her lap. "Six is enough. It'll be nice for them when we're old."

We all gaped at her, but it was Jinx who asked, "Whatever do you mean?"

"Marvin's an only child, and his mother isn't who she used to be. She's…needy. And Marvin, bless his heart, is not a caretaker.

She drives him crazy. Also, he worries about her, and there's no one to share the burden."

I strongly suspected that Daisy shared the burden.

"It'll be nice to have kids to look out for us when we're ga-ga."

I stared at the dummy board. Sybil. Hazel. Millicent. Mabel. Their kids had moved away. They were alone. No one was looking out for them. I was more sure than ever that someone was targeting older ladies. But how had they found their targets?

CHAPTER FIFTEEN

K ay, Teddy, and I sat in the booth at Winstead's. When I'd called to invite Kay to dinner, she'd accepted, told me she didn't feel like dressing up, then asked if Teddy could join us.

"Of course," I'd replied. After all, Anarchy had to be at the station, and Grace, much to my surprise, had accepted another date with Jonathan Kettering. After the grilling Mother gave her, I'd assumed poor, foolish Jonathan would be as appealing as week-old fish.

"We accomplished a great deal today." Teddy had a satisfied tilt to her head. She took a sip of limeade and gave the table three quick raps for emphasis. "The funeral will be next Tuesday afternoon, the obituary will run Sunday, and we've decided to bury Sybil in her navy St. John suit. I'll give the eulogy."

"Oh?"

"I've known Sybil my whole life." Her gaze slid to Kay. "She could be stubborn, even difficult, but she was a wonderful friend."

She might have been a good friend, but she'd been a sub-par

mother. I kept that thought to myself. "You accomplished so much." Meanwhile, I'd gone to the bank, then played bridge.

"Of course, there will be a reception at the club following the service."

"Of course."

Kay's lips twitched at the dryness in my tone. "Teddy has been amazing." My usually chic friend had dark circles under her eyes, and she looked pale underneath her tan. She'd chosen to wear a black tee-shirt, and it seemed to hang too loosely on her frame. "I'm sure the funeral will be just what mother would have wanted."

Teddy ducked her head, hiding a smile. "Where are you in the planning for Althea's service?"

I was guilty of procrastination. Not that I'd admit that. "The funeral is scheduled for the Monday after Sybil's. I'm working on the obituary." Not exactly true. Not remotely true. What was I supposed to say about a woman I barely knew? Did I include John as her husband? Where should mourners send donations in her memory? I pushed those questions aside. "When I looked in Althea's closet, I noticed several light blue dresses. I assume it was her favorite color. She'll be buried in one of those."

"The eulogy?" Teddy regarded me with bright, interested eyes.

Poor Althea had led a lonely life. She hadn't cultivated women friends. Her marriage had ended in an ugly divorce (well, almost ended). And she'd taken up with another woman's husband. I hadn't found anyone who could eulogize her. "The minister will give the eulogy."

"Which hymns?" Teddy asked. "I'd hate to duplicate."

Singing the same hymn at two different funerals was the least of my worries. "I left that to the minister."

"The reception?"

"Cookies and coffee and punch in the church basement." Mother had agreed to help me with that part.

Kay, who had her elbows planted on the table and her head in her hands, looked up. "Did your sister look at Mom's statements?"

Happy not to talk about Althea's service, I replied with alacrity. "She did. There were numerous cash withdrawals from the checking account."

"What's this?" Teddy asked.

"Ellison thinks someone took advantage of Mom. There's hardly any money left."

Teddy jerked backward. "Sybil, too?"

Too? I stared at the woman across the table. "What do you mean, Teddy?"

"Adelaide Forsythe died about six months ago. Barney had left her well taken care of, so you can imagine her children's surprise when there was almost nothing left."

"Did they trace the money?"

"She made regular cash withdrawals, sometimes as much as two-thousand dollars a week. They searched her house to see if she'd stuffed the money in a mattress or her lingerie drawer, but it was gone. They have no idea what she did with it."

"Was she fully in charge of her faculties?" Kay asked.

"She was a bit...muzzy. Her bridge game went to hell. She couldn't remember which suit was trump or how to evaluate a hand. But she knew who everyone was, and she didn't repeat herself. She could still hold an engaging conversation. She often talked about her grandchildren."

Adelaide's children—they were much older than me—I searched my memory for their names and came up empty.

"Addie and Scott," Teddy supplied as if she'd guessed that I'd forgotten people I barely knew. "Addie has two daughters and lives in Phoenix. Scott and his family live in one of those little townships in Connecticut where a one-bedroom starter home costs more than a four-bedroom in Kansas City."

"She never mentioned anything to them?" I asked.

"Not a word."

Ruby, my favorite waitress, served our burgers along with sides of onion rings and extra-crispy French fries.

"May I please have a small chocolate frosty?" I'd resolved to be good, but the day seemed endless and I had yet to write Althea's obituary and I wanted one.

"Yes, ma'am." Ruby made a note on her pad. "Anything else?"

"Another limeade, please," said Kay. Then she offered us an I-know-I-shouldn't shrug. "I don't usually drink two."

"Don't be silly, dear." Teddy patted Kay's hand. "You've had a terrible time of it. Besides, it's a limeade, not a snifter full of brandy or an extra-dry martini."

We ate our burgers in silence.

"Everyone must be hungry," said Teddy. "We got very quiet."

"I was starving." Somehow, I'd forgotten to eat lunch. But now that the edge of hunger was gone, I owed it to the other women at the table to make conversation. "Teddy, remind me where your children are?"

"I got lucky," she replied. "Edward and Sarah both ended up in Kansas City." A smile lit up her face. "I get to spoil my grandchildren rotten, and Edward is a stockbroker, so I let him handle my finances." The smile faltered. "Frankly, I'm surprised Sybil's broker didn't question her spending."

"Maybe he did." I made a mental note to add "calling Sybil's broker" to my to-do list. Mabel Whittier had reacted poorly when I asked about the cash she withdrew from her accounts. Perhaps Sybil had a similar reaction.

"You must be beside yourself, dear. All that money, just gone." Again, Teddy patted Kay's hand.

Kay snatched her hand away. "It's fine."

Teddy blinked at Kay's reaction, then dipped a French fry in ketchup and pointed it at me. "What can you tell us about Althea's murder?"

Couldn't we complain about the weather or discuss the fall fashions that were beginning to appear in stores on the Plaza? Although, bringing up hemlines when Kay had lost her whole family might appear insensitive. "The police are still investigating."

"Is Kay a suspect?"

"I believe they are pursuing other leads." I could give her—and Kay—that much.

"Is that a 'yes' or a 'no?'" Teddy insisted.

"It's okay, Teddy," said Kay. "I didn't kill Althea. Ellison's husband will catch whoever did."

Ruby put my frosty on the table, then added Kay's fresh limeade.

Kay stared into the drink as if it held the secrets of the universe. "I wonder what Althea wanted to tell me."

"What do you mean?" asked Teddy.

"Althea. At the luncheon, before she was murdered, Althea said she had something to tell me, then she changed the subject." Kay looked up from the scoop of lime sherbet floating in her glass. "She accused you of being friends with Hunter Tafft."

"I remember." Althea had broken off whatever she meant to say when she spotted someone in the hallway. I said as much.

"Hmm." Kay tapped her fingers on the table, and I couldn't help but notice that two of her nails were chipped. "Maybe she saw Hunter. Was he at the club?"

"No." Anarchy had shared the list of every person in or near the clubhouse when Althea died, and Hunter wasn't on it.

"Then I wonder what brought on the diatribe," said Kay.

Teddy patted her lips with a paper napkin. "Maybe she spotted another lawyer."

Lawyers were a dime a dozen at the club. It had to be more than that. "Maybe she saw a lawyer from Hunter's firm." I'd review the list when I got home. No. I wouldn't. Reviewing that list meant I'd involve myself in the murder investigation. Something I'd promised not to do. I'd revisit this conversation with Anarchy when I got home.

"How many lawyers are in Hunter's firm?" Kay asked.

"It's one of the big ones."

"So, how many? Fifty?"

"Probably closer to a hundred."

"Edith Bishop!"

Kay and I stared at Teddy.

"Who's Edith Bishop?" Kay asked.

"Lloyd Bishop's widow. His second wife. They married later in life, and Lloyd's children were furious when they discovered their step-mother had spent their inheritance."

"On what?" I asked.

"That's just it," said Teddy. "They didn't know. She didn't travel. Her Volvo was six years old. She seldom ate out. But the money was gone. Just like Adelaide Forsythe."

"How much money?"

Teddy leaned over the table and lowered her voice. "I only know this because Lloyd junior and Edward are friends, but it was more than a quarter million."

"How long ago did Edith die?"

"Two years? Let me think." She closed her eyes. "I went to the funeral, and I needed a raincoat. It was springtime. April of seventy-three!" She sounded triumphant.

"Where are the children?"

"Lloyd's in Los Angeles. Hank is in Houston."

"Do you know how to get in touch with them?"

Teddy nodded. "Edward will have Lloyd's number. I can ask him for it."

"Would you share it with me, please? If you have a number for one of Adelaide's children, I'd like that, too."

"Of course, dear. But, why?"

"It's possible a con artist—"

"You really think someone is taking advantage of lonely widows?"

Lonely widows. I put down my cheeseburger and stared at her. "What are you suggesting?"

She popped half an onion ring into her mouth, and I waited impatiently while she chewed. "Isn't it obvious? Some lothario is romancing these poor women out of their money. That's why they don't tell their children about their spending. They don't want their kids' disapproval."

Could she be right? I tried to imagine Mabel Whittier, with her fluffy white hair and befuddled expression, enamored with a younger man. It might be possible.

Kay wrinkled her nose, and her skin took on a greenish hue. "You mean Mom took a lover?"

"Not necessarily. It could have been companionship."

"You were her best friend." It was my turn to point a French fry. "Wouldn't she have told you if she had a special friend?"

Teddy shrugged. "An older woman. A younger man. Money. Maybe she was too embarrassed."

Kay shoved her plate, which still held half a cheeseburger, toward the middle of the table. "That's just…"

"Awful," I replied.

"You girls. You think sex and love and companionship are meant for the young. You're wrong. Older people still want those things. Perhaps more, because we realize how precious they truly are."

I wasn't about to argue. "Did you see any signs that Sybil had found someone?"

"No. But, I wasn't looking." Her cheeks flushed, and her gaze fell to the table's surface. "I hate to admit this, but as Sybil got more and more confused, I saw less of her. I made a point of visiting every Monday afternoon, but I didn't call for a chat or invite her to lunch or—"

"You were a marvelous friend, Teddy." It was Kay's turn to pat Teddy's hand. "Mom was lucky to have you."

"Where would she have met someone?" It was a reasonable question.

Teddy shook her head. "I honestly don't know."

"Sybil still had a cleaning lady?" I knew the answer. There was no way Sybil could have maintained her house without help. "And the nurses. Maybe one of them noticed a man visiting your mother."

"The nurses came from an agency. I'm not sure there was any continuity. They sent who was available on any given day. And, there were gaps." She scowled. "When I looked at the schedule I found hours in the mid-afternoon when Mom was by herself. But Bernie? She was with Mom for years. We can ask her. Her number will be in Mom's book. I'll call her when I get home."

It was too much to hope that Bernie would know the name of the man who'd taken advantage of Sybil (if he even existed), but I crossed my fingers anyway.

Kay swirled her limeade. "Do you really think there's a man conning widows out of their life savings?"

I nodded. "It makes sense. And, between the three of us, maybe we can stop it from happening to another woman."

I lifted my frosty, and Kay and Teddy lifted their limeades, and the three of us clinked glasses.

CHAPTER SIXTEEN

Anarchy held Finn's leash, and I gripped Max's. The sky above of us was a deep shade of lavender. But the late hour didn't mean a respite from the heat. Sweat trickled between my breasts, and I regretted suggesting that we get the bouncing-off-the-walls dogs some exercise.

We'd met at home after my dinner at Winstead's and decided that a few laps around Loose Park might earn us some peace and quiet.

Peace and quiet at home. The park was home to a million locusts. Each one droned louder than a lawn mower.

The dogs didn't care about the noise. They trotted happily, their tongue lolling from their mouths.

Max tugged on his leash, and I tightened my grip on its handle. I didn't fancy chasing him through the dark park. The path where we walked was well lit. But the park's interior was bathed in shadows. It was the domain of teenagers sneaking beers and amorous couples who hid their canoodling behind the low hanging branches of pine trees.

"Starting tomorrow, we'll be interviewing everyone at the

club a second time, trying to get a minute-by-minute accounting of everyone's whereabouts."

"You're stuck."

"Very stuck. Who do you think did it?" Frustration bled into Anarchy's voice. "I could make a circumstantial case against both Robert and Skip, but I can't prove a thing."

"They both had motive and opportunity, but I have a hard time seeing either one of them as a cold-blooded killer. I'm no help."

"Pick one."

Would Robert kill the woman carrying his child? "Skip. If I have to pick between the two of them, I think it's Skip."

An owl hooted, and Finn stopped dead in his tracks.

"Come on, buddy." Anarchy gave his leash a gentle tug.

Finn didn't move. Not even when Max nudged him. Instead, he growled, as if the owl had thrown down some sort of avian gauntlet.

"Did you hear that?" asked a woman on the path behind us.

I knew that voice. Had she overheard Anarchy and me talking or had the locusts' drones masked our words? Who was I kidding? If we could hear her, she could hear us.

A man grunted.

"Bianca is white. She weighs four pounds. I don't want some great horned monster making her his dinner. Ellison, is that you?"

I turned. "Good evening."

Lois and Skip were right behind us, both wan in the glow cast by the streetlights. Lois clutched a Maltese in her arms.

The owl hooted again, and Finn lunged, somehow breaking loose of Anarchy's hold. He raced toward the interior of the park.

Anarchy cursed softly, before saying, "I guess I'm going for a run."

"If he jumps in the pond, don't follow. The water is disgusting."

He gave me a quick grin. "Good tip. Would you two mind staying with Ellison till I get back?"

"Of course." Skip's expression was pinched. He'd definitely heard us.

We watched the darkness swallowed my husband.

I forced a polite smile. "How are you?"

"Fine," Lois spoke quickly.

"Any idea when your husband might wrap this up?" asked Skip. This. The murder investigation. "I'm getting funny looks at work."

"No idea. It might help if we knew why the killer wanted her dead."

"No one could stand her." Lois scanned the sky above us as if the owl might swoop down on us at any minute.

"I was looking for something a bit more substantive." I was pretty sure the threat in Lois's letter referred to Althea's pregnancy, but I might be wrong. Perhaps Althea had been keeping other secrets. I gave Lois a long assessing stare.

She held my stare for long seconds, then her shoulders slumped, and her gaze shifted to the shadows curling at our feet. "You found it. I knew someone would."

"Found what?" asked Skip.

She took a step away from her husband and seemed to hold more tightly to the little dog in her arms. "I wrote Althea a letter." She gave her lower lip a quick chew, then asked, "Is Anarchy going to arrest me?"

Skip's gulp was audible. "Lois, what have you done?"

"I wrote Althea a letter. I tried to mend fences."

I snorted. I couldn't help it.

"Fine," she snapped. "I threatened her. I wanted her to leave us alone."

A breezed ruffled the leaves of the nearby trees, and Max

whined softly. There was something in the air. I shivered despite the heat.

"Threatened her with what?" Skip's voice was slow and low and measured, as if he were disguising his outrage behind a modicum of control.

"She was pregnant. I told her that if she didn't stop her campaign to get you fired, I'd tell everyone."

Skip pinched the bridge of his nose and audibly exhaled.

"Or worse," I added.

They both looked at me. Sharply. Maybe Anarchy shouldn't have left me with them.

"You said you'd tell her secret or worse."

"I know it looks bad, but I never dreamed she'd be murdered. I was just trying to scare her into stopping."

I believed her. Mainly because Hazel had seen a man. "How did you know about the pregnancy?"

"Our cute little neighbor, Annie Stanton, saw her at the obstetrician's office. Annie brought back a bundt pan she'd borrowed, and I invited her in for a cup of tea. She saw an open issue of *The Independent* on my kitchen counter and pointed out Althea's picture. She said they'd chatted in the doctor's waiting room. Apparently, Althea told her how long she'd been hoping for a baby. Obviously, she didn't know that Althea and I hated each other. If she did, I doubt she would have told me about the baby. Annie's a sweet girl and would never purposefully cause trouble."

Skip stared slack-jawed at his wife. "Who was the father?"

"No idea. But knowing Althea, he was a married man. She always wanted what she couldn't have. Maybe the wronged wife killed her."

Lois didn't know who she was throwing to the wolves.

"Bad dog." Anarchy dragged a reluctant Finn out of the darkness. My husband's hair was mussed, and beads of sweat decorated his forehead. He did not look happy.

At least he'd avoided the pond.

"Ellison, let's head home."

"Sure."

"I know it looks bad, but I didn't kill her. I swear." Lois's declaration stopped Anarchy dead in his tracks.

He tilted his head, and his eyes glittered, even in the darkness. "What have you been discussing while I was gone?"

"My wife admitted to writing Althea Dodson a letter that might be construed as threatening." Construed? Skip sounded every inch a lawyer. "If you'd like to question her about it, we need to have counsel present."

Anarchy shook his head. "I have no questions."

Skip blinked his surprise.

"Ellison?" There was an edge to Anarchy's voice, and Max and I hurried to his side.

"Good night," I told the Worthams. I didn't have time to say more because Anarchy claimed my elbow and hurried us toward home.

When they were far behind us, he asked, "How did that come up?"

"I think Lois was so worried about the letter that she couldn't help but spill the beans. I wondered why someone might have wanted Althea dead, and she just...folded."

"Did Skip know about the letter?"

"No." His shock and anger had been real.

"I shouldn't have left you with them."

"I'm fine."

"He could easily be the killer."

"Even if he is, I doubt he'd murder me in public in front of his wife."

"I suppose you're right." His expression was shuttered, as if he'd seen something that sent the cop cogs in his brain turning.

When we got home, stepping into the air-conditioning was heaven, and I sighed with pleasure.

"Do you want anything to drink?" asked Anarchy.

"Ice water." I pushed the button on the answering machine.

"Ellison, it's Ogden Whittier calling. It's six o'clock, and I apologize for calling during the dinner hour. I've talked to Mom. You won't believe where the money has gone." The edge in his voice hinted at barely contained fury. "At any rate, I'm taking Mom to Chicago. I'll phone you tomorrow."

"Why didn't he just tell me?" I complained.

"He probably wants your reaction." Anarchy handed me an already sweating glass.

I pushed the button a second time and heard Kay's voice. "It's me. I called Bernie, and she thinks she might have seen the man. Late last October, she came in on a Tuesday to help Mom get her winter clothes out of the cedar closet. That's not her usual day. At any rate, she says a man, middle-aged and handsome, was at the house with Mom. Bernie heard him scold Mom about having staff there on off days. She thought that was odd. Sorry it's not more. I'll talk to you soon."

I growled my frustration. "How long was he there? What was he wearing? What kind of car did he drive?" I picked up the phone to return Kay's call but paused. It was nine o'clock, and she'd had an exhausting day. Besides, if Ogden knew who'd taken his mother's money, I might not need that information.

"What's all this?"

I told him about Teddy's lothario theory.

Anarchy kissed the shell of my ear. "We should put you on the payroll. Seems like you'll have this case solved by tomorrow."

"More like Ogden has the case solved."

"He wouldn't know there was a problem if you hadn't called him. You're the one who observed the connections. It's good police work."

"I'll save my observation skills for painting."

Anarchy drained the last of his water, then put his glass in the dishwasher. A man who put his dirty glass in the dishwasher—he really was perfect. Then he wrapped his arms around my waist, pulling me close. "What else are you doing tomorrow?"

"I have to write Althea's obituary. I'm dreading it."

"Can you ask her husband for help?"

"If I get stuck, I'll call him." When pigs flew.

CHAPTER SEVENTEEN

I crumpled the sheet of paper and threw the resulting ball into the near-overflowing wastepaper basket. Around me, cute little pigs stretched their wings. I ignored them, choosing to focus on the view outside the window. The dogs frolicked in the morning sunshine. If I were smart, I'd take them on a walk now before the heat became oppressive, but I couldn't find the energy.

Oink.

I scowled at the pig whizzing around the standing lamp in the corner. "Bacon!"

The pig smirked at me, then rejoined its friends.

I took a sip of coffee, then, with a sigh that seemed to come from the depths of my soul, I looked up John Dodson's phone number.

His answering machine picked up, and I waited for the beep.

"John, it's Ellison Jones. I need your help with something. Would you please call me?" I left my number and hung up.

The smug pigs dissipated into thin air.

Shaking my head (sometimes I had too much imagination), I grabbed my mug and headed for a refill.

In the kitchen, Aggie was pouring marinade into a bag of raw chicken. "Good morning," she said.

"Good morning!" I reached for Mr. Coffee's pot. "How was your date?"

She had gone out last night with Mac.

A happy, dreamy expression settled on her face, and the rosy pink in her cheeks clashed with the mustard of her kaftan.

"That good?"

The pink on her cheeks became almost ruddy as she focused on sealing the bag. "How was your evening?"

"I had dinner with Kate and Teddy Bryant at Winstead's, then Anarchy and I walked the dogs."

"How's your friend?" She opened the refrigerator door, put the chicken inside, and pulled out the cream.

"Struggling." I took the container from her and added a jot of cream to my mug.

"I'm sorry to hear that. How's the obituary coming?"

I groaned. "I have Althea's name, the day she was born, and the day she died. That's it. I broke down and left a message for her husband. Hopefully, John will give me a list of the charities she supported or her hobbies or something."

"I know something that might cheer you up."

"Oh?" I asked, intrigued.

"I was at the market yesterday and heard the Dixon's place sold."

The Dixon's house had burned down right as their marriage imploded, and we'd spent too many weeks staring at a weedy, vacant lot.

"I heard it's a young family," she added.

"Well, that is good news."

Marian Dixon hadn't had enough to occupy her time, and after Henry's death, she'd made spying on me her hobby. Annoying, but even more annoying was her habit of calling Mother to report.

"You're sure you won't miss Marian?" Aggie teased.

"Ha. Ha."

"Every block has one—someone who watches the comings and goings. Like Mrs. Kravitz from *Bewitched*."

I stared into my coffee. Aggie was right. Most every block had someone who nosed into their neighbors business.

"Your wheels are turning," said Aggie. "I can see them."

I settled onto a kitchen stool and told Aggie about the older ladies who had been targeted and Teddy's theory.

She shook her head in disgust. "So you need to talk to the busybodies on their blocks? Hope they saw the man?"

"That, or I need to speak with Ogden Whittier. I think he knows who it is." I glanced at the clock on the wall. It read nine-thirty. "He said he'd call, but I'm tired of waiting." I returned to my desk and dialed the number in Deerfield.

The phone rang only once before a woman answered. "Hello."

"May I please speak with Ogden?"

"He's not here." Her voice held an odd edge.

"May I please leave a message? This is Ellison Jones calling from Kansas City."

"Kansas City? How do you know Ogden?"

"I don't really. Ogden's older than me, but I've known his mother for years. We've worked on a few committees together, and she does her banking at our family bank."

"You're the woman who called."

"I am."

"Oh, thank God. I couldn't remember your name."

Not the reaction I was expecting.

"Ogden and his mother never made it home to Chicago. I called the police, both here and there, but they won't do anything. Not till they've been missing for twenty-four hours. I need someone to go by Mabel's house and check on them. Will you do that? Please?" She sounded desperately concerned.

"Of course. It's only a few blocks away."

"Thank you. I've been up all night. Calling. Worrying. I haven't slept a wink. The only person I know in Kansas City is Mabel, I didn't know who to call when the police refused to help, I nearly lost my mind. I was about to buy a plane ticket."

"I'll go right now." The woman's obvious panic had bled through the phone line. I too was worried. "And, I'll call you as soon as I know something. What's your name?"

"Susan. I'm Ogden's wife."

"Give me thirty minutes, Susan."

"Thank you."

I hung up the phone, slipped Susan's phone number into the pocket of my skirt, and returned to the kitchen. "Aggie, are you up for a quick field trip?"

"Where are we going?"

"Mabel Whittier's house. She and Ogden never made it to Chicago."

"I'll grab my purse."

Aggie's purse was tooled leather with hand-painted yellow smiley faces. She threw it over her shoulder, opened the back-door, and called for the dogs.

They raced inside and immediately sat, their gazes fixed on the box of treats atop the fridge.

She distributed biscuits, and we hurried to my car.

As we sped down the drive, she asked, "What do you think happened?"

"Something awful." The moment Susan said Ogden and Mabel hadn't made it home, a heavy weight had settled on my chest. I'd called Ogden. He'd come to Kansas City because of me. What if…

It took us less than five minutes to get to Mabel's house. I parked in the drive, and we stared at her Georgian-style home.

"The front light is still on," Aggie observed.

I nodded, hurried up the front steps, and rang the doorbell.

No one came.

With the sun beating on the back of my neck, I rang again.

No one came.

The weight on my chest grew exponentially heavier. "Let's try the back."

We followed the driveway to the back of the house.

"That's a rental car." Aggie pointed to the Ford Granada parked in front of the garage.

I swallowed a huge lump of dread and tried the backdoor. The handle refused to turn.

"Who are you?" A woman in a sky blue house dress had joined us.

"Ellison Jones." I tapped my chest. "And Aggie DeLucci."

"What are you doing back here?"

"Susan, Ogden's wife asked me to check the house. Ogden and Mabel were supposed to arrive in Chicago last night, but they never made it."

The woman studied me for a moment, taking in my navy wrap skirt embroidered with lady bugs, my white scoop-neck tee-shirt, and the Gucci handbag hanging from the crook in my arm. Then, she nodded. "Ogden arrived yesterday afternoon. I never saw him leave."

We'd found Mrs. Kravitz. "Did anyone else come by the house?"

She duckbilled her lips and scratched her chin. "Not that I saw."

I glanced at the locked house. "If it's not too much trouble, may I use your phone?"

Her brows lifted.

"I'd like to call my husband."

"He's a locksmith?"

"He's a homicide detective."

Most people paled when I told them that. Not Mrs. Kravitz. Her eyes widened, and she rubbed her hands together with barely containing her glee. "You're the woman who finds bodies!"

"You're famous," Aggie whispered.

"It's like you don't want a Christmas bonus," I whispered back.

She snickered.

"I'm Gladys Crane."

"Pleased to meet you, Gladys. The phone? If it's too much trouble, we can ask someone else." As if Gladys would ever give up the opportunity to crow about being involved in an investigation, even if that involvement was limited to the use of her telephone.

"No, no. You're welcome to use the phone. I live across the street."

We followed her down the drive.

"What do you think happened to them?" she asked as we approached her front door. "Murdered?" Her curiosity was ghoulish.

I gave her a tight smile. "Let's hope not."

She opened the door to her home. We stepped into the air-conditioning. And I barely held back a moan. I was so tired of being hot.

"In there."

Through an open door, I saw a man's desk. I hurried into the study and called Anarchy.

"Jones."

"It's me. I think...you'd better come to Mabel Whittier's house."

"Did you find a body?"

"No."

"I hear a 'but.'"

I glanced at Gladys, who lurked in the hallway, listening to every word I said. "The house is locked."

"When has that stopped you?"

Gladys stopped me. Breaking and entering with a witness? Especially a witness like her? I'd be the talk of the town.

"Please, can you come?"

He heard the deep-seated worry in my voice. "Give me the address."

"Westover Road. The six-hundred block. You'll see my car in the driveway."

"I'll be there in fifteen minutes. Stay safe."

I hung up the phone. "He's on his way."

"May I get you anything while you wait?" asked Gladys. "I have iced tea and Tab, and I can make coffee."

Maybe Gladys wasn't so bad after all.

"Iced tea, please," said Aggie.

"Coffee if it's not too much trouble."

"No trouble at all. Why don't you have a seat in the living room?"

Aggie and I sat in Gladys's living room and stared through the front window at the house across the street. Neither of us were inclined to chat, not when Gladys was probably listening.

It took five minutes for Gladys to return with a tray holding coffee, iced tea, and a plate of Hydrox cookies. "Do you really think something happened to them?"

"I don't know what to think," I replied as I picked up the coffee cup and took a sip. "Does Mabel have any regular visitors?" Does, not did. Have, not had. "It must be so lonely for her with her son living in Chicago."

"I saw a black Mercedes every so often."

"Really?" I tried to sound casual. "Did you know the driver?"

"He always pulled around to the back. I never saw his face. When I asked Mabel about it, she told me to mind my own business." Gladys's tone invited us to be outraged with her.

I gave a kids-these-days shake of my head. An octogenarians-these-days shake?

Aggie took a sip of iced tea and murmured, "Delicious. What kind of tea do you use?"

Gladys gave a pleased smile. "It's red zinger."

"We'll have to buy some," said Aggie. "Rude reply aside, I'm sure Mabel appreciated having you nearby. It's so nice to have someone keeping an eye on the neighborhood."

"I couldn't agree more. Please, have a cookie."

I selected a cookie and dipped it my coffee. Aggie nibbled on hers.

"What model of Mercedes?" I asked.

"You don't think he might have had something to do with this?" Gladys was nearly breathless.

This. A murder. Two murders. "Just curious."

"It was a sedan."

I shrugged as if her answer met nothing. If I was being honest, it did mean nothing. Half the men in the neighborhood drove black Mercedes sedans. "There's Anarchy." I pointed outside where an unmarked police car parked at the curb. Anarchy and Peters (oh, joy) got out, turning their heads, looking for me. I stood. "Gladys, thank you for your hospitality."

"The tea was marvelous." Aggie put her glass on the coffee table and rose from the couch.

Together, we crossed the street to my waiting husband.

"It's not like we don't have enough to do," said Peters.

"It's not like I want someone to be dead inside that house."

Anarchy—ever the peacekeeper—said, "There's not much we can do if the house is locked."

"Ogden told me he was flying back to Chicago last night, but the rental car is still in the drive. Something is wrong." I wiped a trickle of sweat off my temple. "Susan Whittier asked me to come over here and check on things. You can call her and get permission to break the lock." I glanced over my shoulder at Gladys's house. She stood at the front window, watching us with avid interest. "I'm sure Mrs. Kravitz would be delighted to let you use her phone."

Anarchy's lips twitched. "Mrs. Kravitz?"

"Crane. But her first name is Gladys, and she watches everything that happens on the block."

"I love a nosy neighbor," said Peters. "Makes our job easier."

"We'll have someone from the station call and ask Susan Whittier for permission. Do you have her number?"

I handed him the slip of paper. "It's the seven-oh-eight number."

Anarchy slid behind the wheel of the car and spoke into the police radio. Less than two minutes passed before he returned. "We have permission."

"The backdoor might be easier," said Aggie. "You can break the glass."

The four of us tromped around to the back, and I watched as Peters wrapped his hand in his sport coat and shattered a pane.

I flinched at the sound.

Peters carefully broke out the rest of the glass, reached inside, and turned the lock. "You two wait out here." His tone was snide. His eyes were narrowed.

Aggie and I took shelter from the sun under the limbs of a maple tree. We sat on a wrought-iron bench and stared at the back of the house.

"Working for you is never boring."

"I'm just hoping that I'm wrong. Maybe their flight was delayed and they decided to spend the night at a hotel near the airport."

Aggie nodded at the rental car.

"I know, I know, but let me clutch at straws."

Anarchy appeared at the backdoor, and I read his face. He didn't have to say a word. He didn't have to. I knew. Mabel and Ogden Whittier were dead. Murdered. And it was my fault.

CHAPTER EIGHTEEN

Anarchy sent Aggie and me home.

Despite my objections, he gently, kindly made it clear we had no place in the middle of a crime scene.

Peters had been neither gentle nor kind. "We don't need you screwing up the evidence. Leave."

We left.

I slid behind the wheel of the car, turned on the ignition, and blasted the air-conditioner (the interior was hotter than the hinges on the gates to hell). I did not put the car in gear. Rather, I stared out the windshield as my hands gripped the steering wheel.

Without comment, Aggie pulled a Kleenex from her smiley-face purse and handed it to me.

I used the tissue to wipe the tears from my cheeks. "Thank you."

"I can drive," she offered.

"Just give me a minute."

"The man who killed them is to blame, not you." Somehow, Aggie recognized the guilt tearing me apart.

"I called Ogden. He came to Kansas City because I called

him." A sob ripped through my chest, and I pressed the back of my hand to my mouth.

Aggie offered me another Kleenex.

"He must have confronted the man who's been taking Mabel's money. Why would he do that? Why not go to the police?"

"Was taking Mabel's money illegal?" she asked.

I turned in the seat and stared at her.

"I know he was preying on an older lady, but she *gave* him the money, yes?"

"As far as I know."

"It's despicable, but I'm not sure it's against the law."

"Then why kill Ogden and Mabel?" I stared at the heat shimmering on the pavement.

"An altercation? Maybe there was a fight. Ogden accused the mystery man of swindling his mother. They fought, and the man killed Ogden, then he had to kill Mabel to keep her quiet."

I wished Anarchy had told us how Ogden and Mabel died before he sent us on our way.

Aggie twisted in her seat, glancing over her shoulder. "The neighbor is staring at us."

"I'd expect nothing less." I reversed the car out the driveway and headed toward home. "I need to call Kay. I want to talk to Sybil's cleaning lady myself." I'd promised Mother I'd steer clear of the investigations into Althea and Hazel's deaths. This was different. I'd ask every question. Talk to every cleaning lady, housekeeper, gardener, and pool boy in town if it meant I got a description of the man who'd just killed two people.

"What can I do to help?"

"Adelaide Forsythe and Edith Bishop. I'm pretty sure they were victims."

"Were?"

"They passed away."

"Natural causes?"

Oh, dear Lord. Had he drained their money, then killed them? "I'd like to know who worked for them. And for Mabel. House-keeper. Cleaning help. Gardener. Anyone who might have seen him. Mabel withdrew cash from the bank. Presumably, he visited her to take the money."

"At night," said Aggie.

"Oh?"

"That or they met somewhere. If he'd come to her house during the day, Gladys Crane would have noticed."

"You're right. He came at night." Somehow, I doubted the man who'd romanced Mabel wanted to be seen with her in public.

I pulled into our drive, and parked the car. "Let me call Kay, then the phone's all yours."

Aggie was an extrovert. She made friends easily. She knew every housekeeper, every nanny, every lawn guy on the block. She could use her network to find out who'd worked for the dead women.

I hurried to the family room and dialed Kay's number.

She answered on the second ring.

"It's me," I told her. "I need to speak with Bernie."

"Ellison? Your voice is strange. What's happened?"

I couldn't bring myself to tell her. "Please, Kay, the number?"

"Hold on."

I waited, wrapping the phone cord tightly around my fingers.

"Do you have a pen?" Kay asked.

"I do."

She rattled off the number, and I wrote it down, reading it back to her.

"That's right," she confirmed. "Use my name."

"Thank you."

"Ellison, are you okay?"

Not even close. "I'm fine."

"Call me if you need me."

I rubbed my chest. Kay was dealing with so much and offering me her support. "You're a good friend."

"You're a better one. You've all but given me the shirt off your back."

A terrible thought occurred to me, and I rested my head against the back of my chair and stared at the ceiling. "What if Teddy's wrong?" What if it was a woman taking advantage of the older ladies?

"What do you mean?"

"If I asked you for a thousand dollars, would you give it to me?"

"Yes." Her answer was immediate. "But if you asked for a thousand dollars every week, I'd question you."

"What if your short-term memory was gone. What if you didn't remember giving me last week's money?"

"I see your point. I didn't ask Bernie about the women that came to visit Mom."

"I'll call her now."

"Please let me know what she says."

"I will," I promised.

As soon as I hung up the phone, it rang. The only person I wanted to talk to was Bernie, and it was a certainty that Sybil's cleaning help was not calling me. "Aggie," I called. "Would you please pick that up?"

From the kitchen, I heard her say, "Jones' residence."

I closed my eyes and took a deep, cleansing breath, trying to release some of the tension and guilt and sadness that coiled around my chest.

"Ellison."

I opened my eyes and found Aggie standing at the entrance to the family room.

"Your mother is on the phone. She doesn't sound happy."

"Gladys." The name had become a four-letter word.

Aggie gave a sympathetic nod.

I sighed and picked up the receiver. "Hello."

"How could you?"

"How could I what?"

"Two bodies?"

"I did not find them."

"You went to Mabel Whittier's house."

"And stayed outside. I did not find her or her son."

"Ellison—"

"Don't. Just don't. I'm exhausted and stressed and I already blame myself. I do not need a lecture right now."

"You promised."

"And I kept my promise. Someone, probably a man, has been conning older ladies out of their life savings. This has nothing to do with Anarchy's investigation into Althea's death."

"What do you mean 'conning?'"

"Teddy thinks he romances them."

Mother's disapproval traveled the phone line without her saying a single word. "You can't keep doing this."

I pinched the bridge of my nose. "I don't set out to find bodies, Mother. It just…happens."

"Anarchy will investigate these murders, too?"

"I assume so. He was the first on scene." And I got the sense that he'd hit a wall in his investigation of Althea's murder.

"Then he'll miss dinner. Again. You and Grace will join your father and me at the club this evening. We'll present a united front."

Go to the club and endure speculative glances and mean-spirited whispers or argue with Mother? Of the two options, one was exponentially worse. "What time do you want us there?"

"Seven o'clock. Make sure Grace is appropriately dressed." She hung up without waiting for my reply.

I pressed the switch hooks on the cradle for a few seconds.

When I released them, I heard a dial tone. Guilt had fingers flying around the dial.

"Hello."

"Hello. This is Ellison Jones calling. May I please speak with Bernie?"

"You're talking to her."

"Kay Morrison gave me your name, I was wondering if I could speak with you about the people who visited her mother."

"I told her everything I know."

I winced. "Please, Bernie, you've been very helpful, but I have a few more questions."

"I can't talk right now. I have to get to work. I'm cleaning a place at The Sulgrave. If you want to talk to me, you can meet me on the Plaza at four-thirty."

"Where?"

"Wherever you can buy me a good glass of wine. After cleaning for Mrs. Castlebury, I'll need it."

"Nabil's?"

"Swanky. I'll be the woman who looks like she doesn't belong."

"Thank you, Bernie. I really appreciate..." she'd hung up.

I found Aggie in the kitchen. "Grace and I are having dinner with my parents tonight. Will the chicken keep?"

She gave me a pained look.

"Go ahead and prepare it. I imagine Anarchy will be hungry when he gets home."

"You're done with the phone?"

"I am. I'm meeting Bernie at four-thirty."

"Take cash."

I nodded. Apparently motel clerks weren't the only ones who monetized information.

At four-thirty, a skinny woman in blue cotton pants and a faded tee-shirt pushed through Nabil's doors. She blinked, adjusting to the dim light, then brushed aside wisps of hair that had escaped her limp ponytail.

I stood. "Bernie?"

She walked toward me. "You're Ellison?"

"I am." I resumed my seat at the bar. "What are you drinking?"

"Wine. I'm not picky." She oozed into the stool next to mine.

I nodded to the bartender, and he served Bernie a glass of Chablis.

She picked up the glass and drank deeply. How could a woman's spine curve like that? It was as if she'd taken slouching to new heights.

"Long day?"

"She follows me around wearing white gloves. 'Bernie, you missed a spot,' or 'Bernie, don't forget to vacuum behind the couch,' or 'Bernie, the linoleum in the kitchen is looking dull. I think you'd better rinse it again.'"

"Sounds like a nightmare."

Bernie shrugged. "At least she pays well. But you don't want to know about Mrs. Castlebury."

"No."

"Poor Mrs. Morrison. She was a good employer. Fair. Generous at Christmas. I liked her."

"Can you tell me more about the man you saw?"

"Middle-aged, not bad looking, tall." She took another sip of Chablis. "Fit."

"What about his clothes?"

"He wore a suit and a boring tie."

"A boring tie?"

"Yep." She popped the "p." "The men I see, when they get dressed up, their ties are wild and crazy. This guy wore a snoozer. Blue and silver stripes."

"Did you see his car?"

"No."

"Who among Mrs. Morrison's friends visited her after..."

"After she started slipping? Just Mrs. Bryant. She came on Mondays and Thursdays. I know because those are—were—my days there."

"When did she stop coming so often?"

Bernie frowned. "She was still coming twice a week, right up until the end of last month."

I frowned. Why had Teddy lied?

"Ellison?" Chuck Wade had stepped inside Nabil's and approached the bar. "Nice to see you."

I returned the sentiment. "Have you heard from Lindsay?"

"She's on her honeymoon. The last thing she'd do is call her father."

"Fair point."

"How's Anarchy's investigation going?"

I forced a smile. "He doesn't like me to discuss active investigations."

"Of course, I understand. I just..."

I patted his arm. "It's okay. Everyone asks."

"I bet. What brings you out on such a hot afternoon?" His curious gaze landed on Bernie.

She sat ramrod straight and gave the tiniest shake of her head.

"I have a few big parties I'm planning at the house in August and September. We decided we might need some extra help."

"You decided to conduct an interview at Nabil's?" Chuck's gaze took in the two wine glasses on the bar.

Where I conducted fake interviews was none of his business. A bit of annoyance bled into my voice when I replied, "It was convenient for both of us."

"Well, I won't keep you. Stay cool." He strode toward the back of the bar where the maître d' stood waiting to lead him to a table.

When he'd disappeared from view, Bernie grabbed my wrist. "That was him—the man I saw at Mrs. Morrison's."

My stomach sank. "He manages the Morrison trust, he was probably there to discuss business with Sybil."

"If you say so." She swirled the wine in her glass. "Are you really looking for extra help? I'm going to need to pick up some new clients."

"I'm not. But I'll put the word out for you."

"You'd do that? You don't know me."

She hadn't tried to extort money for information. I liked that about her. "I get a sense that you're good people. And there's always someone looking for cleaning help. I can't make any promises, but I'll try."

Lately it seemed like all I did was try. I'd tried to host a nice luncheon for Kay. I'd tried to write Althea's obituary. I'd tried to help Mabel. Trying wasn't working out so well. I needed to succeed.

CHAPTER NINETEEN

I suspected state dinners at the White House took less time than this. I stole a quick glance at my watch. We'd been in the dining room for more than two hours, and Mother was sipping her coffee as if we had all the time in the world.

We didn't.

I'd promised Grace we'd be done by eight-thirty, and she was shooting me increasingly annoyed looks with the passing of each additional minute.

"Grace, tell me more about the Kettering boy," Mother demanded.

"What would you like to know, Granna?"

"He's a year older than you?"

"Yes."

"Where does he want to go to college?"

"Duke."

Mother gave a half-nod. Yale or Harvard or Stanford would be better. "And what about you, have you started looking at colleges?"

"I have some time."

Mother pursed her lips.

"Let it go, Frannie. She's right. She has plenty of time." Unlike Mother, Daddy wasn't annoyed with me. As he saw it, I'd done the right thing. I'd had a hunch and called my husband for help. I hadn't broken into the house on my own. I hadn't put myself in danger. Overall, he approved of my actions.

The dining room was still half-full. Tish and Robert, along with Lois and Skip, sat at a table near the French doors to the patio.

The Brandts dined with the Smarts.

The Wades dined with Jinx and George.

And every single one of them had stopped by our table to speak.

Jinx had been direct. "Is it true? Ogden and Mabel?"

I'd swallowed the lump in my throat and answered her with a brief nod.

Linda Wade had tiptoed around the issue while Chuck talked golf with Daddy. "I heard you had a trying morning."

"I did."

"Such a tragedy."

"More like an appalling crime." I'd heard from Anarchy. Ogden and Mabel had each been shot.

She'd recoiled at that, bringing her hand to her chest and blinking rapidly.

Mother hit me with a withering glare. "What Ellison means to say is that the loss of life pains us all."

Linda had nodded, then asked, "Where's Anarchy, tonight?"

I'd forced a smile. "Investigating."

"Ellison seems to think some modern-day Rudolph Valentino is behind this," said Mother with a dismissive wave her hand.

Daddy and Chuck dropped their conversation—something about Tom Watson, who they both knew, winning the British Open at Carnoustie—and stared at me.

"What's your theory, Ellison?" asked Linda.

"I could be wrong, and really it's Teddy Bryant's theory, but it seems likely that someone has been taking advantage of older ladies who aren't as sharp as they once were."

"That's awful!"

Her husband nodded in narrow-eyed agreement. "Terrible. Do you think that happened to Sybil?" Was that guilt in his voice? He wasn't responsible for her personal estate, but he and his firm made a great deal of money managing the Morrison trust. He could have kept tabs on her finances.

I looked him in the eye and nodded. "That's exactly what I think."

"I could have the firm—"

"That's very kind, but the police are investigating. I'm sure they'll catch the killer."

"Come on, dear." Linda, who was looking distinctly pale, tugged at her husband's arm. "We've kept them from their dinners long enough."

They'd moved on to their table, and Mother had leaned in and whispered furiously, "That's what happens when you talk about murder, Ellison. People turn green around the gills and can't wait to get away from you."

Daddy patted her hand. "Now, Franny, it's not Ellison's fault."

She'd snorted as Daddy rose from his seat to greet Lois and Skip.

"Please sit down, Mr. Walford," Lois insisted.

Of course, Daddy had remained standing.

Lois had smiled brightly—too brightly—and fiddled with a strand of her hair. "What happened today, do you think it's tied to Althea's murder?" She was nervous. Obviously so. But she looked lighter, as if telling Skip about the letter had lifted a weight from her shoulders.

The weight had definitely shifted to Skip. Dark half-moons hung beneath his eyes and his shoulders slumped.

"Anarchy's investigating," I'd replied. That seemed to be my new catchphrase.

Skip straightened his shoulders. "Not every killer is caught."

"My husband has an impressive clearance rate."

We stared at each other for long seconds. Was Skip posturing to protect his foolish, letter-writing wife? Or, was he a murderer?

He looked away first. "Let's go, Lois."

They'd left us, and Mother had drunk her coffee. Slowly.

When the last sip was gone, Grace stood. "Thank you for a nice dinner."

"Of course, dear," said Mother. "Please remember to stand when an older woman comes to the table. Otherwise people will think your mother raised you in a barn."

What would I do without Mother's thinly veiled criticisms?

Grace shot me an apologetic look. "You're right, Granna. I forgot. It won't happen again." Then she kissed Mother and Daddy's cheeks, gave me a quick hug, and flew out of the dining room.

"Where is she going?" Mother demanded.

"She's meeting her friends."

"Which friends? Where?"

"Peggy and Debbie. And they're just going to chill out at Debbie's house."

Mother blinked. She hadn't expected me to have an answer. Or maybe my use of slang threw her. "Her dress was too short."

"It's the style, Mother."

"And your hair, don't you think you're too old to wear it down like that?"

Daddy stood and helped pull out Mother's chair, winking at me over her shoulder. "I think you both looked very pretty."

"If Ellison is going to keep long hair, she should put it up when she's in public. As for Grace, too much leg." She sniffed. "Her table manners are passable, but how does one forget to stand when an older woman stops by the table? You need to work on that, Ellison."

"Yes, Mother." She wasn't wrong.

She paused and scanned the club's dining room. It had emptied quickly, and only a few tables were occupied.

"Any news on the carpet in the lounge?" I asked.

"Not yet." She sniffed. "This room could do with a refresh, too."

Chippendale-style chairs with seats covered in a muted gold damask sat on a gold-hued carpet decorated with laurel wreaths. The walls were cream. The sconces were brass. The dining room was neutral for a reason, but I kept that opinion to myself.

"Come on, Frannie. Let's go home." Daddy tucked Mother's hand into the crook of his arm. "Ellison?"

"I'm going to stop by the ladies' lounge."

"We can wait. I know you worry about the parking lot."

With good reason. "I'm parked under the light near the door. I'll be fine."

"You're sure ?"

I lifted on my tiptoes and kissed my father's cheek. "Positive. Thank you for dinner."

They left, and I cut through the quiet clubhouse, making my way to the ladies' lounge where I hadn't found a body (recently).

When I finally stepped outside, the parking lot was near empty. I paused, giving myself a moment to adjust to air so humid that it pooled in my lungs. Then, keys in hand, I walked to my car.

I heard the scrape of a shoe on the concrete behind me, but before I could turn, pain exploded across the back of my head, and the world turned black.

SOMETHING WAS TERRIBLY, HORRIBLY WRONG.

I was upside down.

Bouncing.

And my head felt like someone had smacked me with a two-by-four.

The haze of confusion cleared, and I remembered the parking lot. Someone *had* smacked me.

I slitted my eyes taking in my surroundings. I was on the golf course, and the hard thing pressing into my abdomen was someone's shoulder.

I fought the urge to scream or struggle. Some don't-be-an-idiot voice in my brain insisted I was better off if whoever was carrying me thought I was unconscious. *Also,* said the voice, *if you survive this, you are never ever going into that parking lot by yourself again.*

If I survive. My heart beat so loud, it was a wonder the man carrying me didn't hear it. If Anarchy was in this position he'd be calm and analytical, biding his time for his best chance. I needed to be like Anarchy.

Whoever was carrying me grunted, shifting his grip as if I were slipping.

If he dropped me, I had to be quiet. I couldn't react.

When he dropped me.

The way this night was going the worst-case scenario seemed inevitable.

My abductor swore under his breath but managed to keep hold of me by tightening his grip on my thighs.

Where were we? If he meant to kill me, why not do it in the parking lot?

If he didn't mean to kill me, why haul me out onto a deserted golf course?

My blood ran ice cold, and it took everything I had not to stiffen and give my fully conscious state away. What if I'd made the wrong choice? Maybe I ought to struggle and yell and scream in hopes that someone from the clubhouse heard me.

He shifted my weight again, and, to my left, I spotted the cabana that ran the length of the pool.

He skirted around the structure and stepped onto the pool deck.

Please don't let him drop me on the concrete.

He didn't.

He did something worse.

He walked to the edge of the pool and threw me in.

I contained a gasp, and, somehow, kept my head turned just enough to breathe through my nose. Thank heavens my hair shielded my face.

I floated, limbs loose, hoping he'd leave.

He didn't.

I *felt* him, standing at the edge of the pool, watching me drown.

Didn't he know that lingering at the scene of a murder was a bad idea? I thought that was chapter one in the killer's handbook.

The pain in my head was horrendous, nausea-inducing. I probably had a concussion.

I floated.

Who'd thrown me in the pool? Skip? If so, why?

I inhaled through my nose.

Where was Lois? Did she know her husband had tried to murder me?

I floated.

How long did I need to stay in the water? Was he gone? I didn't feel his presence anymore, but my survival instincts refused to let me turn my head.

I wanted Anarchy.

I wanted the safety of his arms.

I wanted him to brush a soft you're-okay kiss against my temple as I nestled with him in our bed.

I wanted his strength.

I wanted his fingers to wipe away my tears. A Biblical flood prickled behind my eyes, just waiting for a moment's safety to appear.

How did opossums do this? Playing dead was hard.

I floated.

How long had I been in the water? Two minutes? Five minutes? Ten minutes?

My head throbbed. My stomach roiled. My heart raced.

I floated.

"Ellison!" My name was a roar followed by a splash.

Strong arms wrapped around me, pulling my face from the water.

"Ellison." Anarchy's hand cupped my cheek.

"I'm okay. I'm okay." Now that he was here, now that he'd saved me, that was true.

"How?" He held me close, his eyes searching my face.

"He thought I was unconscious when he threw me in the pool. I wasn't." The tears had arrived, mixing with the pool water already wetting my skin.

I shook. My hands. My legs. My whole body. Someone had tried to take me away from Anarchy. From Grace. From Beau.

"Let's get you out of the water."

The strength had left my limbs. There was no way I could swim to the ladder at the side of the pool.

"I've got you." With one arm (the other was wrapped tightly around me), Anarchy swam to edge, then lifted me to the pool deck.

I lay on the still-warm concrete and shook as if I were soaking wet in a blizzard and not a hot July evening.

"Where are you hurt?" He brushed my wet hair away from my face.

"Someone hit me over the he…he…head." My teeth chattered too hard to speak. I burrowed into Anarchy's arms and drew hot humid air into my lungs, imagining its warmth spreading through my limbs. "He knocked me unconscious."

"Attempted murder. If you hadn't awakened before you hit the water, you'd be dead." His voice was steely, even as his gentle fingers explored my scalp. "That's quite a lump. We need to get you to the hospital."

I moaned and fresh tears washed my cheeks.

"What's wrong, sweetheart?"

"Mother's going to kill me."

CHAPTER TWENTY

I blinked myself awake. My eyes opening onto a hospital room. Despite my objections when we arrived, the doctors and my husband had insisted I spend the night for observation.

"You're up."

I turned my head and winced as the pillow pressed against the lump on the back of my head. "Karma."

My sister sat in the armchair next to my bed. "How are you feeling?"

"Like someone tried to kill me." My headache was of the T-Rex variety. Huge. Vicious. Obliterating.

"The nurse said we should call if you need pain meds."

"Yes, please."

Karma dug through the bed sheets for the call button and pushed it.

I closed my eyes against the killing brightness of the overhead lights.

"We're awake? How are we feeling?" The new voice in the room sounded chipper.

I decided I hated Chipper. Chipper was too loud. Chipper was too cheery.

"She needs something for her pain," said Karma.

I slit my eyes and watched as the nurse (who didn't look much older than Grace) made a note on the chart hanging at the end of my bed. "On a scale of one to ten, with ten being the worst, how bad is our pain?" she asked.

"A nine."

She made a sympathetic face. "Doctor already approved hydrocodone. I'll be back in a jiff."

When the door closed behind her, I asked, "Where's Anarchy?"

"He went home to change. The hospital gave him scrubs to wear because his clothes were wet, but..."

"But he wanted actual clothes."

"He should be back soon."

I nodded and winced as an ice pick attacked my brain. "Mother and Daddy?"

"They went to the coffee shop."

"Grace?"

"She's in the coffee shop with your mother and Dad. She mentioned something about pie."

I licked my dry lips.

"Here." She held out a plastic cup with a bendy straw.

I sipped cold water. "Thank you."

"When you're feeling better, I want to talk to you about Sybil's statements."

"Did you find something?"

"No, but some of the statements are missing."

I just stopped myself from shrugging. "She threw them in a laundry basket. It's possible a few got tossed."

"As far as I can tell, up until a few months ago, she wrote weekly checks to herself for up to three-thousand dollars. The memo line on every check reads, 'Cash.'"

"How did she get them cashed?" I murmured.

Karma tilted her head and frowned at me. Was my head injury so bad I'd forgotten how to cash a check?

"How did she get to the bank? She couldn't drive. Who cashed the checks for her?"

Karma's worried expression cleared. "Do you think her daughter would know?"

I closed my eyes and resisted the urge to shake my head (nodding had been painful enough). "Kay wasn't in town."

"Althea?"

My eyes flew open. "I need to look at Althea's diary." Although, the thought of reading Althea's tiny script made my head hurt worse.

"Here we are." Chipper had returned, and she held out a tiny plastic cup.

I stretched out my hand, and she dumped two pills into my palm.

I swallowed them immediately, then took a sip of water when Karma offered the cup.

"You'll feel better soon," Chipper promised.

A weak smile curled my lips. "Promise?"

She winked. "I got you the good stuff. Do you need anything else?"

Just my husband. "No, thank you."

"I'll let you rest."

Karma and I watched the door close, then she asked, "What's in Althea's diary?"

"Althea felt guilty about something to do with Sybil. She wrote that she hoped Kay wouldn't blame her. I wonder if Aletha took Sybil to the bank without realizing how much Sybil was withdrawing." Truly, my head ached too badly to think about who took Sybil's money. I should be using my feeble brain power to figure out if it was Skip who'd tried to kill me.

The door opened and Anarchy stepped into my hospital

room. Dark smudges marred the skin beneath his eyes and stubble covered his jaw. "You're awake."

My eyes filled with tears.

He crossed the room in three steps and wrapped me in his arms. "I could have lost you."

I swallowed around the lump lodged in my throat.

"I'll give you two a minute." Karma disappeared into the hallway.

A sob made it past the lump.

Anarchy smoothed my hair. "We'll catch him. I promise you. We'll catch him. He won't ever hurt you again."

"I…I'm getting your shirt wet."

"I don't care about my shirt, Ellison. I just care that you're with me."

I sniffled. "May I have a tissue?"

Anarchy handed me the box.

"Thank you." I mopped my eyes.

"Can you tell me what happened?"

"I walked into the parking lot and heard someone behind me. Before I could turn, whoever it was hit me and I passed out. When I came to, he had me in a fireman's hold and he was cutting across the golf course to the pool."

"Did you see his face?"

"No."

"Did you get the sense that he struggled to carry you?"

"Not really. He slipped once; I guess the grass was wet. But he righted himself. Also, he didn't drop me in the pool. He threw me."

"So he was fit."

I understood what Anarchy wasn't saying. Skip Wortham was in good shape. Robert Hart lifted martinis, not weights.

I yawned. "I'm sorry, all of a sudden I'm exhausted."

"Did they give you something for the pain? It can make you drowsy."

Now that he mentioned it, my eyelids seemed impossibly heavy. "You'll stay?"

"I'm not going anywhere. When you wake up, we'll figure out who did this."

Secure in the knowledge that Anarchy would keep me safe, I let myself sleep.

~

"MOM?"

I forced my eyes open.

Grace sat in the chair next to my bed and held my hand.

"Hi," I croaked. My throat was dry as dust. "Is there any water?"

She reached for the cup with the bendy straw.

I pushed up onto my elbows, relieved that the pain in my head had receded to a dull roar.

"Here. Let me help." She gave me the cup, and adjusted the mattress so that I was sitting instead of lying on my back.

"Thanks." I drank every drop in the cup.

"You had me scared."

"I'm fine. It'll take more than a dip in the pool—" I stopped when I saw the tears standing in her eyes. "Honey, I really am fine, and Anarchy will catch whoever did this."

She responded with a watery smile.

"Is your grandmother still here? Karma said you went to the coffee shop together."

"That was hours ago. Right now, she's out there." Grace waved toward the hall. "Granna is terrorizing the nurses. She says they must have given you too much painkiller for you to sleep so long."

I bet Chipper wasn't so chipper after Mother's wrath.

"I needed the sleep. I feel better."

"Good. That's good." She glanced at her hands that she'd clasped in her lap. "I wish these things would stop happening."

"You and me both."

"I guess it's a good thing you're tough."

I didn't feel tough. I felt like ten miles of bad road. But I donned a fierce expression. For her. "Toughness runs in the family. Just look at your grandmother."

She hiccupped a half-laugh half-sob.

"Are they going to let me go home?"

"They want to keep you for a second night. For observation."

"We'll see about that."

"Please, Mom. If the doctors want you to stay, stay."

For her, I'd stay. Especially if me staying wiped the tight, worried expression off her face. "Where's Anarchy?"

"Detective Peters is here. They're huddled in the waiting room. Granna demanded an update, and Detective Peters told her to mind her own business."

"I wish I could have seen that."

Grace smiled (not a hint of tears in this one). "It was off the hook. He told her to leave, and Granna looked down her nose at him and scowled. You know how she does."

All too well.

"But Detective Peters didn't seem to care. So, she shifted her scowl to Anarchy and demanded an update. He asked her what was more important, her update or catching the man who'd done this to you. She...deflated. By the way, Anarchy is scary angry. I wouldn't want to be the man who did this when Anarchy catches him."

"Is Karma still here?"

"She went to the police station."

"Why?"

"She's reviewing Althea's financial statements. She wants to help catch who did this to you."

The door from the hallway opened, and Anarchy peeked his

head in. The dark smudges remained, as did the stubble. But now his hair was mussed, as if he'd been raking his fingers through the strands. Despite all that, he was still the most handsome man I'd ever seen. Especially when he smiled at me. "You're up."

"I am."

He stepped into the room, crossed to the bed, and gave me a gentle kiss.

"What's wrong?" I demanded.

"What do you mean?"

"You have that look."

"What look?"

The look. Slightly narrowed eyes, a tautness in his mouth, a hard set of his jaw. The look. "Skip has an alibi?" As guesses went, it was an easy one.

He rubbed the back of his neck. "Lois swears they were together."

Lois had lied before. "What are you going to do?"

"Bring them in for questioning."

"Both of them?"

His answering nod was grim.

"I don't understand why Skip would try to kill me."

"Your mother says he stopped by the table at dinner."

"That's right."

"Did you say anything that might have set him off?"

"I don't think so. I don't remember." My memory of the whole night was a bit fuzzy.

"Mrs. Wortham asked if Mr. Whittier and his mother's deaths might be linked to Althea's, and Mom said you were investigating. Then she bragged about your clearance rate. Mr. Wortham went kinda pale and told Mrs. Wortham they needed to leave. I think he was mad about her question, like you and Mom wouldn't have put that together without her help, because he practically dragged her out of the dining room."

We stared at Grace.

"You're observant, like your mother."

She shrugged. "I try."

"What if Lois is right? About the murders, I mean."

"The M.O.s are different," Anarchy replied. "Althea was stabbed. Hazel was killed with a fireplace poker."

We all drew sharp breaths. I was so, so lucky that my skull hadn't been crushed.

Anarchy rubbed his palm across his chin, hiding the furious set of his mouth. "The Whittiers were shot."

"I think Althea's murder was planned. The killer knew she'd be at the club and brought the knife."

Anarchy nodded.

"I'm not sure he meant to kill Hazel. Something happened, and he picked up the closest object that could be used as a weapon."

"What about the Whittiers?" Grace's eyes were as big as saucers, and it occurred to me that sixteen was too young to be part of this conversation.

"That message Ogden left on our machine. He sounded angry. I can't help but wonder if he confronted the man who'd been swindling his mother."

"And he came to her house and killed them?" Grace sounded more curious than horrified.

"It's a good theory," said Anarchy. "But Peters and I can't figure out how the deaths might be linked." He smoothed a hand over my forehead. "You should rest."

"What time is it?"

"Five o'clock."

"I just woke up from a six-hour nap."

"You have a head injury."

"They let me sleep uninterrupted. It couldn't be too bad." A hospital letting a patient sleep was a minor miracle (probably wrought by Mother). But if the doctors thought I had a concussion, Chipper would have been waking me up on the hour.

"What do you expect to do from a hospital bed, Ellison?"

"I don't know. I can help Karma review Althea's statements."

"Are you allowed close work?"

"As far as I know."

Which is how, an hour later, four bankers' boxes arrived. Anarchy stacked them in front of the window sill. "If your headache gets worse, you stop."

"Promise."

He'd kissed me and left us.

Meanwhile, Karma settled into the Naugahyde chair and flipped through Althea's brokerage records.

Two hours passed as we poured over each document.

"I don't see anything out of order here." She sounded frustrated, as if the answer to the puzzle hid in Althea's papers.

I'd been stuck flipping through bank statements. Althea and John had maintained separate accounts, and it was easy to track her spending. She's paid the utilities, her credit card, and carried a health insurance policy that she paid monthly. She'd visited a salon every four weeks, bought groceries, and given herself a weekly allowance of a hundred dollars. That was February. And March. And April. And May.

I flipped to the next statement and my fingers froze. Quickly, I flipped to the next statement. And the next. "I found them."

Karma looked up from the sheet of paper she was reading. "Found what?"

"Sybil's missing statements." I quickly reviewed the canceled checks for February. Sybil had paid her utilities, the staffing company that sent her nurses, and her insurance. She'd also written four checks to herself totaling five-thousand dollars. I glanced at the memo line and saw that Karma was right. Each one had a notation that said, "Cash."

Karma put down whatever she was looking at and joined me on the bed. "This is just like the other statements I saw. But with less money. Maybe the Casanova knew she was nearly bled dry.

There were no cash withdrawals in May or June. Taking advantage of someone like that—it's just evil."

"This is it." I tapped the bank statement.

"What do you mean?"

"The link between Althea and Hazel's deaths and Ogden and Mabel's."

"How so?"

"Althea was an accountant. She knew someone was taking Sybil's savings. What if she wasn't murdered because she threatened Skip's job, what if she was murdered because she knew who'd taken Sybil's money?"

Mother, who was less than pleased with my decision to investigate from my hospital bed, chose that moment to bustle into my hospital room. "It's been hours. You need your rest."

"We found Sybil's missing statements in Althea's papers."

Mother looked less than impressed.

"Maybe Althea knew who took Sybil's money. Maybe that was what she meant to tell Kay at the luncheon. Maybe that's what got her killed."

Mother sniffed. "That's a lot of 'maybes.'"

I was on to something. I was sure of it. "I need to speak to Anarchy. Is he still here?

Mother gave me the look. "I sent him home with Grace. The poor man needed a decent meal, and Grace needed a break from the hospital.

My heart stuttered. They'd left me? He'd left me?

Karma reached for my hand. "There's a police officer stationed outside your room, and Anarchy will be back soon."

I exhaled.

Mother's eyes narrowed, as if she'd heard my terror in that one breath. "Nothing will happen to you, Ellison. Your husband and I will make sure of it."

CHAPTER TWENTY-ONE

A narchy pushed my wheelchair through the hospital's main doors.

"Please stop."

He did as I asked, and I stood. The nurses had insisted I leave in a wheelchair, and I'd agreed, knowing I'd be out of the dang thing the moment we hit the sidewalk.

Grace, who had been sitting in the idling car's driver's seat, moved to the back as Anarchy opened the passenger door for me. Once I was safely buckled in, he circled the car and slid behind the wheel.

"Peters is talking to the judge this morning?"

Last night, when I told him my theory, he'd decided the next step was to subpoena Adelaide and Edith's bank records.

"A uniformed officer is at Hazel's house now, collecting her statements."

"Do you really think Mr. Wortham killed all those people?" asked Grace.

I hated to believe it, but Skip was big enough, strong enough, to carry me from the parking lot to the pool. "He does drive a Mercedes sedan."

"So? Half the people you know drive Mercedes'."

"We brought him in for questioning and kept him overnight. But, if Lois continues to swear up and down that he was never out of her sight, we'll have to cut him loose."

My heart gave a nervous flutter.

Grace shifted in her seat. "So, what now?"

"Now I gather evidence."

"I meant, 'what do we do?'"

I turned in my seat and stared her down. "There is no 'we.' I will sit on the couch and read or watch TV (or lose my mind worrying), and you will walk the dogs, or hang out at the pool or go to your tennis lesson. You and I will stay far, far away from anything to do with this case."

"But, Mom—"

"No, Grace. You and I are done. We're out. This is a police matter." I pretended not to notice the slight twitch at the corner of my husband's lips. I'd done what Grace was doing now—gotten involved in things I shouldn't.

When we pulled into the driveway, Aggie opened the front door wearing a bright yellow kaftan embroidered with daisies. Her face was wreathed in smiles, and her curly red hair sproinged with extra energy. She practically bounced as we got out of the car. "Welcome home!"

"Thank you."

"People have been calling all morning," she told me.

Oh dear Lord. I sighed, one of those feel-it-all-the-way-to-my-toes sighs. "That's very kind of them, but I don't have the energy for it."

"I'll tell anyone who calls that you're resting."

We stepped into the foyer and some of the tightness in my chest relaxed. "It's good to be home."

"Where to?" asked Anarchy.

"The family room. Where are the dogs?"

"Backyard," Aggie replied.

They were probably digging their way to China.

"Let's get you settled, then we'll let them in." Anarchy led me to the family room and sat me down in my favorite corner of the couch.

"Coffee?" asked Aggie.

"Please. And the dogs."

She left us, and a moment later, the dogs tore into the room, tripping over each other in their eagerness to be the first to greet me. I gave them pets and kisses, telling them how much I missed them.

Aggie appeared with my coffee, and I gratefully accepted the mug.

"Would you like anything else?" she asked.

"Not a thing," I replied with a tired smile.

"Ellison?" Libba's voice carried through the house.

"You're supposed to rest," said Anarchy.

"It's Libba."

"She's not restful."

"She's just checking in on me. She won't stay long." A bold-face lie, and we both knew it. "Besides, what else am I going to do? Watch soaps?"

Libba appeared at the entrance to the family room. "Would it kill you to answer me?" She crossed the room, put a bouquet of snapdragons on the coffee table, and flopped down on the other end of the couch. "I swear, Ellison, you're going to give me gray hair."

"Sorry."

"'Sorry' means you won't do it again." She eyed me critically. "What happened to your head?"

A dip in the pool followed by two nights in the hospital had not done my hair any favors.

She turned to Anarchy and lifted her left brow. "I heard you arrested Skip Wortham. Are you sure he did it?"

Anarchy crossed his arms over his chest. "We're gathering evidence."

"I don't think he did it," she said. "He's not ruthless enough. He might steal from little old ladies, but murder? He's not mean enough."

"Not even to conceal his crimes?" I asked.

Libba shook her head. "He doesn't have it in him. So, who are your other suspects?"

When no one answered, she tsked. "You do realize, if you're wrong, the man who tried to kill Ellison is still out there."

Grace, who was crouched next to Max, petting his silky ears, gasped.

"That's enough," I told my friend. "Grace, why don't you get the dogs out before it gets too hot?"

I expected an argument, but she gave a brief nod and left us.

"Seriously," said Libba. "Who else?"

I hesitated before responding, "Chuck Wade."

"Chuck?" Libba asked, incredulous. "You think Chuck did this? How hard did the assailant hit your head?"

I ignored my friend and looked at my husband. "He drives a black Mercedes. And Bernie saw him at Sybil's."

"Chuck?" Libba stretched out her legs and crossed her ankles. "I am not convinced."

"That wedding was over-the-top expensive. And, the memo lines, they all read, 'Cash.'"

"Which is what people write when they're getting cash."

I did not acknowledge Libba's excellent point.

"Hmm." Libba tapped her index finger against her lips, leaned back, and gazed at the ceiling. "He's ruthless enough."

"What?"

"You've heard the whispers, right?" Libba sat up straight as her gaze bounced between Anarchy and me. "Mafia ties."

I laughed, shaking my head. "Chuck Wade and the mafia?

The man's an estate planning attorney for one of the largest firms in Kansas City. He's not in bed with the mafia."

"Why not?" Libba said. "You think the mafia doesn't need tax planning? Isn't that how they got Capone?"

Anarchy, rubbing his hand across his chin, finally spoke, "We'll bring him in for questioning. But regarding the murders and the thefts—not the mafia."

Libba wrinkled her nose and huffed, "Poo."

My husband got me situated to his satisfaction, then left for the station.

Libba stayed till my eyelids grew heavy. "Rest." She patted my knee. "I'll come by later."

I let her go and napped.

Ding, dong.

"I'll get it!" Aggie called. Over the past several hours, the doorbell had been in constant use—florist deliveries, Bundt cakes, and even a stack of newly-released novels. I had remained curled up in the corner of the couch, letting Aggie handle everything. She brought me chicken salad for lunch, kept my glass filled with iced tea, and the scent of home-baked chocolate chip cookies perfumed the air, making my mouth water.

"She's resting," Aggie said, her voice uncharacteristically loud.

"I don't care! Where is she?"

Oh dear Lord... Linda Wade.

Linda stormed into the family room, and her furious gaze zeroed in on my nest. Her face was flushed, and the stench of bourbon hit me from across the room—she smelled like downed a whole bottle. "How dare you!"

My hand instinctively slid between the cushions of the couch, where Anarchy had stashed my gun.

"Your husband went to Chuck's office." She was practically shaking with rage, and I realized she really might be dangerous. "He took Chuck in for questioning. It's humiliating!"

"For whom?" I asked, my voice calm despite the crazy woman in front of me.

"For *me*," she spat, her eyes narrowing into slits.

"Chuck has been taking advantage of vulnerable older ladies, hasn't he?" The accusation rolled right off my tongue.

"He hasn't done anything illegal." Linda's voice grew increasingly shrill with each passing word.

"You admit he did it?"

"I admit nothing!"

"How do you live with yourself?" The question was genuine.

She glared at me. "Those ladies, their children abandoned them. Chuck brought them happiness!"

"You knew the whole time, didn't you?" I said softly. "You knew it wasn't right."

Her expression faltered for a split second before rage retook her features. "It wasn't illegal."

I wasn't so sure about that. There had to be *some* kind of law protecting people from their own foolishness. What had Anarchy called it? Stealing by deceit?

"What about Althea?" I threw out the question, never dreaming she'd react.

Linda retreated a step as her face flushed a deep crimson. Gotcha!

"Yes, Chuck killed her. She threatened to tell Kay, to tell everyone. Right before the wedding, after all that planning... Do you think Chuck would let her ruin Lindsay's day?"

She was justifying murder, plain and simple.

"And Hazel?" I asked.

"She turned on Chuck. He listened to her complaints about her children, about her late husband, about her life. A whole daily litany. Then, when he took care of Althea, she turned on him. She tried to extort money. From us."

"What about Ogden and Mabel?"

Her expression twisted into something cruel. "That's your

fault. If you hadn't called Ogden, he never would've come to Kansas City."

"I didn't kill him."

"But you made it happen. Don't worry—it was quick. Painless."

"Is that so?"

"Shots to the heart."

Had Linda and Chuck had discussed the murders over dinner? *I shot Ogden Whittier through the heart. Would you please pass the peas?*

"How do you know how they died?" My hand slipped deeper into the sofa.

"Ogden called the house. He was furious. He demanded to speak with Chuck. When I said Chuck wasn't home, he told me exactly what kind of man I married. He promised to see Chuck in jail. I couldn't let that happen."

"You killed them."

She shrugged as if the death of two people mattered little.

"Why, Linda? Why take money from little old ladies? Why murder?"

"When Chuck and I got married, I felt like the luckiest woman in the world. Every girl on campus wanted him, and I got him. I was sure he was destined for great things."

"He's done well." Chuck was a partner in a well-respected law firm. Their daughter had attended private schools. They took lovely vacations. They belonged to a country club.

"Pfft. We could never afford a second home or—" her lips curled into a snarl "—a month of vacation in Italy." Her gaze lowered to the floor where I'd kicked off a pair of Gucci loafers. "I can't afford to wear Chanel or Gucci or Hermès."

In essence, she'd wanted to keep up with the Joneses.

She shook her head and fumbled with her handbag. "You ruined everything."

The days of villains pointing guns at me in my own home

were over. I pulled the gun from the couch and pointed it at her. "Put down the handbag, Linda."

"You won't shoot me."

"Try me."

She did. She pulled a small gun from her bag.

I pulled the trigger, shooting her in the arm.

Linda dropped her bag and her gun and clutched the wound.

"Aggie! Call Anarchy. Now!"

My housekeeper appeared in the doorway holding a cassette recorder. "Already done. I called him the minute she barged in here. And I recorded most of your conversation."

Linda, who was already bleeding all over my carpet, leaned over and vomited half a bottle of bourbon.

I didn't mind. I needed a new carpet anyway.

CHAPTER TWENTY-TWO

I sat between Kay and Mother, listening as Teddy Bryant eulogized Sybil Morrison.

"Sybil was a woman of strong convictions." Teddy's voice was strong and clear.

There were a few chuckles from the congregation, and I imagined the women seated behind me nodding their heads in agreement.

"For those of us lucky enough to call her a friend, she was a loyal advocate, a shoulder to cry on, and a bringer of chocolate Bundt cakes and laughter."

Next to me, Mother gave a tiny smile.

"Sybil wasn't one for grand expressions of emotion. One never got an 'I love you' from her. Instead, she showed how she felt. She showed up, or in the case of her daughter Kay, she bragged endlessly."

Kay clutched my hand.

"Kay, she was endlessly proud of you. But, being Sybil, she didn't always know how to express it."

I reached for the handkerchief in my pocket, offering it to Kay as her eyes filled with tears.

She nodded a watery thank you.

"While today is about Sybil and how much we will miss her. It's also a reminder to hold our loved ones close. Sadly, I think Sybil died with regrets. And I know she'd want all of you, her dear friends, to learn from her mistakes." Teddy paused, giving the congregation a moment to consider her words. "Tell the people you love that you love them. Sybil, I offer you my favorite blessing.

"May the road rise up to meet you. May the wind always be at your back. May the sun shine warm upon your face, and rains fall soft upon your fields. And until we meet again, may God hold you in the palm of His hand."

Next to me, Mother stiffened. I already knew how she'd rank this funeral—too maudlin and too ethnic.

Kay squeezed my hand, her grief palpable.

I turned and whispered in Mother's ear. "I love you, even if you do give this service a five out of ten."

A smile curled her lips as she reached for my free hand. "I love you, too, and I give it a solid seven."

THE RECEPTION AT THE CLUB WAS IMPECCABLE. THERE WAS NO way Mother could find fault. Top-shelf liquor. Lovely food. Teddy had even hired a harpist to strum in the corner.

Jinx grabbed my arm and guided me to quiet spot. "Spill."

"It's a long story."

"You shot Linda Wade?"

"I guess that part is short."

"She and Chuck killed four people?"

"Two each."

"They'd been taking advantage of lonely widows?"

"You don't really need me for this." Obviously, Jinx already knew everything.

"I like confirmation."

She had taken me to the motel, I owed her for that. "What else do want to know?"

"Skip Wortham?"

"Completely innocent."

Jinx shook her head and lit a cigarette. "Poor Lindsay."

"I guess his family doesn't seem so bad, now."

Jinx barked a laugh.

"Listen, I need a drink."

She nodded, then blew a plume of smoke. "Is Anarchy here?"

"I came with Mother."

"Ah." One word said so much. "What did she think of the eulogy?"

"A seven."

"That surprises me."

"Me, too." I took a first step toward the bar and the wine spritzer that was calling my name.

"When does Beau get home?"

I couldn't help but smile. "Sunday." I planned on following Teddy's advice and telling him just how much we all loved him.

"Think you can avoid finding bodies for the rest of the summer?"

"I sure hope so." We both knew I wasn't that lucky.

SOMEWHERE IN THE NIGHT

BONUS NOVELLA

JULIE MULHERN

CHAPTER ONE

November 1975
Kansas City, Missouri

The holiday season might bring people together, but family dinners also drove them round the bend.

Or was that just me?

One of Mother's cherished customs was rushing through our Thanksgiving meal so we could see the Plaza lights come on. Each year, more than 100,000 colored lights decorated the Plaza's Spanish-inspired buildings. Towers looked like delicate lace. The buildings looked fit for fairies. Even the parking garages were transformed.

Simply put, the Plaza during the holidays was magical.

Less magical was the stress of arriving in time to see the lights come on. It wasn't as if we didn't have other opportunities to see the lights. They shined brightly until after New Year's.

But Mother insisted. Which is how I found myself packed in

a limousine with Mother, Daddy, Anarchy, Grace, Beau, and Karma.

As I thought about the mess we'd left with Aggie, my housekeeper, I clenched my hands until my nails dug into the heels of my palms.

"Ellison," said Mother, who'd never once concerned herself with the amount of work she'd left for her help. "That's a sour look you're wearing."

"Is it?" We could be at home right now, drying the last of the dishes, getting ready to curl up in front of the fire in the family room with mulled wine or hot chocolate. Instead, we were racing around like chickens with our heads cut off.

"There are people who'd give their eye teeth for your Aunt Matilda's view. She's kind to invite us." Mother gave a put-upon sigh. "Even if she did give her guest parking spaces to Jane's family. She knows your father refuses to park anywhere else."

Hearing the clear censure in Mother's voice, Daddy, who'd undoubtedly rather be home watching the Cowboys play the Lions, patted her knee. "Parking down here is a zoo. Besides, the limousine is nice." He took a sip of his very stiff scotch and leaned back into his seat.

Mother pursed her lips and shifted her gaze to my half-sister, who'd relocated from San Francisco to Kansas City over the summer. "The holiday lights are spectacular. You'll love them."

"I'm sure I will." Karma and Mother were always scrupulously polite.

"Have you ever seen the lights come on, Beau?" asked Karma.

"Yes." He sounded nowhere near as enthusiastic as Mother.

"It's very exciting," Mother insisted.

As exciting as flipping a light switch.

I batted down that uncharitable thought. It was Thanksgiving. I refused to be negative. Not even in the privacy of my head. Where was my holiday spirit? The Plaza lighting ceremony was the official start of the Christmas season. I needed good will toward men, or at least good will toward Mother. "Who else will be at Aunt Tilly's?"

Mother scrunched her nose as if she'd smelled particularly pungent trash. "Jane and her brood. They were invited for dinner." It ate at Mother's craw when Jane's family was asked for dinner, and we weren't.

"Mother, if you dislike them so, why go?" It was a reasonable question. Another reasonable question? Why drag us with her?

She shook a finger at me. "Ellison Russell—"

"Jones," I corrected.

"Jones," she ceded. "Don't take that tone with me. Your aunt looks forward to this every year, and I can hardly decline an invitation just because we don't care for her in-laws."

Mother called Aunt Tilly's in-laws outlaws. She was convinced Aunt Tilly counted her silver when they left.

"Who's Jane?" asked Karma.

"Aunt Matilda is my father's sister," Mother explained. "She married George Webster. Jane is George's niece."

"And Aunt Tilly's," I added.

"Only by marriage." Mother dismissed my excellent point.

"Jane married a man named Kowalski," I added. The mere mention of the name annoyed Mother.

"Like Stanley?" asked Karma. I didn't miss the amusement dancing in her eyes.

Mother scowled. Deeply. To her waspy ear, Kowalski sounded so very ethnic.

"Yes," I replied. "Exactly like Stanley. Except Jane's husband's name was Mike."

"Was?" asked Anarchy.

"He had a heart attack a few years back." Probably from the stress of getting to Aunt Tilly's apartment in time for the lighting ceremony. "Mike and Jane had two children, Clover and Mike junior. They're both married."

Mother sighed as if Clover and Mike were heavy weights to bear. "Clover's husband's name is Wyatt. Mike's wife's name is Karli."

Anarchy chuckled. "Karli Kowalski? That's very alliterative."

Mother's lips curled in distaste. "The fool woman did it to herself. As for her first name, it's spelled with a 'k' and an 'i.'"

"We see them once or twice a year," I told Karma.

"Which is more than enough." Mother might have said more, but the limousine pulled to a stop next to the glass front door, and we all piled out of the car and headed to the elevator.

As we waited for the elevator to arrive, Daddy asked, "Anarchy, what are your family's holiday traditions?"

Anarchy reached for my hand and gave it a quick squeeze. "An annual argument about serving turkey instead of tofu." My husband had a Bohemian upbringing. He'd rebelled by becoming a meat-and-potatoes-eating, straight-arrow police detective.

"And you, Beau?" Dad shifted his gaze to the latest addition to our family. "Do you have a favorite holiday tradition?"

I held my breath. Beau's whole life had recently been upended, and the last thing I wanted was to upset him.

"Pie," he replied. "We ate pumpkin pie for breakfast on the day after Thanksgiving."

Mother jabbed at the elevator call button as if hitting it a second time would make it arrive faster.

"That's a great tradition," said Anarchy. "I say we continue that one."

Beau grinned.

"It's not healthy." Mother was in a mood, and we hadn't yet interacted with Jane. It promised to be a long evening.

"It's one day out of the year." I kept my tone mild.

She eyed me critically. "You do realize most people gain ten pounds over the holidays?"

First off, I was fairly certain she'd made that up. Secondly, I was not the one who planned on eating pie in the morning. I offered her a tight smile. "I wonder how many calories are in a scotch and soda."

"One-hundred-and-forty," said Karma. "Although the way this family pours, the number is probably higher."

Unlike Mother's ten-pound-holiday-weight-gain number, Karma's sounded legitimate.

"How do you know that?" asked Mother.

Karma smiled brightly at Mother. "I had a diet coach back in California."

Mother pursed her lips and closed her eyes, and I could see the wheels turning. Three times one-hundred-forty. She paled as she added four-hundred-twenty calories to her daily tally.

"A slice of pumpkin pie has around three-hundred-and-twenty calories." Karma flashed me a quick grin, so quickly Mother couldn't see.

I adored my sister. Truly, I did.

The elevator doors slid open, and we pressed inside.

A moment later, we knocked on Aunt Tilly's door, and her houseman, Hudson, welcomed us inside. He'd added a sprig of holly to his white coat and wore a silk bow tie decorated with tiny turkeys. He looked quite festive.

When Hudson had our coats draped over his arm, he asked, "A scotch and soda for you, Mrs. Walford?"

Mother offered him a grateful smile. "Yes, please." It might cost her one-hundred-plus calories, but there was no way she could deal with Jane and her family without scotch.

Hudson gave a brief unsurprised nod. "A scotch for you, Mr. Walford?"

"Please."

"Mrs. Jones?"

"Sparkling water with lime." Anyone else's house, I'd ask for wine, but Aunt Tilly poured Lancer's.

"Mr. Jones?"

"The same."

"And you, miss?" Hudson smiled at Karma.

"Scotch and soda."

"Miss Grace?"

"Scotch and soda."

"Grace!" Mother sounded scandalized.

My daughter, who wore a Laura Ashley dress she loathed to please her grandmother, grinned. "Just kidding. May I please have a Tab with two limes?"

Aunt Tilly's houseman nodded, then turned to Beau.

"Hudson, this is Beau. The newest member of our family."

"Pleased to meet you, Beau. What may I get you to drink?"

"A soda, please, if it's not too much trouble."

"No trouble at all." Hudson nodded toward the living room with its wall of windows. "They're just finishing dinner. They'll join you in a moment."

"Thank you, Hudson." Mother swanned into the living room and perched on a brocade covered fauteuil. Aunt Tilly's apartment was furnished in dainty French antiques and shaded in soft blue, pink, and gilt. The paintings were Dutch still lifes in ornate frames. It was the most feminine room imaginable, and it made Daddy itch.

No surprise, he stepped outside onto the balcony. He wouldn't last long. Not without his coat. The temperature had reached forty this afternoon, but with the sun long since set, it was cold outside.

"Frances, you're here!" Tilly had mastered the art of sounding thrilled to see everyone she met. Her tone suggested Mother's arrival was the best thing to happen since sliced bread. Which was lovely until you heard her use the exact same tone with the plumber or the woman who came every Monday and did her laundry. "And Ellison. How pretty you look." She held out her manicured fingers to Anarchy. "We met at the wedding. Call me Aunt Tilly."

"A pleasure to see you, again." Anarchy gave her the grin that made my knees turn weak.

Aunt Tilly swayed and fluttered her eyelashes at my husband before switching her focus to Karma. "You look so much like Marjorie. The two of you could be sisters."

They were sisters. Well, half-sisters.

Karma managed a polite smile. "Dad's genes."

"I suppose that must be it." Tilly turned to Beau and caught his chin in a vise-like grip. "And you're Beau. Frances told me about you. What a handsome boy you are."

Beau, who wore a navy blazer and rep tie, did look handsome. "Nice to meet you." He cast me a desperate glance.

"You may call her Aunt Tilly."

"Nice to meet you, Aunt Tilly."

"Aunt Matilda," Mother corrected.

My great-aunt was tall and thin and chic and looked twenty years younger than her actual age. She was feminine and fun and, because she spent most of her time in Palm Springs, we didn't see her often enough. "Aunt Tilly is just fine," she told Beau as she released his chin. "Now that you're all here, the party can start. You all know Jane." She nodded to her niece, who wore a rust-colored pants suit with a turquoise blouse. Jane had once been a pretty woman, but decades of cigarette smoking had cut deep lines into the skin around her mouth. Tonight, her lipstick had bled into those lines. Not a good look. Nor was her frosted blue eyeshadow.

Aunt Tilly shifted her gaze to a stranger. "And this is her husband, Earl."

Husband? When had that happened?

Earl wore a handlebar mustache, long sideburns, and an

open-collared shirt. No tie. No jacket. Also, he was at least ten years younger than Jane. Maybe fifteen.

Mother's disapproval rose like mist from a morning meadow. She stared with singular focus.

Uncomfortable in the silence, I cleared my throat.

Anarchy held out his hand. "I'm Anarchy Jones, Ellison's husband."

The two men shook.

"How long have you been married?" Mother's eyes were narrowed to mere slits.

Jane giggled. "Two weeks. It was a whirlwind romance."

"We got hitched in Vegas." Earl possessed a country twang.

"You got hitched." Mother's voice was dry as dust. She and Jane didn't like each other. Mother believed Jane maintained a relationship with Aunt Tilly in hopes of inheriting money that belonged, at least in Mother's mind, to our family. "How romantic."

Jane blinked in the face of Mother's sarcasm.

Not that I'd argue the point with her. Getting "hitched" in Vegas sounded about as romantic as a colonoscopy.

"It was beautiful." Jane was starry-eyed. "The chapel was filled with flowers, and the minister's wife sang *We've Only Just Begun*. She sounded just like Karen Carpenter."

I forced a smile. "Best wishes to you both."

"I see you've met Earl." Clover, who'd entered the living room a moment after her mother, sounded less than enthused about Jane's new husband. She took after her mother. Pretty. Blonde. And Clover's face wasn't ravaged by cigarettes. Although...her mouth was tightly pursed.

"Just now," I replied.

Clover leaned forward and ghosted a kiss near my cheek. "Sorry about this," she whispered. Then, she held out her hand to Anarchy. "Clover Bowman. Nice to meet you." She glanced over her shoulder. "And this is my husband, Wyatt."

The two men shook.

Wyatt Bowman was a bean counter. A straight arrow. He and Anarchy had that in common. They also had to put up with family craziness. There, the similarities ended. Wyatt was slight, with thinning hair and a tremulous smile. Meanwhile, Anarchy was tall and strong and had eyes the color of perfectly brewed coffee.

Hudson appeared with a tray of drinks.

As I accepted my club soda, I wished I'd requested something stronger. "What time is it?" The real question? How long until we could politely leave?

"We have fifteen minutes until the lighting ceremony." Aunt Tilly waved at the wall of windows. "Grace, why don't you show Beau the TV room? The other children are already there. We'll call you when the lights are about to go on."

Grace didn't need telling twice. She grabbed Beau's hand and disappeared.

As they left, Karli and Mike arrived. Her cheeks were flushed, and her eyes were shiny. Either they'd been kissing or arguing. Given the unhappy tilt of her lips, I guessed the latter.

Except for Jane and Earl and Aunt Tilly no one looked happy. I glanced toward the door to the balcony. Daddy was still out there. Probably freezing. Lucky, lucky man.

"Everyone has a drink?" Aunt Tilly held up a glass of scotch and water. "Wonderful. Let's sit."

Mother resumed her perch on the fauteuil and offered Jane a tight smile. "How did you two meet?"

"My car broke down. The mechanic said it would cost five-hundred dollars to fix it. Which is more than it was worth. So, I decided to buy a new car." She giggled again. "Well, a new-to-me car. Earl was the salesman."

Mike, who sat next to me on the couch, made a funny noise, like pieces of gravel rubbing against each other.

I added two and two and got four. A new-to-her car. A salesman. Jane had married a used car salesman. No wonder Clover and her brother wore bemused, angry expressions.

"Did you attend the wedding?" I asked Clover.

"Mother surprised us," she replied coolly. "She didn't tell us she was dating."

What was that strange noise Mike was making?

I glanced his way.

His jaw worked. The man was grinding his teeth. Hard enough for me to hear. Mike was a big man. Tall. Beefy. And starting to go soft around the middle. We'd never had much use for each other. But I didn't need to know him well to sense the barely contained fury radiating from his person.

Earl, who had his arm draped around Jane's shoulders, gave Mother a slick grin. "When you know, you know. Right, babe?"

Jane snuggled closer to her new husband. "It was love at first sight."

Mike ground his teeth harder. If he kept it up, he'd break a molar.

"What a charming story." Mother sounded anything but charmed.

"Did you buy a car?" asked Karma.

Jane nodded. "Earl got me a good deal on a Pinto."

Oh, dear Lord.

The door from the balcony opened, and Daddy stepped inside.

"Harrington," said Mother. "Meet Jane's new husband, Earl. I'm sorry, I don't believe I caught your last name."

"Hicks."

Mother closed her eyes as if the name pained her. "Meet Earl Hicks."

Daddy stepped forward and extended his hand. "Pleasure to meet you, Earl. I'm Harrington Walford."

The two men couldn't look more different. In his charcoal-gray suit paired with a crisp white shirt and festive red tie,

Daddy could have modeled for Brooks Brothers. Earl looked like...well, a used car salesman. But they shook.

"Harrington--" Mother pointed "--Hudson left your drink on the console."

Daddy claimed his scotch with alacrity, then he bent and brushed a kiss against Aunt Tilly's rouged cheek. "You get prettier every time I see you."

She swatted at his arm as her face flushed with pleasure at the compliment. "I do declare, you say the nicest things."

"Nothing but the truth."

Silence fell. Uncomfortable silence. And I fidgeted in my seat. "Did you all have a nice dinner?"

Earl rubbed his belly and tipped a glass of what looked to be straight scotch at Aunt Tilly. "Good eats. A first-class spread."

Oh my. What came next? Loosening his belt or a belch?

I didn't want to know the answer. "Do you have family in town, Earl?" There was an outside chance the newly married couple would split holidays. If we were lucky, they'd go someplace else for Thanksgiving next year.

"Just me. I was an only child, and my folks are gone."

Hope died a quick death, but I forced a smile. "So, where are you living, Jane?"

"Earl's apartment was too small for us. He moved into my house." Her hand traveled from his knee to high up on his thigh, and she fluttered her eyelashes. "Our house."

Next to me, Mike snorted, loud enough to draw all eyes.

"Mom." Grace hovered near the entrance to the living room. "Can you come?"

I stood. Grateful for the interruption. "Of course. Is everything all right?"

She nodded, but her gaze was shifty.

Something was wrong. Beau? Were the other kids being mean to him?

"Excuse me." After I sorted whatever was happening with

the kids, I'd find Hudson and ask for a real drink. The evening definitely called for scotch. I followed my daughter into the hallway. "What's wrong?"

"Mikey locked himself in the bathroom."

Mikey was sixteen. And not my child. How had he become my problem?

Then, I smelled it. Pot. "Are you kidding me?"

"I knocked, and he didn't answer. I'm worried."

Not my problem. Not my problem. But Grace was looking at me as if I had the power to solve this problem. I rapped my knuckles against the bathroom door. "Mikey?"

Mikey remained stubbornly silent.

I twisted the locked handle. "Mikey?" I rapped once more. Harder.

There was no answer, and the silence seemed ominous.

Grace clasped her hands. "What if he smoked pot laced with LSD?"

I winced. I hated that my daughter knew to worry about things like that. I prayed she was wrong as I said, "Go get Anarchy."

She didn't move. "But…"

I understood her reluctance. Anarchy was a police detective. If he found Mikey doing drugs, there might be criminal charges. But if Mikey was dying, Anarchy was the best person to help him. "Tell Anarchy there's a problem, Grace. Mikey may need his help."

She nodded, then disappeared down the corridor, and again I rapped on the door.

Again, there was no response.

Anarchy arrived with Mike, who shouldered past me and hammered on the door. "Mikey, open the door, son. Now."

The other children gathered around—Beau, Mikey's younger sister Gina, and Clover's daughters, Heather and Ivy.

I offered them a weak smile. "Why don't you go back to the television room?" It wasn't a question, more like a suggestion.

Gina, who'd paled to the color of fresh fallen snow, shook her head. "I'm staying here."

I planted my hands on my hips, channeled Mother, and gave them a fearsome scowl. "Grace, take everyone to the TV room. Now."

The children took giant steps backward, and Grace gave a short, unhappy nod, before herding the kids, including a reluctant Gina, back down the hall.

"We need to take the door off the hinges," said Anarchy. "Does your aunt have a screwdriver?"

"I'll ask Hudson."

I raced to the kitchen, where Hudson was handwashing Aunt Tilly's Haviland china.

If he was surprised to see me barging into the kitchen, he didn't show it. "What may I do for you, Miss Ellison?" he asked.

"We need a screwdriver."

Hudson wiped his hands on a dishtowel then reached for the vodka.

"No, no. An actual screwdriver."

Ever unflappable, Hudson opened a drawer, revealing both a flathead and Phillips.

I took them both. "Thank you, Hudson. When you get a moment, may I please have a scotch and soda with a twist?"

He nodded as if my sudden request for alcohol came as no surprise. "Yes, ma'am."

I hurried back to the bathroom and held my breath as Anarchy and Mike removed the door. Then, I peered inside.

Mikey lay on the tile floor, not moving.

CHAPTER TWO

———————————

"Call an ambulance." Anarchy used his cop voice, the one that demanded immediate action.

Mike stumbled backward, away from the entry to the bathroom, then took off down the hallway, presumably to call for help.

Anarchy and I stepped into the tiny room, and he fell to his knees and checked for a pulse. "He's alive."

"Thank heavens." I took my first full breath since he and Mike had gone to work on the hinges. "What can I do?" Mikey's skin was the color of dirty Silly Putty, and his eyes remained firmly closed.

"He's breathing on his own." Anarchy sat back on his heels. "Any idea what he might have taken?"

"My son does not do drugs." Karli spoke from the doorway to the bathroom. A crowd of concerned adults surrounded her.

"Someone was smoking pot in here." The smell hung heavy in the air. I pointed to the roach on Aunt Tilly's tiled floor. "Who else?"

Her mouth puckered as if she'd been sucking lemons, and she planted her hands on her hips. "Not Mikey."

Denial wasn't just a river in Egypt.

"Grace thinks the pot was laced with something."

I heard a gasp and knew it was Mother's. "How does my granddaughter know what a marijuana cigarette smells like?" Because she was a teenager in the 1970s. Recognizing something and using it were two different things. I said as much.

Mother pressed a palm to her forehead. "Harrington, I need another drink."

Karli joined me next to her son's body. "Mikey, honey, wake up."

Mikey didn't move. Maybe she should lean closer? The overwhelming smell of her Charlie perfume mixing with gin on her breath was as good as smelling salts.

I blinked my watering eyes.

Karli tapped her son's cheek. "Mikey, it's time to wake up now."

No one said a word. Especially not Mikey.

"The ambulance is on its way." Mike pushed his way into the bathroom and joined his wife at his son's side. "What can we do for him?"

"We wait," Anarchy replied. "His breath is shallow, but he is breathing."

"But his color," said Clover from her spot just outside the door. "He looks like a corpse."

True, but not helpful.

Karli sobbed, and Mike patted her shoulder as if he didn't know what to do to comfort his wife.

"Don't fall apart when your son may need you." Jane sounded judgmental—as if she couldn't abide Charlie perfume, copious gin, or her daughter-in-law's narcissism.

Karli turned and gave her mother-in-law a vicious glare. "Don't talk to me about being there for your children."

Jane's face flushed an ugly red, and her fingers stretched as if she longed to slap Karli across the face.

"Someone should go to the lobby and wait for the ambulance," I suggested. It would help clear the crowd spilling into the bathroom. And clear some of the tension, too.

"I'll go." Wyatt went so far as to raise his hand when he volunteered.

Everyone shuffled around, and he disappeared down the hallway.

A long—endless—moment passed, then Mother said, "Well, we've missed it."

"Missed what?" asked Jane.

"The lights."

I stared at Mother. A boy was unconscious on the floor, maybe dying, and she was worried about missing the lights come on?

"How can you say such a thing?" Jane demanded. "That's my grandson."

"A delinquent who—"

"Come on, Frannie." Daddy tugged on Mother's elbow. "Let's get you a drink."

Mother allowed him to remove her from what promised to be a nasty argument.

"How long will it take the ambulance to get here?" Karli wrung her hands.

"St. Mark's is only a few blocks away." I didn't add that the driver would have to get through the craziness and traffic on the Plaza.

"He's still breathing?" she asked.

"He is," Anarchy confirmed.

Mike wrapped an arm around his wife. "He'll be okay, honey."

She pushed him away. "You don't know that. How could this happen?"

"Mom?" Grace stood in the hallway near the doorway. "How's Mikey?"

"Breathing. An ambulance is coming. Do the girls know what he was smoking?"

"Pot. He offered to share. We all said 'no.'"

"Thank God," Clover whispered.

Karli gave her sister-in-law a scowl that could peel paint, then she turned her glare on Grace. "You didn't try and stop him? You didn't come and find an adult?"

I would not allow her to blame my daughter for her son's choices. "This is not Grace's fault, Karli."

"She let my son take drugs."

"Your son chose to take drugs. He needs more parental supervision, not a mother who blames everyone else."

Karli's fingers curled into claws. "How dare you?"

"Let's all calm down." Anarchy's voice was even. Authoritative. It demanded calm.

"Make way." An EMT pushed through the bottleneck at the bathroom door.

Anarchy and I stood, allowing room for someone with actual medical training.

"If you folks would step back?" said the EMT. "Give us some room."

Everyone but Mike and Karli retired to the living room, where Aunt Tilly had the lights turned low. Outside, the Plaza blazed with color. Everyone took a cursory glance then perched on delicate chairs. Everyone except Mother. She took her fresh drink onto the balcony and stared at the lights.

Daddy offered Jane an apologetic smile. "Frances was worried that Ellison had found another body. She's a bit sensitive about that." He took in Jane's horrified expression, and added, "I'll keep Frannie company." He escaped onto the balcony, leaving Anarchy and me with Jane, Clover, Wyatt, and Aunt Tilly.

We watched a second EMT push a gurney down the hallway to the bathroom, and Jane pressed her palm to her mouth.

I frowned. "Where's Earl?"

Jane tilted her head as if she was puzzled by his absence. "He must be with the children."

That hardly seemed likely.

"I don't know about you, but I could use another drink." Aunt Tilly tapped her foot on the Aubusson beneath her favorite rose-hued bergère. "Hudson will be here shortly."

Hudson, God love him, arrived almost immediately.

"Another round for everyone," she told him.

"Yes, ma'am." He disappeared into the kitchen to make our drinks.

As we waited, the EMTs rolled a still unconscious Mikey to the front door. His parents followed behind.

"Karli is going to ride in the ambulance," said Mike. "I'll follow in the car."

"Do you want us to come?" asked Clover.

"No. We'll call you when there's news." He slipped out the front door.

Aunt Tilly offered us a tight smile. "This is a Thanksgiving we'll never forget."

Jane winced and stood abruptly. "I'm going to find Earl."

When her mother left, Clover shook her head. "I've been telling them for months. That boy needed help. Would anyone listen to me? No. Mother told me to mind my own business. Mike refused to see the truth. And Karli? She called me names. This is the first time I've let the girls near their cousin since the Fourth of July."

"He's a regular user?" asked Anarchy.

Clover shrugged. "We haven't seen him since July, but he was stoned at the family picnic. His eyes were mere slits, and he ate a whole bowl of potato salad. Enough for ten people."

Mother and Daddy, both shivering, stepped inside from the balcony just as Jane returned to the living room. "Earl's not with the children," she said. "They haven't seen him."

"He must be here somewhere," said Clover.

"He's not. I checked every room."

"Would he leave without telling you?"

"Never."

An uncharitable thought glided across my brain. Had Earl supplied the pot that sent Mikey to the hospital? Was that why he disappeared? I stood.

"Ellison?" Anarchy looked up at me from a chair that didn't look sturdy enough to hold him.

"I need some air."

"And a coat," said Mother. "It's freezing out there."

"They're in the guest bedroom," said Aunt Tilly.

"I'll get it," said Anarchy.

While he was gone, Hudson appeared with our drinks, and I took a grateful sip.

"What do we do?" said Clover. "I know Mike said to go home, but they shouldn't be alone. What if—"

"Don't talk that way." Wyatt patted her knee. "Mikey will be fine."

Anarchy draped my mink around my shoulders, and together we stepped outside.

He wrapped an arm around my shoulders. "There's a plaid topcoat on the bed."

I dragged my gaze away from the lights. "Pardon?"

"A plaid topcoat. Rust and mustard. Is that something Wyatt would wear?"

"No." Wyatt worked for a large accounting firm. He wore navy or gray. Period.

"Mike had on his coat when he left, so the plaid coat must belong to Earl."

"He left without his coat? In this weather?" What possessed me to look down? Intuition? Bad luck? I didn't mind heights, but seventeen floors was a long way down. For whatever reason, I looked, and Aunt Tilly's Waterford glass slipped through my fingers and shattered against the concrete balcony.

"What's wrong?" Concern etched Anarchy's handsome face.

I swallowed bile, clutched the guardrail, and closed my eyes. "I found Earl."

CHAPTER THREE

Mother was not pleased. Not with me. Not with Anarchy. Especially not with Earl. She demonstrated her displeasure with pursed lips, narrowed eyes, and an icy stiffness in the set of her shoulders. "Ellison," she said as she rose from the rose silk fauteuil.

"Yes, Mother?" I barely contained a sigh.

"It's Thanksgiving."

That was indisputable. "Yes, Mother."

"We're at your Aunt Matilda's."

Technically, Tilly was my great aunt, but I wasn't about to quibble.

"And you found a body."

"Anyone might have noticed it," said Anarchy.

Mother turned her bone-chilling gaze his way. "Harrington and I were out there, and we didn't see a thing. But Ellison? It's like she's a beacon for corpses."

Anarchy's lips quirked.

Fortunately, Mother didn't notice.

He adjusted his tie, a red silk we'd bought on our honeymoon in Italy. "To be fair, Ellison finds only a small percentage of the murder victims in Kansas City."

Ice flowed from Mother's fingertips, turning Aunt Tilly's living room into a walk-in freezer.

"Hicks might have fallen." Wyatt pushed his glasses up his thin nose. "He'd had plenty to drink."

All eyes shifted to the balcony and its railing that reached four-and-a-half feet. No one fell over the railing.

"Or he jumped," he added, but his tone was doubtful.

Jane, who hunched on the sofa, lifted her tear-stained face from her hands. "Earl would never do that."

"How do you know?" Mother sounded genuinely curious.

Jane flushed. "I just know. We had so much to live for. We were happy and—" she glanced around Aunt Tilly's antique-packed living room, then lowered her head to her hands.

I tended to agree with Jane. Not because I believed he was deliriously happy. Not at all. I doubted he'd jumped because Earl had struck me as a slick operator, not the kind of man who'd take his own life.

"Well," said Anarchy. "If he didn't fall, and he didn't jump, someone murdered him."

Earl's widow gasped.

"I've already called the station. Peters will be here soon." Peters was Anarchy's irascible partner.

"You'll investigate with him?" Daddy stood at the entrance to the living room.

Anarchy gave a brief nod.

"Harrington," Mother stood. "I'd like to go home."

"I'm sorry, Frances, but you'll have to stay until Peters questions you."

She pressed her clasped hands to her chest. "Peters? Questioning me?" Mother and Peters were like oil and water, they didn't mix.

"He'll question everyone. Even me."

"It's a waste of his time. I didn't kill that dreadful man."

"I know, Frances." Anarchy's tone was placating. "But it looks like someone here did. And you may have noticed something important."

Jane let out a low miserable moan.

I couldn't blame her. I was one hundred percent sure my family was blameless. Which meant that one of her children or one of their spouses killed her husband. Or...she had.

Anarchy rubbed his chin. "We'll need to recreate the past hour. Aunt Tilly, may we use your office for interviews?"

"Of course, dear boy." She frowned. "But are you certain he didn't fall? He did drink rather a lot."

Anarchy's assessing gaze returned to the balcony. "I'm sure."

What a night this was turning out to be. Mikey on his way to the hospital, and a man murdered.

Peters, wearing a furious you-interrupted-my-turkey-coma expression and an irredeemably wrinkled raincoat, arrived a few minutes later. He and Anarchy asked Mother to join them, then they all disappeared into Aunt Tilly's study.

Fat tears ran down Jane's cheeks, and she rubbed her eyes, smearing her mascara.

Clover and Wyatt held hands.

Aunt Tilly shook her head as if the whole disastrous evening was a giant misunderstanding. "He fell. He must have. No one here is a killer."

I stood, eager to escape Jane's low sobs. "I'll check on the children. Karma, would you like to join me?"

She gave a grateful nod, and, together, we walked toward the TV room.

"I feel sick," she said. "Positively green."

"I know."

"You feel this way every time, don't you?"

The awful thing was...I didn't. I'd found so many bodies that I'd grown a protective shell. "It's always terrible."

She reached out and squeezed my hand.

"Still glad you moved here? I bet if you were in San Francisco, you'd be at some marvelous dinner in a fabulous house with a spectacular view of the bay."

She shrugged. "Maybe. But the company is better here."

We entered the TV room, where Gina huddled in the corner of a squishy couch. Her eyes were red-rimmed but dry, and her hands were clenched in her lap. Her cousins, Heather and Ivy, sat on the floor with their backs against the couch. Grace and Beau squeezed together in an oversized club chair.

"Gina, how are you?"

"How do you think?" she snapped. "My brother's dying, and my parents left me here." She swiped angrily at a tear.

I sympathized. I did. But there were problems bigger than hers. "Was Mikey taking anything?"

The question earned me a glare.

"Please, Gina. Knowing what's in his system may save his life."

She wrapped her arms around her knees. "He swiped a bottle of Mom's Valium."

"I see." I moved to the far end of the couch, picked up the telephone receiver, and dialed the operator. When she answered, I said, "Would you please connect me with St. Mark's Hospital? It's an emergency."

A moment later, I was on the line with a nurse in the emergency room. "This is Ellison Jones calling." I glanced at the ceiling, then added, "I'm Frances Walford's daughter." Mother was the board chairman, and dropping her name got immediate results.

"How may I help you, Mrs. Jones?"

"You have a patient, Mikey Kowalski. I've just been informed he may have taken Valium. I thought the doctor would want to know."

"He will. Thank you. Is there anything else?"

I lifted my brows and gazed pointedly at Gina. "Is there anything else they should know?"

"No."

Ivy's hand snuck around the side of the couch and she pulled out a half-empty bottle of bourbon. "He drank."

I eyed the level. "Half a bottle?"

"No," she replied. "Just a couple of swigs."

"He also drank bourbon," I told the nurse. "We're not sure how much."

"I'll tell doctor. Thank you, Mrs. Jones. Happy Thanksgiving."

"To you as well." I hung up the phone and said, "Thank you, girls, for telling the truth."

"You're not mad?" said Ivy.

"No."

"She's disappointed," said Grace. "That's worse."

"I assume the bottle is Aunt Tilly's?"

Heather and Ivy gave identical nods.

Gina stared into space. "You didn't ask how he was?"

"Giving information was more important than getting it."

She glared at me with you-couldn't-possibly-understand disdain.

"Beau, how are you doing?" I asked. The poor boy had been dragged into another family mess.

"I'm okay." His eyes were at half-mast. "Can we go home soon?"

"Anarchy and Detective Peters are asking everyone a few questions. When they're done, we'll go."

He nodded, yawned, and snuggled closer to Grace.

I glanced at the TV where Lucy pulled away the football just as Charlie Brown tried to kick it. Then I held out my hand for the bourbon bottle. "I'll take that." From the slightly glazed looks in Mikey's cousins' eyes and the level of bourbon left in the bottle, I strongly suspected he wasn't the only one who'd been tippling.

Karma and I returned to the living room at the same time as Mother.

She glared at me, and said, "They want to talk to you next."

I nodded, gave Karma the bourbon bottle, and headed into the study.

Like everything else in Aunt Tilly's house, her study was feminine and delicate and decorated with French antiques.

Peters looked slightly ridiculous sitting behind a gilt desk.

I smiled at him. Brightly.

He grimaced at me. "We need a timeline."

I took a seat. "I'm pretty good with the sequence of events, but I'm not sure about the times."

He grunted.

"Just tell him what you remember," said Anarchy.

"All the adults were in the living room when Grace came and got me. We knocked on the bathroom door. When Mikey didn't answer, I sent her to get Anarchy."

Peters made a note. "And then?"

"Anarchy and Mike arrived, and Anarchy sent me to get a screwdriver. They took the door off the hinges, then Mike went to call an ambulance. He must have said something as he passed through the living room because everyone crowded into the hallway."

"Everyone?"

I nodded. "I think so."

"You saw Hicks?"

I closed my eyes and recreated the chaotic scene. "No. I guess I didn't."

He made another note. "What next?"

"We sent the kids back to the TV room, and Wyatt offered to go downstairs and wait for the ambulance."

"Did anyone go with him?"

"I don't think so."

"After that?"

"The EMTs arrived. Quickly. They must have been parked nearby in case there was an emergency during the lighting ceremony. Then, everyone returned to the living room to get out of their way. That's when we realized Earl was missing."

"Did anyone besides Wyatt leave the group in the hallway?"

"I don't know. I was in the bathroom with Anarchy and Mikey. There seemed to be a lot of jockeying for position."

"Position?"

"A better view."

Peters nodded. People's fascination with tragedy no longer surprised him.

"When you told everyone you'd found Earl, how did they react?"

"Clover and Wyatt looked shocked. Jane collapsed."

"Sounds dramatic," Peters observed.

"It was. She pressed her palms to her cheeks, then she fell onto a couch and sobbed. But..."

"But what?"

"I didn't see any tears." Jane had covered her face with a handkerchief.

"Did you ever see her leave the crowd outside the bathroom?"

"I'm sorry. I don't know."

He grunted. "Tell me about them."

"What do you want to know?"

"What do they do? Do you like them?"

"Jane is a bookkeeper for a commercial builder. Mike sells plumbing parts. Wyatt is an accountant. Neither Clover nor Karli work outside their homes."

"Do you like them?"

I glanced at Anarchy. "Clover and Wyatt are okay."

"The rest are too blue collar for you?"

"Peters!" Anarchy sounded outraged.

"What? Your wife hangs out with the country club crowd, not bookkeepers or plumbers."

"That's not why I don't care for them."

"Then why?"

"Jane takes advantage of my aunt. Mike gives me the heebie-jeebies. And Karli is a mean drunk." I stood.

So did Anarchy. He dropped a kiss on my cheek, then said, "When you go back to the living room, would you please send in your dad?"

"Of course."

"We'll talk to him, then Karma, then Grace. After that, you all can go home."

"What about you?"

He grimaced. "I'll be late."

I lifted up onto my tiptoes and kissed his cheek. "I'll wait up for you."

"It could be after midnight."

I gave him a wry grin.

"What?"

"Our first Thanksgiving as husband and wife."

"And of course you find a body," Peters grumbled. He and Mother had more in common than either one would ever admit.

I gave him my best scowl and returned to the living room.

THE LIMOUSINE DRIVER TOOK US HOME. WELL, US WITHOUT Anarchy. He'd catch a ride with Peters when they finished questioning Jane and her family.

The kids and I went to the kitchen and let the dogs out in the backward. Max took off like a shot, burning with the need to protect the yard's perimeter from squirrels. Finn followed behind.

"Are you guys okay?"

Grace yawned. "We're fine."

"You're sure?"

Beau pushed a lock of blond hair away from his face. "I know we should feel sad, but we never saw Mr. Hicks. Never met him. It doesn't seem real."

"You never saw him?"

"Aunt Tilly sent us to the TV room," he explained.

"Wasn't he in the hall outside the bathroom?"

"Nope." Grace popped the "p."

What had Earl been doing while his family gathered round that door? Was he already dead?

One of the dogs scratched on the back door, and I let them in and passed out biscuits.

"Mom."

I turned to my daughter. "Yes?"

"Let's never do this again."

Find a body? I could make no promises. Despite my best efforts it kept happening. "What do you mean?"

"Aunt Tilly's on Thanksgiving. Next year, just tell Granna we're not going. We see the lights at least twenty times during the holidays. We don't need to see them on the busiest night. And we can go see Aunt Tilly another time when her other relatives aren't there."

"Done."

Her eyes widened as if I'd surprised her. "Just like that?"

"I spent my evening wishing I was curled up in front of the TV in the family room. If you two don't want to go, we'll skip it."

"What will Granna say?" Grace raised an excellent question. Mother would not be happy.

I'd deal with her displeasure. Easily said when it was a whole year away. "We'll stay home." Mother and Daddy could go without us. I glanced at the clock on the kitchen wall. "You two should head to bed."

Grace crossed her arms and tilted her chin. One of her brows lifted. "What about you?"

"I'll wait up for Anarchy."

"He could be hours."

"I'll make coffee."

Grace gave a slow nod, then she and Beau began their climb up the backstairs to the second floor.

"Grace," I called.

Her steps slowed. Beau's did too.

"Did any of the girls go off by themselves?"

"No," she replied.

Well, that was a relief. "Thank you."

They continued their climb, and I leaned against the counter.

The day had been endless. I'd prepared for our little dinner party (Aggie had done the cooking, but I'd set the table with the Francis I sterling and Spode Gloucester china I'd received on my first marriage). I'd arranged flowers. I'd made a run to the grocer for more butter. I'd taken the dogs for an extended run, so they'd be calm when Mother arrived. I'd argued with Grace over what she was wearing. I'd realized we were out of Daddy's favorite scotch and driven to three liquor stores before I found one open. I'd kept a nervous eye on my watch throughout dinner, because, if we were late to Aunt Tilly's, Mother would blame me. And I'd found a body.

Fatigue made my eyes gritty. Gathering the remains of my energy, I filled Mr. Coffee's reservoir with water, then gave him a fond pat.

Tired? Mr. Coffee was always solicitous.

"Exhausted." I spooned coffee grounds into the filter.

Holidays can be that way.

"I found a body at Aunt Tilly's. Someone at the party is responsible." I waited for Mr. Coffee's response, but I'd rendered him mute. Only the orange glow of his on button let me know he was thinking. And perking.

That's why you're waiting up for Anarchy. You want to talk about it. But he'd want you to go to bed. Get your rest.

Mr. Coffee was right on both counts. I did want to talk. One of Tilly's extended family members was a murderer. That required discussion. And Anarchy would want me to rest. But I didn't want to go to bed alone on our first Thanksgiving as husband and wife.

I poured myself a cup of coffee, added a jot of cream, and settled on a kitchen stool.

The dogs flopped onto their mats in the corner, dropped their chins to their paws, and closed their eyes.

Looks like it's just us.

"You won't find me complaining."

What happened tonight?

"Jane remarried. Her new husband fell from the balcony."

Fell? You made it sound like murder.

"He didn't exactly fall. There are guard rails. Either he jumped or someone pushed him."

You and Anarchy think he was pushed. Mr. Coffee saw things clearly.

"Yes."

Your mother was there?

"She was. She was even on the balcony before me." I stared into the depths of my cup. "I was the one who looked down and spotted the body."

I'm so sorry. Mr. Coffee got me. He understood the horror of looking down on a man who'd plummeted seventeen stories. He also understood the painful tension that tightened my neck and shoulders when I seriously disappointed Mother. And finding bodies made for serious disappointments. *Anyone could have looked down and seen him.*

"Anyone could have. I did." I was starting to sound like Mother.

Not your fault. How did your Aunt Tilly react to a murder at her party?

"She was resilient as always. When we left, she was comforting Jane." I swirled the remaining coffee in my cup and frowned. "She looks thinner." My great-aunt had always maintained a waspish figure, but tonight she'd looked almost gaunt. "She's amazing. She's in her mid-eighties and still plays golf." And she sported the Palm Springs tan to prove it.

More coffee?

"Thank you."

When my mug was full and I had resumed my perch on the stool, Mr. Coffee asked, *Why would someone kill Jane's husband?*

"I think Earl believed he'd found himself a rich woman."

Hadn't he?

"Jane's not rich. Not at all. Sometimes Aunt Tilly helps." Much to Mother's chagrin, Aunt Tilly had provided down payments on houses, and paid Clover and Mike's college tuitions, that sort of thing. "Maybe Earl thought Jane was Aunt Tilly's heir."

Is she?

"I don't know."

What does Jane do?

"She's the bookkeeper for a construction company. Aunt Tilly got her the job."

What did Earl do?

"He was a used-car salesman."

Mr. Coffee gave an amused gurgle. *I bet your mother was thrilled with that.*

I chuckled softly. Poor Mother. Being even shirttail related to a used-car salesman was enough to justify the one-hundred-and-forty calories for an extra scotch.

You think a member of Jane's family killed him?

"Earl and Jane got married in Vegas without informing her children." I thought back to Mike's grinding teeth.

Did any of them have an opportunity to throw Earl off the balcony?

"Mike was on the phone when everyone gathered round the bathroom door. He could have killed Earl before he returned to the bathroom."

Anyone else?

"Wyatt volunteered to go to the lobby and wait for the ambulance. He could have killed Earl before going downstairs."

Their wives?

"Anarchy will find out."

CHAPTER FOUR

I contemplated the unslept in half of our bed, wrapped the warm wool robe I bought on our honeymoon over my nightgown, jammed my feet into leather slippers, and went in search of coffee.

Having stayed up late waiting (in vain) for Anarchy, I needed a jolt of caffeine. Two jolts. Possibly three.

When I reached the kitchen, Mr. Coffee winked at me. *Aggie filled me up, just push the button.*

"Where's Aggie?" I pushed his button.

Shopping.

"That's right." Aggie and her sister got up at an ungodly hour the day after Thanksgiving, hit the stores (and the sales), and finished their Christmas shopping in time for brunch.

To me, it sounded like a close approximation of hell. Crowds of hungover shoppers fighting for deals? No, thank you.

I settled on the kitchen stool to wait for the beverage that would get me through my day, or at least my morning. "Did Anarchy come home?" It was possible he'd come late, decided not to disturb me, and slept in the guest room.

I didn't see him.

I lowered my head to my hands and stared at the countertop. I'd never say this to Mr. Coffee, but some mornings I wished he'd perk faster.

A literal horde on the backstairs had me turning on my stool, and Beau, with the dogs on his heels, burst into the kitchen.

"Good morning." I managed to smile for him. "Pie?"

"Yes, please." He frowned. "Where's Anarchy?"

"He's still investigating Mr. Hicks's death."

"He didn't come home?"

I swallowed a sigh but couldn't help the slump of my shoulders. "Not yet."

"You're sad." He wrapped his arms around me and squeezed.

Emotion clogged my throat, so rather than argue, I smoothed his blond hair. Long seconds passed before I asked, "Do you want whipped cream on your pie?"

"Yes!"

"Me, too." If I was standing in for Anarchy and eating pie for breakfast, I might as well go all out.

"Your coffee is ready." Beau nodded toward Mr. Coffee's full pot.

The clouds above my head parted, the angels sang, and I stumbled toward nirvana, splashing ambrosia into my mug and sipping without even taking time to add cream.

"You sure do love your coffee," Beau observed.

"I do."

I released my hold on the coffee mug and pulled leftover pie and whipped cream from the refrigerator. "How big a slice?"

"I'm hungry."

I cut a huge wedge and put it on a plate, then dipped a spoon into the whipped cream and dropped a dollop in my coffee. "How much whipped cream?"

"I love whipped cream."

"Tell you what." I pushed the bowl and the spoon over to him. "Help yourself."

He grinned. "I need my pie."

"Oh. Right." I picked up Beau's slice and set it in front of him. "You also need a fork."

"I can get it."

"It's right here." I opened the drawer.

"Starting without me?" Anarchy stood in the kitchen doorway wearing his clothes from last night. Stubble shadowed his jaw, and dark circles hung beneath his tired eyes.

"You made it!" Beau sounded absolutely thrilled.

"Hey, I wouldn't miss the start of a tradition."

My eyes filled with tears, and I turned my back so they wouldn't see me cry. This was a happy moment, not a weepy one. "Coffee?"

"Please." He came up behind me and dropped a kiss on my neck as I poured.

"I'll let you cut your own pie."

"Who cut Beau's piece?"

"I did."

"I like the way you cut."

"Fine." A smile took over my whole face as I cut a slice of equal size for Anarchy and watched as he took a seat next to Beau at the kitchen island. They dug into their pie like they hadn't had an enormous dinner the night before, like their stomachs were bottomless pits, like they were men who didn't need to count calories or watch their waistlines.

"You're not eating?" asked Anarchy.

I held up my coffee cup. "I added whipped cream."

"Not the same," said Beau.

"I'm happy with my coffee." Which needed to be refilled.

"May I please go skating with Joey this afternoon?"

Joey's parents belonged to a club that maintained an ice rink.

"Of course."

Beau grinned then forked another enormous bite.

Woof! Finn, who sat at Beau's feet, stared at him with soulful eyes.

"Ellison says I can't feed you from the table."

Sure, make me the bad guy.

Anarchy stood. "More coffee?"

It was as if he could read my mind.

He took the cup from my hands and poured. "This is a great tradition. We should do it the day after Christmas, too. What do you say, Beau?"

He looked worried. "Do you serve mince?"

"Pecan."

His face cleared. "I love pecan pie."

Ding, dong.

The dogs scrambled to their paws and raced to the front door, barking like lunatics.

"It's eight-thirty," I observed. "It can't be Mother." She wasn't an early riser, and, if she wanted access to our house, she simply barged in.

"Karma?" Anarchy suggested.

Ding, dong.

The dogs lost their ever-loving minds.

"Not Karma. She wouldn't ring twice."

"Libba?"

"Ha." Like Mother, she barged in.

"Are either of you going to answer the door?" asked Beau.

I sighed. "I suppose."

When I reached the front door, I scolded the dogs. "Quiet! Sit!"

In what was a holiday miracle, they both listened. Only then did I open the door.

Clover stood on the other side.

The poor woman looked like death warmed over.

I grabbed the dogs' collars and said, "Please, come in."

She slipped inside. "I'm sorry to come so early." And

without calling first. "But I needed to talk to you. Your husband and his partner think that Earl was murdered." She looked at me expectantly, as if she expected me to tell her Anarchy's thoughts.

"I don't discuss my husband's cases."

"But we're family."

I must have reacted—a tic near my eye, a wrinkled nose, a curled lip—because Clover's face flushed with sudden anger. "You think you're better than us."

Mother definitely thought that. Me? Not so much.

"No," I replied. "Not at all. But I wouldn't have much of a marriage if I compromised my husband's cases by discussing them." I discussed them with Aggie all the time. But Aggie was different. She really was family.

Clover snorted.

I forced a polite smile. "May I offer you coffee?" She looked like she needed a cup.

She sagged as if that small kindness had broken her. "Please." She raked her fingers through her already messy hair, and a mulish expression settled on her tired features. "Maybe you can't talk, but you can listen."

"Yes," I agreed. "I can listen, but I can't promise I won't tell Anarchy everything you tell me."

"I'm counting on it."

I held out my arm. "Let me take your coat."

She shucked out of a navy peacoat and gave it to me.

I led her to the living room. "I'll hang this up and get us some coffee. Make yourself at home."

When I returned, carrying a tray with two coffee mugs, a pitcher of cream, and a plate of cookies, Clover was slumped in a wingback chair picking at her cuticles.

"Cream?" I tried to sound chipper. Tried and failed.

"Black." She accepted the coffee and for long seconds she stared into the mug's depths. "I didn't kill Earl. Neither did Mike or Wyatt. That leaves Karli."

I was struck with the sickening certainty that Karli would soon be knocking at my door, equally eager to throw her sister-in-law to the wolves. "Why would Karli kill him?"

"I don't know. I just know I didn't do it. Neither did Mike or Wyatt."

When I'd gone to the kitchen for coffee, Anarchy had urged me to talk to Clover, certain I'd be able to get more information from her. This wasn't information, it was casting blame where it hurt the least. I tried a different tack. "What do you know about Earl?"

Her upper lip curled. "He was after Mom's money."

I raised my brows.

"I know. I know. She doesn't have any. But she told him she was Aunt Tilly's heir."

"Is she?" Mother would have kittens.

"She wants to be. She says your side of Aunt Tilly's family is already rich as Midas." Her gaze traveled my living room, as if my furnishings made her point.

"What else can you tell me about Earl?"

"He smoked too much, drank too much, and Mom paid for that trip to Vegas."

"A real gem."

"Mom can pick 'em. Do you remember her last boyfriend?"

"I can't say as I do."

"Vinny." She shuddered. "Turns out, Vinny got the money to take her out by robbing liquor stores. She visited him in prison. Regularly. She'd still be taking the bus to the pen, but he died."

"Died?"

"He started an argument with a man holding a shiv."

A story I prayed Mother never heard.

"The one before Vinny cleaned out her bank accounts and disappeared. Aunt Tilly had to pay all Mom's bills until Mom got a job."

"The bookkeeping job?"

"That's the one." She stared at the hands she had clasped in her lap. "We didn't like Earl. How could we? But he wasn't the worst man she'd been with. Wyatt and I didn't kill him. And it couldn't be Mike. My brother doesn't have a violent bone in his body."

I wasn't so sure about any of that. They'd all looked ready to wring Earl's neck. Tossing him off a building wasn't a stretch.

"It had to be Karli."

"I'm sure the police will figure it out."

She bit her lower lip.

"How's Mikey?" I asked.

"He'll be fine. When they release him from the hospital, Karli and Mike are sending him to a rehab facility. Aunt Tilly is paying for it."

Aunt Tilly paid for an awful lot. I kept that thought to myself. "I'm so glad he's better."

"I blame Karli. She can't be bothered to mother." Clover drained her coffee mug and stood. "I should go. The girls need me."

I rose from the settee. "I'm so sorry this happened to your family."

Clover pressed her palm to her lips and nodded. "It's been less than a day, and it's tearing us apart."

"Murder does that."

On that cheery note, she left.

I closed the door on her and returned to the kitchen, where Anarchy was putting rinsed plates into the dishwasher. "Where's Beau?"

"He mentioned ice skating and went upstairs to change. What did Clover say?"

I told him everything.

"Do you think your aunt made Jane her heir?"

"No idea. Why?"

"If she is Tilly's heir, one of her family might have killed

Earl to keep him away from the money. I should have asked your aunt about it last night."

"Why didn't you?"

"Your aunt looked tired and...frail. I decided to let her rest."

"That was kind." I studied my husband. "You look like you could use some rest, too."

He closed the dishwasher door. "I wish I could. I came home for pie with Beau and a shower." He glanced at his wrist. "I'm due at the medical examiner's office in an hour."

"You haven't slept."

He grimaced as he leaned against the edge of the counter. "I was present when someone was murdered. My captain wants this solved quickly."

In my experience, being exhausted and clear thinking did not go together, but I refused to nag. "Is there anything I can do to help?"

"If you talk to your aunt..."

I imagined that conversation. *Aunt Tilly, it's absolutely none of my business, but we think someone may have murdered Earl over your money. Who's your heir?*

"Does it matter who inherits?" I asked. "If Jane and her family believe they're the beneficiaries, does it matter what Aunt Tilly's will says?"

"Maybe. Maybe not. I'd still like to know." He studied my expression. "I'm not asking you to call her or go by her apartment."

I exhaled.

"But if you see her—"

"Of course."

A smile tugged at his lips. "Come here."

I went, melting into his chest as he wrapped his arms around me.

"Best Thanksgiving ever," he whispered against the shell of my ear.

"Earl was murdered."

"The first Thanksgiving that you're my wife. Of course it's the best."

I tilted my head and stared into his eyes. "How did I get so lucky?"

"I'm the lucky one."

Max nudged us, and Anarchy smiled at him. "You want in on the hug, buddy?"

Max wanted his breakfast.

I swallowed a sigh and left the comfort of Anarchy's arms. "Go take a shower. I'll feed the dogs then take them for a walk."

"And after that?"

"Beau's skating. Grace will hang out with her friends. I may paint."

He nodded. "I'll try to be home early."

I wasn't holding my breath.

CHAPTER FIVE

The right shade of green eluded me. Either there was too much yellow or too much blue.

"I give up."

Finn, who curled on his mat in the corner of my studio, gave his tail an encouraging wag. Max, who was on his own mat, didn't bother. He was too accustomed to my fruitless searches for the perfect hue. He even yawned, knowing that I'd find the right color tomorrow when I wasn't stressed about a murder.

"You're right."

My dog yawned again. He knew he was right. He was always right.

I washed my brushes in the sink, put them in a mason jar to dry, then, in search of coffee, descended the stairs to the kitchen.

Aggie, who wore a muumuu the exact shade of green I'd been hoping to mix (somewhere between split pea and asparagus), was dicing leftover turkey. The orange pom-poms on her cuffs bounced as she worked. "I'm prepping Turkey Tetrazzini."

"That sounds delicious."

"Coffee?" She nodded at Mr. Coffee's full pot. "I just made some."

"I'll help myself. How was your shopping trip?"

Max scratched on the back door. I opened it, and the dogs rushed out into the cold.

"Successful," she replied.

Brnng, brnng.

I picked up the receiver. "Jones's residence."

"Ellison." Mother's voice boomed through the phone line.

I winced. "Good afternoon, Mother."

Aggie put down her knife, poured me a cup of coffee, and put it in my hands. What would I ever do without her?

"I need you to go to St. Mark's immediately."

"Why? What's wrong?"

"It's your Aunt Tilly. She's been admitted."

"What happened?"

"She's not well."

I snuck a restorative sip of coffee. "Could you be more specific?"

"No. Now get down there before Jane and her brood descend like a pack of locusts. It's undoubtedly their fault she's there. I'm sure the stress of that horrid man going off the balcony is what put her in the hospital." Mother gave a martyred sigh. "I'd go myself, but I'm expecting ten for dinner."

I glanced at the kitchen clock. It was just after four, the kids would be home soon, and I hadn't seen them all day. "I'll go in the morning."

"Ellison." Mother's voice was honed to a don't-you-dare-argue edge. "Go see your aunt."

"Why is she in the hospital?"

"I already told you, I don't know. Hudson called. The poor man was beside himself with worry."

How would I feel, being in the hospital alone during the holidays? "Fine. I need to change clothes, then I'll go."

"Don't dally."

"Goodbye, Mother." I hung up the phone before I could snap at her.

"Everything okay?" Anarchy had slipped into the kitchen without me noticing.

I offered him an I-wish-I-could-stay-home-and-snuggle-on-the-couch smile. "Aunt Tilly is in the hospital. Mother wants me to go see her."

"I'll go with you."

If Anarchy didn't look so tired, I'd be tempted to say yes. But he looked wan, and his lips drooped in an uncharacteristic frown. "You should rest. If I go now, I'll be home for dinner."

"Leftovers?" he asked.

Aggie held up a wooden spoon. "Turkey Tetrazzini."

"I can't wait, Aggie. And I can't go looking like this." I waved my hands over my paint clothes, then headed upstairs.

Anarchy followed me. "I'm happy to take you."

I glanced over my shoulder at his tired face.

"You should nap."

We reached the bedroom, and Anarchy closed the door behind us.

"Did you learn anything at the autopsy?"

"No."

I heard a hesitation in his voice. "But?"

"Jane took out a fifty-thousand-dollar policy on Earl's life last week."

"What!"

"We found a copy of the policy among his things. In fairness, he insured her life for the same amount."

I toed off my sneakers. "What did Jane say?"

"She claims the policies were Earl's idea."

I perched on the edge of the bed and stared at the carpet. "Jane isn't my favorite, but…"

"You don't think she's a killer." Anarchy joined me on the bed, stretched his long legs, and rolled his shoulders.

I gave him a quick kiss on the cheek, stood, and shimmied out of my jeans. "I've been wrong before. Was she unaccounted for last night?"

He winced and rubbed the back of his neck. "The only people I'm certain had an opportunity are Mike and Wyatt. But the situation was so chaotic, Jane could have stepped away without anyone noticing."

I pulled a pair of gray wool slacks from the closet and paired them with a cream cashmere sweater. "Did Clover or Wyatt know about the policy?" Fifty-thousand dollars, especially when it was payable on a man they loathed, was a good motive for murder.

"She says they did not."

"Hmph." Jane was a mother, and mothers protected their children.

"Exactly."

I pulled the sweater over my head then studied my reflection in the mirror that hung above my dresser. I added a string of pearls. "Do you still want me to ask Aunt Tilly about her will?"

He made to stand. "I'll come with you."

"No. Rest. You've been up since seven yesterday morning."

"You're sure?"

I returned to our bed, rested my hands on his shoulders, and stared down into his tired eyes. "Positive. Take a nap. That's an order."

"Okay, boss."

I leaned forward, kissed his forehead, then headed for the door. "I'll see you at dinner."

"Ellison."

I looked over my shoulder.

"I have a bad feeling. I think I should come with you."

"You have a bad feeling because you're so tired you can't see straight." I pointed to the pillows. "Rest."

I parked in the visitor lot and entered the hospital through its main doors, which made for a nice change. Far too often, I arrived at the hospital via the emergency room.

The volunteer at the information desk, a woman whose white hair was looking distinctively lavender, peered through thick glasses and shuffled papers when I asked for Aunt Tilly's room number. "Here it is." She jotted the number on a piece of paper.

"Thank you. I wonder if you'd also give me Mikey Kowalski's room number."

After more shuffling, she added Mikey's room number to the paper. "Have a nice holiday weekend."

Too late for that. I wished her the same.

I rode the elevator to Aunt Tilly's floor then walked an oatmeal-hued corridor. Was there anything more depressing than a hospital during the holidays? Undoubtedly. But eyeing the string of construction paper feathers tacked to the nurses' station, I was hard-pressed to think of a sadder place.

The door to Aunt Tilly's room stood open, and I peeked my head inside. "Aunt Tilly?"

"Ellison!" She sounded delighted to see me. "You're just in time."

I stepped into the room, gave my great-aunt a kiss on the cheek, and said, "Good afternoon, Hudson."

Aunt Tilly's houseman held a silver cocktail shaker in his hands, and a black liquor suitcase stood open on the window ledge. He'd brought vodka, vermouth, olives, and glasses.

"You'll have a martini," said Aunt Tilly. A statement, not a question.

"What do the doctors say about martinis when you're in the hospital?"

Aunt Tilly, who wore a pink quilted-satin bed jacket to which she'd pinned a diamond brooch, wrinkled her nose. "What do they know?"

There was no point in arguing. Aunt Tilly would do exactly

as she pleased. I took the path of least resistance, and said, "I'd love to have a drink with you."

"This is why you're my favorite. You know when to pick your battles."

I accepted a martini glass from Hudson, settled on the Naugahyde chair next to Aunt Tilly's bed, shrugged off my jacket. "I'm your favorite?"

Aunt Tilly's cheeks flushed the same soft pink as her bed jacket. "Jane needs me, it doesn't make her my favorite."

I sipped, letting the vodka roll across my tongue as I took in my great-aunt. Her color was off, but her hair was perfect. Her eyes were tired, but her lipstick was expertly applied. A dark bruise peeked beneath her sleeve, but she'd covered it with a diamond wristwatch. "How are you feeling?"

"Right as rain." She offered up a bright smile.

"Now, Miss Tilly." Hudson's voice held a scolding tone. "You fainted."

My octogenarian great aunt rolled her eyes. "You worry too much."

"Aunt Tilly?"

"Earl's death came as a shock." She took a restorative sip of vodka. "It upset me more than I thought. To think, the man stumbled off my balcony."

I stared at her. Did she believe Earl tripped on his shoelace and fell over a four-foot railing? "Earl didn't stumble off the balcony, Aunt Tilly. He was mur--"

"Poor, poor Jane. She's a bad picker." Apparently, Aunt Tilly did not want to discuss murder.

"So I've heard."

Aunt Tilly shifted her gaze to Hudson. "You go on home. Be with your family. If I need another martini, Ellison can make it."

"I can stay," he offered.

She smiled at him. "I'll be fine, Hudson. Thank you for everything."

He gave a slow nod. "You take care, Miss Tilly."

"I will. I promise."

"Happy holidays to you, Miss Ellison." Hudson collected his coat from the small closet and slipped out into the hall.

Aunt Tilly took another sip of her drink. "What was I saying? Oh, yes. Jane's terrible taste in men. Earl came back from Las Vegas, called an insurance agent, and took out a fifty-thousand-dollar policy on her life. Who does that?" She swirled the liquor in her glass. "A man who might kill his wife, that's who. Well, I told her that she should take out a similar policy. I even offered to pay for it."

"Was the policy in force?" Fifty-thousand dollars was a strong motive for murder.

"I wrote the check for the yearly premium last week." With her free hand, she smoothed the blanket on her bed, and I couldn't help but notice a dark bruise near her wrist.

I swallowed. Hard. This was my chance to ask Anarchy's uncomfortable question. "Clover suggested that Earl might have married Jane for...your money."

Tilly chuckled. "Wouldn't that have sent your mother around the bend? If Earl Hicks ended up the beneficiary of my estate." She shook her head. "She doesn't have to worry now."

"I hate to ask this, but..."

"Who gets it all when I die?" Aunt Tilly looked amused. "The bulk of my money will go to a charitable trust. It will support the arts and children's organizations here in Kansas City."

"That's lovely."

"I named you and your mother co-trustees."

I choked on a sip of vodka. All this time, I thought Aunt Tilly liked me.

"Of course, I remembered Hudson. The man is a saint for putting up with me for all these years. Your mother and Sis get my homes and their contents. I figured Frances would want the family real estate and antiques to stay in the family." She wasn't wrong. "Jane gets seventy-five-thousand dollars. You get my jewelry." She patted the brooch she'd pinned to her bed jacket. "Marjorie, Clover, and Mike get twenty-five thousand each. My great-great nieces and nephews get five-thousand, and I've put another fifteen thousand in college funds for each of them."

"That's very generous of you."

"I suspect, of all my family members, you're the only one who'll think that. I'd appreciate it if you'd keep the details to yourself."

"May I tell Anarchy?"

She sank deeper into her pillows (Hudson must have brought them from home, because they were far too fluffy to belong to the hospital). "If you must."

I nodded my thanks. "You fainted?"

"I did." She pursed her lips in annoyance. "And Hudson over-reacted. I should be at home now, in the TV room with my feet up. Instead, I'm here." Her displeasure was palpable.

"Tilly?"

I turned in my chair and spotted John Milbank in the doorway.

His brows lifted as he took in the martini glasses in our hands. "Ellison, nice to see you." His voice was as dry as our drinks, and Hudson mixed an arid martini.

"Likewise." Why was John visiting Aunt Tilly? He was an oncologist. Surely fainting called for a neurologist.

"You brought cocktails?" He entered Tilly's room and picked up the chart that hung from the end of her bed.

"I arrived and was served a cocktail. It is five o'clock."

"It's also a hospital."

"Pish," said Tilly. "When a woman reaches my age, she should do as she pleases."

"Even if it affects her medications?" His gaze scanned her chart.

"Aunt Tilly?" My tone invited an explanation.

She gave a put-upon sigh. "Something else I'd like you to keep to yourself, dear. I have cancer."

My stomach sank. "No."

"Yes," John replied. "And she's declined chemotherapy." His disapproval was evident in the set of his jaw.

"Chemotherapy would buy me a year? Maybe two? Or it might kill me. I've had a marvelous life. I don't mind dying. Especially not when it's on my terms."

John huffed.

Aunt Tilly pointed at him. "That's enough out of you, doctor. I've made my choice."

"Fine, Tilly." He didn't sound happy. "How are you feeling?"

"Ready to go home."

"We need to run some tests."

She pursed her lips. "You and I both know there won't be any testing on a holiday weekend. Let me go home. I'll come back on Monday."

"Tilly, you blacked out. You're lucky you didn't hit your head or break a bone when you fell."

They stared at each other. Neither willing to cede an inch.

John blinked first. "I'll make you a deal."

"I'm listening."

"Stay the weekend, and I'll make sure you're first for testing on Monday."

"It's a good deal, Aunt Tilly."

"Fine." She wrinkled her nose at both of us, then drank. Deeply. "But, Ellison, you and that handsome husband of yours will bring me dinner tomorrow night. I want Winstead's. A steakburger with cheese and grilled onions, French fries, and a frosty malt."

"Done."

For a moment, I thought John might argue for healthier food, but he'd already won one battle. He wouldn't win a second. He seemed to realize that, because he gave an unhappy nod. "I'll see you when I'm on rounds in the morning." He nodded my way. "Ellison, always a pleasure."

"Likewise." I waited till he was gone to ask my aunt, "How long have you known?"

"Months."

"Aunt Tilly..."

"My terms, Ellison. I want to go on my terms. Do not tell your mother. She'll do nothing but treat me like an invalid." Aunt Tilly wasn't wrong. Mother would hover. And fuss. And manage. And Aunt Tilly would hate every second.

"I won't tell her. I promise."

"Thank you, dear." She held out her glass. "Would you top this off."

I added more vodka to her glass and swallowed a sudden lump in my throat. "How long have you got?"

"The doctors say a few months, but what do they know?"

"Aunt Tilly..."

"Don't," she said. "Don't. I went to Paris last month. I walked the streets George and I visited on our honeymoon. I sat on a park bench and watched the Bateaux Mouches on the Seine. I ate my favorite meal. Then I went to Palm Springs and played golf every day. And bridge with women I've held dear for more than half my life. I celebrated Thanksgiving with family—even if that despicable man did his best to ruin it—and I'm having unexpected cocktails with my favorite great-niece."

I lifted my glass and smiled at her over the rim. The smile was watery. God broke the mold when he made my great-aunt, I'd never meet anyone else like her again. "I'll miss you."

"Of course you will." She held out her free hand, and I took it in mine. "Ellison, if there's one thing I've learned, it's that one must seize opportunities. They don't always knock again. I've had a wonderful go, and my only regrets are things I didn't do. I didn't let George buy me that strand of Akoya pearls from

Cartier on our twenty-fifth anniversary. He wanted to, and I told him, 'no.' I didn't go on that spa trip your mother planned."

"Don't regret that." I had gone on that trip. With Mother, Aunt Sis, and my sister Marjorie. Mother bossed her daughters and bickered with her sister. Aunt Sis drank. And Marjorie sniped. At me. Endlessly. I'd come home exponentially more stressed than before I left.

Aunt Tilly laughed softly. "I'd have liked for us all to be together."

"Maybe I can..."

She held up a hand. "No, dear. Look at me. I'm spending the holiday weekend in a hospital bed. My days of traveling are over." She looked me dead in the eye, then drained her glass. "Remember, no regrets."

"More?"

She grinned. "Need you ask?" I poured, and she shooed me toward the door. "Go home and spend time with your husband. I'll see you tomorrow night."

"Are you sure? I can stay."

"Go."

I collected my jacket, kissed her cheek, and left without letting her see the tears in my eyes. Rather than heading immediately home, I descended a floor and poked my head into Mikey's hospital room.

The patient was propped up in bed with his nose in a book. His father sat in the Naugahyde chair next to the hospital bed.

"Good evening." I ventured.

"Ellison." Mike stood. "What are you doing here?"

Who said chivalry was dead?

"I thought I'd stop by and see the patient."

Mikey looked at me over the top of his book, then went back to reading.

"I'm glad you're feeling better."

"Yeah." Mikey sounded bored. And annoyed. And totally ungrateful.

"Ellison?" Mike nodded toward the hallway. "A word?"

"Of course."

We stepped out of the room.

"Any word on the investigation?"

"I can't comment on my husband's cases."

"So, it was murder."

"I didn't say that."

"Your husband is a homicide detective. If it's his case, it's murder." Mike made an excellent point. "It must have been Wyatt."

Interesting how Clover and Mike were so willing to blame their sibling's spouses. I shrugged. "I don't know anything."

He leaned against the wall and raked his hands through his hair. "I've been sitting in that chair all day, trying to figure out what happened. When we took the door of the hinges, everyone gathered around. Everyone. All of us on top of each other, right until Wyatt left to wait for the ambulance."

Not everyone. Why hadn't I seen it before?

CHAPTER SIX

"Anarchy?" I called his name as soon as I set foot in the house.

The dogs raced toward me, their stubby tails working so hard their butts shook.

I offered pets and scratches behind ears and asked, "Where's Anarchy?"

Woof. Max trotted toward the back of the house.

I followed him through the kitchen to the family room where Anarchy was stretched out on the couch with his eyes closed.

Max flopped onto the carpet in front of the fireplace, and Finn snuggled next to him.

I chewed on my lower lip. Should I wake Anarchy? The man was exhausted, but...

"I can hear you thinking." His lids remained closed.

"I didn't want to disturb you."

He pushed up on his elbows and gave me a sleepy grin. "You never disturb me."

My knees went weak.

"How's your aunt?"

"May I?" I joined him on the couch and rested my clasped hands in my lap. "We need to talk."

"That sounds ominous."

"Maybe. Where are the kids?"

"Beau is spending the night with Joey, and Grace is out with her friends."

"Aggie?"

"On a date with Mack."

"Dinner?"

"Warming in the oven. There's a salad in the fridge." He studied me. "Do you want a drink?"

"Hudson brought Aunt Tilly's liquor case. I had a martini with her."

His brows rose.

"That was her doctor's reaction, too."

"I bet."

I squared my shoulders. "When we were in the bathroom, where were Aunt Tilly and Hudson?"

"In the kitchen. Hudson was doing the dishes."

"Why was Aunt Tilly there?"

"With all the hullabaloo, she needed a drink."

"Hullabaloo?"

"Her word."

"And she went to the kitchen?"

Anarchy frowned as he nodded. "Yes."

There were two call buttons in Aunt Tilly's apartment. One near her chair in the dining room, the other near her favorite chair in the living room. Each rang directly to the kitchen. If Aunt Tilly wanted a drink, she'd call for Hudson, not go to him.

"What if they killed Earl?"

He stared at me. "Why would they do that?"

"Let's assume Earl married Jane with the belief that she'd inherit Tilly's money."

His gaze sharpened. "Will she?"

"Aunt Tilly remembered her. Generously." Mother would have a fit. "But it's not the millions Jane is counting on."

"Who gets the money?"

"The bulk of her estate will go to a charitable trust." My shoulders sagged under the weight of being a co-trustee with Mother. "Back to Earl. No one ever saw him in the hallway outside the bathroom."

"They did not."

"That leaves him in the living room. Alone with Aunt Tilly. I know my great-aunt. She wouldn't leave a guest to fetch a drink, no matter how much she might dislike him."

"She disliked him?"

"She paid the premium for the policy Jane carries on Earl's life."

"So, Tilly and Earl are in the living room, then what?"

"They went out on the balcony to see the lights come on."

"Aunt Tilly pitched him over the edge?" He reached for my hand and squeezed my fingers. "I don't think she has the strength."

"What if they struggled?"

He shook his head.

"What if Hudson joined them on the balcony?"

Anarchy opened his mouth, then closed it as he sat back against the couch cushions. "That's possible. But why?"

"Aunt Tilly has a terrible bruise on her wrist. What if Earl tried to throw her off the balcony?"

"And Hudson came to her rescue?"

I nodded enthusiastically. "Exactly."

"Then they should have told us."

"Even after Aunt Tilly paid for a fifty-thousand-dollar life insurance policy?"

"Don't take this the wrong way, but your great aunt doesn't seem the type to worry herself over that amount of money. If that's what happened, she should have told us."

Everything was black and white for Anarchy. "There's something else."

Anarchy grimaced.

"Aunt Tilly is dying of cancer. No one knows, and she's refusing treatment." Aunt Tilly adored Hudson. She wouldn't want him to face repercussions when she was gone.

My husband pulled me onto his lap. "I know you're fond of her. I'm sorry."

"Me, too. What do we do?" In regard to Earl, not Aunt Tilly's cancer.

"Tonight, we have dinner and go to bed early. I'll talk to her tomorrow."

"I promised her we'd bring Winstead's."

"Sounds like you're coming with me. Now, Mrs. Jones--" he pulled me close and kissed the corner of my lips "--I want you to put murder and cancer and whatever is bothering you about Tilly's estate out of your mind."

Easy to do when his lips moved against mine. "And?"

"How hungry are you?" He nibbled on my earlobe.

Starving. "Not very."

I felt his smile against the curve of my cheek. "I was hoping you'd say that. Dinner can wait."

"Ellison! Anarchy! I'm so glad you're here." Aunt Tilly was in her hospital bed wearing a white satin bed jacket (again with a diamond brooch pinned near the shoulder) and a broad smile. "There's nothing duller than a hospital on the weekend. And you brought Winstead's! Thank heavens! The food here is abysmal."

Anarchy put the Winstead's bag on the table that spanned Aunt Tilly's bed. I deposited the frosty.

"You're wonderful. Both of you. Now sit." She'd somehow finagled an extra chair. The room was crowded but Anarchy and I both had a seat. "Tell me what you've been doing."

"Nothing exciting," I replied.

She wrinkled her nose as if she didn't care for my answer. "Your mother came to see me. And Jane."

"At the same time?"

"Sadly, yes." She reached for her frosty and the sleeve of her bedjacket rode up, revealing a bruise that matched her other wrist.

"Aunt Tilly, what happened?"

"I'm old. I bruise easily."

I tilted my head and pursed my lips.

"I'm fine, Ellison."

"It looks like someone grabbed you," said Anarchy.

"Is there a spoon?"

"In the bag," I replied. "Did Earl cause those bruises?"

Aunt Tilly put the frosty on the table and dug through the Winstead's bag for a spoon. "Life is short. Eat dessert first."

I winced but stuck to my guns. "Did he?"

"Aha!" She held up the spoon.

"I think you and Earl went out on the balcony to see the lights and he attacked you." I nodded toward her bruised wrists. "You struggled. Hudson, who was in the living room picking up glasses, saw you and came to your rescue. Somehow, Earl went over the edge."

Aunt Tilly spooned a bite of frosty.

"Am I right?"

"Ellison." Her voice held a warning.

"Jane's family is tearing itself apart."

She stared at me for long seconds before transferring her gaze to Anarchy. "You're half right. Hudson was never on the balcony."

"What happened?"

"We stepped outside to see the lights..."

Seconds passed as Aunt Tilly stared sightlessly at the oatmeal-colored wall.

"You stepped outside," Anarchy prompted.

"Earl told me I had a lovely home. I thanked him." She pressed a hand to her chest. "Then he grabbed my wrist." Aunt Tilly held out her right hand. "His grip was so tight. I told him he was hurting me. He didn't care. He said everyone had noticed how much I'd been drinking. No one would doubt that I fell off the balcony. He and Jane had talked, and they didn't want to wait for my money."

"Oh, Aunt Tilly." The tears in her eyes were at odds with the determined tilt of her chin. "Jane would never..."

She waved off my sympathy. "I know that now, in the moment, it broke my heart. I fought him, but he dragged me to the railing and leaned us both over the edge. I refused to die like that. I have my ending planned, and it's not splattered across the roof of a porte cochère. I linked my foot around his ankle and yanked. He lost his balance, then he was the one falling."

"What happened next?" asked Anarchy.

"I went to the kitchen and asked Hudson for a drink."

My husband dragged his palm across his chin, hiding a pained expression. "Why didn't you tell us?"

"I was in shock."

"And yesterday?"

"I was hoping you'd determine he fell."

Anarchy gave a slow unhappy nod. "How long has Hudson been with you?"

"Thirty-five years."

"He's like family."

"Hudson had nothing to do with what happened on the balcony." Aunt Tilly spoke quickly. Decisively. And I didn't believe her. "You'll never prove otherwise." She dug her spoon into her frosty like the frozen treat was responsible for the world's misfortunes.

"Even if he did, no charges would be filed. It was self-defense."

She stared at Anarchy with narrowed eyes. "I assume Ellison has told you my situation?"

"She has."

"Then you know I won't be here long."

Anarchy gave a tiny nod.

"Even if Hudson was on that balcony, which he was not, I wouldn't tell you. I won't be here to protect him from an overzealous prosecutor who charges a black man with throwing a white man to his death. I won't be here to defend Hudson's claim on my estate when Jane claims wrongful death. I won't do that to him." Her gaze shifted to me. "You know better than anyone in this family that there's more than blood. The family we choose can be more precious than the family we're born with. Hudson is family."

The expression in Anarchy's brown eyes was grave. "No one will believe you threw a man forty years your junior off a balcony."

"Adrenaline is an amazing thing. I was reading just the other day that a man picked up a car and pulled a child from beneath its wheels."

Anarchy leaned forward, resting his elbows on his knees. "You're certain about this Tilly?"

"I've never been more certain. This holiday is about gratitude. I've had a marvelous life, for which I'll be eternally grateful. I had the love of a wonderful man. I've had marvelous friends. I even have a few family members whom I adore." She winked at me. "And, I've had Hudson. Through thick and thin. He saw me through my husband's death, held my hand when the doctors told me about my cancer, and acted as my protector." She held out her hands. "Please. Let me give him this."

My breath caught in my chest as I stared at my by-the-book-homicide-detective husband.

He closed his eyes and laced his fingers together.

I didn't dare breathe. Didn't dare try.

Worry furrowed Aunt Tilly's brow.

"You're willing to swear an affidavit that Hicks was drunk and fell over the railing?"

"If that's what you want."

I exhaled. Loudly.

A tiny smile curled Anarchy's lip. "I'll come by tomorrow, and we'll write out a statement."

My heart overflowed with appreciation for the man sitting next to me.

We sat with Aunt Tilly as she ate her steakburger and fries and frosty, then I kissed her on the cheek, and we stepped into the hallway.

"Thank you," I told Anarchy. "I am forever grateful. But why?"

"Because your aunt was right. About everything. About what might happen to Hudson. About gratitude. About family."

"But justice?"

"A venal man tried to murder your aunt and died for his trouble. I'd say justice was served."

I raised up on my tiptoes and kissed his cheek. "Thank you. And since we're talking about gratitude, I am grateful for you. Every day."

"I feel the same way." He gazed into my eyes. "Will you make me a promise?"

I nodded. "Anything."

He leaned closer and whispered in my ear. "No bodies at Christmas."

I laughed softly. "That's a promise I can't make."

ALSO BY JULIE MULHERN